WAYWARD WISTERIA

Wisteria Witches Mysteries

BOOK #14

ANGELA PEPPER

CHAPTER 1

Saturday, January 14th

Two days after Zinnia Riddle's 49th Birthday

The magic of my aunt's birthday was still lingering in the air.

I was hanging out on the lower bunk bed in my aunt's spare bedroom when she, the owner of the house I was living in, popped her head in to chat.

"I'm heading out for lunch with Dawna from work," Zinnia Riddle said. "She wanted to treat me, but so did Margaret, so it will be the three of us."

"Have fun with the girls," I said. "Don't do anything I wouldn't do."

She pressed her lips into a flat line. Her pregnancy hormones were straining her sense of humor.

"Or go hog wild," I said. "If the girls are treating you, order the full menu."

"You should come along," she said. "We're going to Lucky's Diner. You love that place."

"Pass." I got up from my spot on the lower bunk, where I'd been reading, and stretched. "I've got a bunch of spy novels to catch up on, plus you could probably use

1

a break from," I pointed to my face, "looking at this goofy mug all day, every day." I'd been crashing there, along with my mother, my daughter, and my pets, while I searched for other accommodations. Though it had only been ten days, sometimes it felt longer. Like when the hot water tank couldn't keep up with our showers.

She didn't leave the doorway.

"Aunt Zinnia, I'll be fine on my own for a few hours." I shooed her away with my hands but it didn't work.

She kept standing there, pressing her lips flatter and flatter.

I said to her with exasperation, "Why are you being so weird? Is it because it was your birthday two days ago? It isn't a big deal. Just because you turned the big four-nine, and you got yourself knocked up by your dear old friend whom you keep pushing away for no good reason, that doesn't mean everyone's going to ask you a bunch of intrusive questions, does it?" I pretended to slap my face in surprise. "Oh! That's why you want me to come with you to lunch. You want me around to deflect attention away from you, and your... *situation*."

I waved at her midsection, and the growing baby bump. She had begrudgingly begun to wear the maternity jeans her friend Margaret Mills had given her. Margaret was quite a bit shorter than my aunt, so the two had extended the leg length using magic.

"No," she said icily. "That's not it at all. I just have a funny feeling you might get up to something that I wouldn't approve of." She looked over at the bedroom's window, scowling with suspicion.

"Why would I do that?"

"I don't know." She kept looking at the window, as though she saw something out there. "Don't go digging around in the back of the refrigerator."

"I wouldn't dare," I said. "You keep way too many jars of eyeballs in there."

"And don't reorganize my bookshelves. I have my own system."

I held both hands up. "I learned my lesson. I promise I won't touch your bookshelves ever again. My word is my bond."

She still wasn't moving. Her gaze kept darting to the window.

I gave her a quick hug then pushed her out of the room.

"Go to lunch," I said firmly. "Don't make Margaret and Dawna wait. Have an extra piece of pie for me. With ice cream."

She muttered one last order for me to behave myself, then she left and made her way down the stairs, admonishing the cat for darting around her feet as she went.

Once I heard the front door close, I opened the bedroom window.

Maisy Nix, who'd been waiting on the roof, jumped in through the window.

"Brrr," she said, tossing her glossy black hair to shake out snowflakes. "It's cold out there." She floated her broomstick into a corner.

Maisy Nix was a fellow coven member, and the owner of Dreamland Coffee. She was a striking, tall woman with masculine energy and a fiery temperament. Arriving by broomstick in the broad daylight was such a Maisy thing to do.

Maisy was there to help me prepare for the party we had planned. Zinnia made me promise not to throw a surprise party for her birthday, but she hadn't said anything about not throwing a *belated* one two days later, on Saturday, when all our friends were available.

Maisy stamped her boots on the floor and shook herself dramatically.

"The air is so cold today," she said. "Plus the wind chill factor makes flying feel even colder."

"You could have taken your car," I said.

"And fill up all the nearby parking? Oh, Zara." She leaned down—she was over six feet tall—and patted my cheeks like I was a small, naive child. Her fingers were icy. "That won't be much of a surprise for Zinnia if she sees the vehicles of everyone she knows lining the streets before she even walks in."

"I know, but should you really be flying around in the middle of the day?"

Maisy sniffed. "Don't," she said, pressing one long, icy finger on my lips.

I swatted her hand away. "Don't what?"

"Don't act like a martyr. Like you're everyone's savior. Just because you quit practicing magic, and it's working for you, that doesn't mean your way is the only way, or that you have to save the rest of us from ourselves." She was referring to my recent vow to be more careful with my powers, and to only use magic when absolutely necessary.

Before we could get into it, a big, handsome man in a red velvet tuxedo climbed in through the window. His tuxedo was accented with a green bowtie.

"I see your *pet* is still rocking his Christmas outfit," I said to Maisy. "You need to take him shopping for something more casual."

"But he looks so cute in his tux," she cooed, holding her lips in an exaggerated kiss shape as she gazed lovingly at her attractive pet/companion. "Like a delicious slice of red velvet cake. Isn't that right, Humphrey?"

He grinned at the sound of his own name.

I shook my head. "You know I love a colorful wardrobe that expresses one's personality, but if you keep dressing him up like a pet, people are going to get suspicious."

Maisy rolled her eyes. "Fine. I'll get him some jeans." Her espresso-brown eyes brightened. "And a leather jacket." She pointed her finger at me. "Now we're talking. For once, Zara, you've had a good idea."

The man stood by patiently. When Maisy and I stopped discussing his new wardrobe, he offered me his hand.

"Hello, Zara," he said. "My name is Humphrey. We have met. Your head broke my nose. I forgave you."

"Hi, Humphrey." I shook the komodo-dragon-to-human shifter's hand. "I remember you. We've met a few times now, and I always remember you."

Maisy nudged me. "Say something nice. He lives for a few kind words."

"Your nose looks like it healed perfectly," I said.

Maisy nudged me again.

I said to him, half-joking, "You're a good boy, Humphrey."

He grinned.

Next to come in through the window was Fatima Nix, Maisy's niece who talked to animals and worked at a veterinary clinic. The short, dark-haired young woman was carrying a stack of catering trays for the party.

"Hi, Fatima," I said. "How's it going with your side project to get rid of the common flea?"

She gave me a blank stare. "You don't have to pretend to be interested," she said, and she immediately left the room with the trays. No interest in chit-chat.

I said to Maisy, "Xavier was right about your niece. She does *not* like me."

Maisy replied in a deadpan voice, "*Nobody* likes you, Zara."

The comment was so over-the-top mean, I had to laugh. Maisy joined me, giggling and wiping a tear from the corner of her eye. Our relationship was... special.

Humphrey stepped back out to the roof that ran over the porch, retrieved some boxes that the three of them must have flown in with, and took them down to the kitchen where Fatima had presumably headed.

I wasn't able to conceal my awe over how much stuff Maisy had flown in on her broomstick.

"Maisy, how did you get everything here in one trip? New spellwork? Does the handle on that broomstick telescope? Did you use a dustpan as a trailer, and tow it behind you through the sky?"

"All of the above." She bounced her elegant dark eyebrows and gave me a smug look.

"You really are something," I said.

"Sometimes I surprise myself. It seems the most reliable way for me to boost my powers is to completely drain them from time to time. I have *you* to thank for that discovery."

"You're welcome."

I closed the window, since we weren't expecting anyone else to arrive by broomstick. Margaret Mills was currently with my aunt, at lunch, and Ambrosia Abernathy was off hanging out with my daughter.

In fact, the two teen girls should have been back already to help set up for the surprise party, but I wasn't too worried. I imagined they were picking up a last-minute gift for my aunt.

Maisy grabbed my arm and said, "Humphrey has learned some new skills. He's shaping up to be a better human than most humans."

I sensed that she wanted to tell me about his skills in great detail.

"Maisy, I really don't want to hear about your sexual escapades," I said, because I didn't.

However, I knew it was pointless to fight it. Objecting to Maisy's stories only made her more excited about telling them. She was like my mother in that way. The thrill wasn't just in the escapade but in the regaling of the tale later on.

My best frenemy blocked the room's exit, and jumped right into a story that left nothing to the imagination.

Ten minutes later, my ears burning, I finally got away to help the others with the snack preparation in the kitchen.

Fatima and Humphrey had things under control, so I went to the living room to put up the decorations. I was tempted to use magic, but I had to stick to the pledge I'd made, even if it wasn't convenient. I used a stepladder and double-sided sticky tape, like a regular person.

The front door burst open, and my daughter and her best friend came running in like someone was chasing them.

"Hi, girls," I said from the top of the stepladder.

They must not have realized I was there, because they both screamed and grabbed onto each other.

"That's odd," I said. "Am I truly that menacing on a ladder, or do you both have a guilty conscience about something?"

They froze. Two sets of teen girl eyes went wide. Then both of them ran past me without a word, up the stairs, and into the bedroom with the bunk beds. The door slammed shut.

Maisy, who'd wandered in to check on the decorations, asked, "What was that all about?"

"Beats me," I said. "Teenagers."

"You're the mother. Shouldn't they report in to you?"

I stifled a laugh. Maisy didn't have any children. She was in her mid-forties, and had never expressed much interest in them. She had strange ideas about how parenting worked.

"If it's important enough, it will come out eventually," I said. "You have to let them think they're getting away with stuff at least some of the time, or they'll rebel even harder."

Maisy sniffed the air. "I smell alcohol."

"Mystery solved," I said. "They probably ran upstairs to brush their teeth and chew strawberry bubblegum. It's happened before."

"You know about this?"

"I'm afraid young Ambrosia has a taste for the hooch. I've been meaning to talk to her mother about it." I sighed. "Actually, I've been hoping it would go away on its own. Some problems do that."

"Terrible habit," Maisy said with a tsk-tsk. "I'm so glad I'm not addicted to anything."

"You don't think you're addicted to....?" I nodded in the direction of her pet, who was working diligently in the kitchen.

She blinked rapidly. "Addicted to what? Coffee? No. I can take it or leave it."

"I meant... the attention of men."

She gave me wide eyes. "I beg your pardon? Are you implying I'm a sex addict?"

"I believe the term is *sex and love addiction*."

She flung her glossy black hair aggressively.

"You're one to talk, Zara," she spat out. "I saw you yesterday at the coffee shop, leaning all over Chive Bacon. Putting your hand on his arm suggestively. Flashing your eyes at him every time you said the word *broomstick*. You couldn't have been more suggestive if you'd flat out offered to..." She made a crude gesture of someone waxing a broomstick.

My jaw dropped.

I *had* seen Chive Bacon the day before. We had talked about our chance meeting at City Hall, when he'd oh-so-conveniently left a flight-ready broom in the hallway for me to use.

But Maisy was wrong about our interaction. I hadn't been flirting. I'd just been trying to get to the bottom of whether or not the broom had been left there by accident. He'd all but admitted that the mayor, a time paladin, had arranged for it to be there so that events would play out a certain way.

Maisy gave me a smug grin, as though my silence was evidence she had won.

She turned, swinging her glossy black hair over her shoulder, and strutted back to the kitchen.

Oh, that hair of hers. How good it would feel to grab onto a thick handful and give it a good yank.

I stopped myself from running after her to find out.

Perhaps she did have a point.

Without the use of my magic, I had been resorting to other tactics lately. Perhaps I'd laid on the natural charm a bit heavy with Chive the day before. But he knew I had a boyfriend, so he must have known it was just my way of being friendly.

The Happy Birthday banner I'd been hanging up fell down at the other end.

I climbed down the stepladder, moved it over, climbed up again, and taped the other end of the banner.

Then the other end fell down.

I looked around to make sure nobody was watching, and then used a simple fixing spell to tack both ends in place.

A little voice said, "Ham."

I turned around to find Boa, the cat, watching. She had only regular feline intelligence, as far as we knew, yet she seemed to be giving me a very knowing look.

"Never you mind," I said.

Then I used magic to blow up the balloons and hang all the other decorations in five minutes flat. *Zara tries to be a magic-free witch, but double-sided tape is not nearly as effective as advertised.*

A few more guests arrived. Everyone had either come by foot, or had car-pooled and parked their vehicles a block away.

When I got the phone call from Margaret that Zinnia was on her way, everybody hid in their places behind the floral-print sofas and chairs. Zoey and Ambrosia had come downstairs, and Zoey was in fox form for easier hiding. Both of the girls were avoiding me. Ambrosia's breath reeked of alcohol and strawberry gum.

I said to all the people hiding, "And, just a final reminder, nobody is to use the terms *over the hill*, or *geriatric pregnancy*. Got it?"

Everyone muttered that they understood.

"Also, the term *medical miracle*," I said. "She hates that."

One woman raised her hand tentatively and said, "Speaking of miracles, how about inspiring stories from the Bible? Like Sarah, who bore Abraham a son at age ninety?"

"No inspiring stories, period," I said.

Everyone agreed to be on their best behavior.

Zinnia walked in the door, took one look at the banner, and walked back out again before we'd even finished yelling, "Surprise!"

Everyone looked at me.

"She'll be back," I said. "Give her a minute."

We waited.

The door didn't open.

I ran outside, where I found Zinnia standing on the sidewalk with a lost look on her face.

I took her hand and said, "It's not happening again, is it?" I was referring to the depression that had come over her last Halloween, when she'd been haunted by her past, and the stepson she'd lost.

Her eyes focused on mine, to my relief.

"I didn't know you had this planned," she said. "You... surprised me."

"That's sort of the whole point of a surprise party."

"I know, but... how did you do this? How did I not know? I always know, when it comes to things like this."

"Maybe it's because I'm good at surprises."

"No," she said, shaking her head. "That's not it."

"Maybe it's because you've never had a forty-ninth birthday before."

"Maybe."

I took her arm and tugged her back toward the house. "Come on in. The whole coven is here, plus a few other people who love you. And Riverflow is here to give everyone a free maternity yoga session as her birthday gift to you."

Zinnia hesitated. "Maternity yoga?"

"There's a lot of squatting. She said it'll be important to know if you go into labor somewhere far from a hospital."

She grimaced, but followed me despite her hesitation.

We walked in, everyone yelled "Surprise!" again, and the party got started.

An hour into the party, my aunt admitted to me that she was enjoying the celebration. "You've taken a difficult day and made it special," she said. "Thank you."

"Wait until you see the cake," I said, and I went to the kitchen to get the next big surprise.

It was a custom cake made to look like a giant teapot, with one of my aunt's favorite floral designs on the side.

I was testing a piece of icing to make sure it tasted as good as it looked when a shadow slipped across the edge of my vision and disappeared behind me.

I whirled around to find my vampire boyfriend, Theodore Bentley, standing casually in the corner.

I put my hand on my hip and greeted him with one of my usual jokes. "Who invited *you* in here?"

"Something's happened," he said.

"It's Wisteria. Something's always happening. Is it big? Do you need Persephone? At least let her stay until the cake's been served."

"There's been an incident at the museum," he said. "I need to speak with Zoey immediately."

"Why Zoey?"

"A fox was involved."

"Zoey's not the only fox in town."

He stared at me, his silver-gray eyes as cool as steel. "Bring her to me here. I don't want to disturb your aunt's party."

I gave him a wary look. "Does she need a lawyer?"

He wouldn't answer.

CHAPTER 2

Bentley didn't offer any further details, but I agreed to send Zoey in to talk to him.

I picked up the teapot cake, and brought it out to a roar of applause. There were many cries of delight.

It was exactly the level of reaction that anyone who has dropped half a paycheck on a custom cake wants to get.

"Wait until you taste it," I said.

Everyone demanded to know what spellwork I'd used to create such a marvelous replica.

"No magic," I said. "Chloe made it."

The group oohed and ahhed in appreciation.

Chloe was the gorgon who ran The Gingerbread House of Baking. She was quite busy with her baby, but spent some time in the bakery working on select projects. She enjoyed making fancy cakes, the more complex the better. I'd asked for a simple cake with floral decorations, and she'd talked me into the three-dimensional teapot.

I didn't know how I would outdo myself the following year, for my aunt's fiftieth. But that was next year's problem.

While everyone gathered around the formal table in my aunt's dining room, I got Zoey's attention, pulled her aside and discreetly told her that Bentley needed to speak with her in the kitchen.

Her happy expression grew serious. "Why? Am I in trouble?" Her breath reeked of strawberry gum.

"Only if you did something wrong at the museum today."

"The museum?" She frowned. "That's weird. I haven't been there since I went there with Mr. Caine, during the Christmas break." Mr. Caine was her genie father, who had since died. Sort of. He'd been liquified and sent to another world.

"Then tell Bentley that," I said.

"But I can't lie. He'll know. He's got those freaky silver vampire eyes that see right into you."

I was confused. "You don't need to lie. Just tell him you weren't at the museum today. He doesn't care if you were there a couple weeks ago, but go ahead and tell him about that, if you want to."

"Oh." Her pupils were larger than usual. She glanced in the direction of the kitchen but didn't go.

"Zoey, is there something you want to tell me?"

She frowned. "I think so, but I don't know. Can I get back to you?"

"Absolutely. We can talk later tonight. That's one nice thing about being bunked up together, roomie."

She nodded and went to the kitchen.

Everyone else was happily watching my aunt as she did the honors, cutting through the fondant into the elaborate cake. There were more oohs and ahhs when all the multicolored layers were revealed.

I put my hand around my mouth and called to my aunt over the din, "Keep going all the way around, like a clock! Chloe put every flavor in there, in different sections!"

With that taken care of, I grabbed Ambrosia by the shoulder and said, "Hey, we haven't spoken much lately."

She gave me a wary look. Ambrosia Abernathy had a round, pale face, accented by dark eyebrows, thick eyeliner, and nearly-white, bleached hair. My daughter and I joked that she looked exactly like someone who could see ghosts. She and I had similar witch specialties, so I'd been mentoring her whenever I could. Plus I'd been getting her to do my grunt work. Interns were great.

"How's the arm?" I asked.

The youngest witch in our local coven had been bitten by a baby wyvern, and while the wound wasn't fatal, it had sapped her powers.

"It's okay." She chewed her lower lip.

"Can I see it?"

Her head dropped back limply, as though the prospect of rolling her shirtsleeve up a few inches was an extremely arduous task. But she did it.

The bite was completely scabbed over, which I hoped was a good sign. Magical injuries weren't the same as regular ones. This one in particular had resisted attempts by myself and the rest of the coven to heal it with magic.

"You might have a scar," I said.

"Scars are cool," she said nonchalantly.

"I'm glad you have such a good attitude. Now, about what you and Zoey were getting up to earlier—"

She cut me off. "Did you really get that cake from the gorgon? How did she learn to do that?"

"Yes, Chloe made it, and I guess she went to pastry school."

"How come some people have cool jobs?" She gazed up at me earnestly, all her teen swagger gone. "If people can just go to pastry school and then spend all day making fancy cakes, why does anyone ever become an undertaker?"

"That would be a good question to ask your parents," I said. Ambrosia's parents, a couple who didn't have magical abilities, ran a funeral home.

Ambrosia said, "Do you think that when you become a grown-up, you forget who you really are?"

I'd been planning to interrogate the girl about where she'd been, and how much she'd been drinking, but I was taken off guard by the depth of her questions.

"I don't think you ever forget who you are," I said. "Maybe you change a bit, but not on the inside. For example, I feel the same way I did when I was your age. Or at least I do whenever my mother's around." I glanced over quickly to make sure my dear vampire mother—my aunt's older sister—hadn't heard me. She hadn't. She was too busy telling the other party-goers about the fancy high-tea desserts her wealthy undead friends served in Venice.

"You don't count," Ambrosia said. "I was asking about other grown-ups. Regular ones." She raised her cartoonishly dark eyebrows, forming a triangle. "Boring ones."

"You got me, Ambrosia. I don't speak for the entire union of grown-ups."

Her eyes became shiny. She bit her lower lip. In a hoarse whisper, she said, "I don't ever want to forget who I am."

Just then, my daughter returned from her meeting with Bentley in the kitchen.

I looked her over. "No visible bruises," I said. "That man does a good interrogation."

Before I could ask her how it went, she handed me her phone.

It was live with a call.

I held it to my ear. "Hello?"

A familiar voice—my father's—said, "Hello, Sunshine! I bet you're happy to hear from your dear old dad. I can picture you smiling!"

"Rhys Quarry," I said. I rarely called him Dad. "Let me guess. Are you in town?"

"I am! How did you know?"

"I have my sources." Like my daughter, my father was also a shifter. His animal form was a red fox. The fox who'd been spotted at the museum that day must have been him. "Hang on a minute," I said.

Zoey was still standing there. I held the phone away and said to her, "I knew you didn't do anything bad at the museum. I hope Bentley wasn't too hard on you."

"He's just doing his job," she said neutrally.

"Was he hard on you? Did he make the scary face?"

She looked away.

Was she frightened? Had Bentley used his scary face to question my daughter? My blood started to boil. Why had I sent her in there without an adult advocate? I couldn't get anything right. I hadn't been using magic—much—but I was still screwing up.

"It doesn't matter if he was a bit intense," she said. "Someone stole something from the museum, and he's got to get it back."

"He'll have to get it back from your grandfather," I said. "What got stolen?"

Zoey gave me a blank look. "Bentley told me, but I forgot." Her face scrunched up. "It was... I don't know."

I patted her on the shoulder. "You're a bit rattled," I said. "It's perfectly understandable." I looked her in the eyes. "If something like this ever happens again, you don't have to talk to Bentley without me at your side. Okay?"

She rolled her eyes, then patted my shoulder in a mirror image of what I was doing.

"I'll be fine, Mom," she said. "I just need cake. Did Chloe really make one section pistachio with raspberry sauce?"

"As per your request," I said. "Go get some before it's all gone."

She gave me a smile to let me know she wasn't too rattled, and went over to get a plate of cake.

The party was going well.

Now I had a new goal. I had to get the museum's stolen goods back from my fair-weather father.

"I'm back," I said into the phone.

"What are you doing? Do I hear a party in progress? Never mind. It doesn't matter. Whatever it is, you need to drop everything and come out for a drink. There's someone with me you need to meet."

"Oh, goody. Let me guess. Is it another half-sibling?"

"What makes you say that?" He sounded hurt.

"Isn't that how you operate? A family in every port?"

He laughed. "It's nothing like that, Sunshine. Come and meet me for a drink! I'm at the hotel. The nice one."

"You're staying at a hotel?"

"Well, sure! I would have called you, but something told me there wouldn't be room for me at the ol' inn that I helped you purchase." He laughed at his joke before deadpanning, "What with you having burned it down."

"I didn't—" I cut myself off. "I'm at a birthday party right now. I can be there in twenty minutes. Don't go anywhere."

He laughed again. "I wouldn't dream of it. We're having a wonderful time. You can find us in the bar, by the piano."

"I'm sure I'll find you," I said. Along with whatever he stole from the museum.

CHAPTER 3

After I ended the call with my father, I finished eating my cake—priorities!—then I located my half-sister and pulled her aside.

"Our father is in town," I said.

Persephone Rose didn't look at all surprised. "He did mention something to my mother about paying us all a visit in the new year."

"He did? Are those two getting back together?"

"No way. But they do keep in touch. Does he not call your mom regularly?"

"I don't think he ever did, and definitely not after she faked her death. They're not in touch, that I know of."

She gave me a pitying look. "I'm so sorry he wasn't there for you like he was for me. I wish I'd known about you sooner, Zara."

"You've got to stop apologizing for that man. He made his choices."

Persephone nodded. "Speaking of your mother, is she still, um, seeing the zookeeper?"

"Yes, but I believe he's free to date other people. Why? Are you still interested?"

"Nope." She shook her head. "I already made that mistake once or twice." She wrinkled her nose. "Or five times. Who's counting? But not anymore. I'd like to date someone who's good for me."

"What about Chive Bacon? He's a little older, but he's sort of cute."

"Sort of cute?" She raised her eyebrows. "Are we talking about the guy who works with Mayor Paladini? The guy with the red beard and the shaved head?"

"That's the one. Why? Have you already ruled him out? Does he have some sort of red flag, like he's way too into making his own beeswax candles?"

Persephone pressed her lips together and smirked. "Oh, Zara. You don't see it, do you?"

"Don't see what?"

"Never mind," she said.

I poked her in the side. "Tell me."

"Doesn't Chive Bacon look a little bit familiar?"

"What do you mean?"

"He looks exactly like our father."

"He does not!"

"Swap Dad's hair around. Give him a beard, shave his head, and that's Chive Bacon."

"You're being ridiculous. Not everyone with red hair looks the same. You're being prejudiced about redheads."

She shrugged. "Fine. Don't believe me. But please don't try to set me up with him. I don't want to date our father."

We paused our conversation to talk to Riverflow, the yoga instructor.

She was in the process of moving people back into the living room for the maternity yoga demonstration. Everyone was full of birthday cake and snacks, which she said would make for an even more effective demo.

After Riverflow left us, Persephone said to me, "This should be interesting. I don't normally care for yoga. It's not nearly as much fun as running, but I'll give it a shot. Are you joining in?"

"Actually, I'm going to meet Rhys at the hotel for drinks. I just talked to him on the phone before I came to you."

"He called you?"

"Not exactly. Zoey tracked him down, and handed me the phone. He says he's got someone with him he wants me to meet."

"Lucky you."

"You should come with me. He's your dad, too."

"And miss out on squatting and grunting with a belly full of cake?" Her eyes twinkled. "No way. Send him my love."

"You can give it to him yourself when you bail him out of jail," I said, and I told her how Bentley, her detective partner, was currently investigating an incident at the museum involving a red fox. Persephone had the day off, so she'd been left out of the loop until now.

"So, obviously the red fox wasn't Zoey," I said in conclusion.

"Dad isn't a criminal," she said, frowning.

I had the urge to strongly disagree, but I bit my tongue. My half-sister had enjoyed a very different upbringing. Her experience of my father was not the same as mine. Her truth wasn't my truth. But there was no point in getting into a fight over it.

"I'm not saying he is," I said, which was sort of true. I'd only been implying it. Heavily. "But, just to be safe, I'll go meet him for drinks, and make sure he has a good alibi."

"I'm sure it wasn't him," Persephone said. "We aren't the only foxes around."

"Right."

I glanced around at the people who'd come to the party. They were happily catching up with each other, wishing each other a belated Happy New Year, and wishing Zinnia a happy birthday.

The crowd was mostly women. I'd invited Ethan Fung, but he hadn't been able to make it. He'd claimed he was needed at the police station. I had a feeling that wasn't the real reason. My aunt had recently informed him she was expecting his baby, and they'd been talking about co-parenting, but the nature of their relationship hadn't been ironed out. I sensed that his not coming to the party was his way of giving my aunt space.

"This party could go on for hours," I said. "Persephone, do you mind if I sneak out and put you in charge?"

"Sure," she said. "If things get out of control, I've got riot gear and tear gas in my car."

I gave her a hug, and quietly slipped out the back door so I didn't drain the energy from the party.

It was chilly outside, which made me aware of how hot it had been inside the house. Unlike my former home —rest in peace, Red Witch House—Zinnia's place didn't expand itself or add extra ventilation when it was filled with people.

I jumped into my car, Foxy Pumpkin. The old 1986 Nissan 300ZX, custom-painted orange, purred happily as I drove toward the nicest hotel in town.

My father had been the car's previous owner, and the magically-enhanced vehicle seemed happy about a reunion. At least one of us was.

Don't get me wrong.

I was happy to see my father. Our relationship had improved significantly once I'd learned that him not being in my life hadn't been his decision, but I still felt how I felt. I didn't trust him. I didn't appreciate him teaching my daughter how to pull scams. I especially didn't appreciate him getting into trouble in town while in his fox form, and dragging Zoey into his shenanigans.

I parked in the visitor parking lot of the Cerulean Lagoon Hotel and Spa.

The famous pond at the front, which was always full of black and white swans during the summer, was frozen over but still lovely.

I barely gave it a glance as I marched my way into the hotel, past the decadent winter floral arrangements, and into the bar.

I found my father leaning on the grand piano, chatting to the young woman playing light jazz.

"And here she is now," Rhys Quarry said warmly. "One of my two beautiful daughters. This is Zara. She's the older one."

The piano player smiled politely at me and continued playing. There were a couple dozen people in the lounge, socializing over drinks and nodding their heads in time to the music.

"Rhys, let that young woman do her job," I said. "She doesn't come into your workplace and... What is it you do, exactly?"

He laughed and said to the pianist, "I told you she was funny. A real wildcard. That's my Zara."

He dropped a folded bill into the musician's tip jar, and guided me over to a table by a crackling fireplace.

I noticed immediately that his wardrobe had been upgraded. My father usually wore shabby-looking suits in shades of brown. My mother had disdainfully called it the Used Car Salesman look. We both suspected he could afford nicer clothes but chose to look that way on purpose, perhaps to catch people off guard and improve his position in negotiating the various deals he was always involved with.

That Saturday, however, he looked like the sort of person who could afford a suite at the town's nicest hotel. His suit was gray, modern, and had a flattering cut. He looked downright handsome.

As I studied his face, I took note of the many ways he did *not* look like Chive Bacon. I planned to report to Persephone Rose how wrong she had been. Our father and

Chive did share the same gold-green eyes and rust-colored hair. Their eyebrows were identical, but eyebrows weren't that different from person to person. They had similar face shapes, but Chive was taller, and his nose wasn't as bulbous, plus he didn't make all those rubbery expressions my father did when he told stories. Probably because, unlike my father, he wasn't a pathological liar.

"That's a nice suit," I said. "Did you rob someone with the same measurements?" I looked around the lounge. "Is your mark here right now? What's the con? Counterfeit room keys?"

Rhys slapped his knee. "You are too funny! I'm glad Zozo called when she did. I was planning to see you tomorrow, but this is a lovely surprise." His rubbery facial features contorted into an exaggerated I-just-remembered-something expression. "Wait. Today is the fourteenth. It was someone's birthday on the twelfth. How is our dear old Ziti Noodles?"

"Aunt Zinnia is fine. She's forty-nine, and pregnant."

His eyes nearly popped out of his head. "It wasn't me," he said. "I always did have a soft spot for your aunt, but your mother would kill me."

"Nobody thinks it was you."

His rubbery face changed to an expression of deep sorrow. "Nobody?"

"Never mind about her. Do you have an alibi for today?"

"Are you offering?"

"What do you think?"

He grinned. "It doesn't hurt to ask." He leaned back and studied me. "You really think I stole that amulet from the museum, don't you?"

"Hah!" I pointed at him. "I never said it was an amulet."

The grin didn't fade. "You didn't, but your sparkly gentleman friend did."

"My sparkly gentleman friend. You mean Bentley?"

"If the fangs fit..."

"He doesn't sparkle," I said. "That's just an urban legend. Did he talk to you already?"

"He's been and gone. I gave him a few ideas about which bushes he might like to whack with a stick. That should keep him busy for a while."

My heart sank. I'd been so certain that my father had committed the museum heist. I'd been so ready to give him heck, but apparently Bentley had already cleared him as a suspect. Now what?

A young man in a hotel staff uniform came by with a bottle of champagne and three glasses.

My father paid, giving the young man a generous tip. Seeing him hand off the folded bill reminded me of the annual outings he'd taken me on when I was a child. He was always paying off security guards to let us into places we shouldn't have been.

His visits were always a whirlwind of excitement. Then, after a full day of showing me the secret side of the world, he would disappear from my life for another year. Of all the lives I imagined him having outside of our special day, I never would have guessed he led a normal, domestic life raising my half-sister.

"Penny for your thoughts," he said.

"No, thanks," I said. "What do you know about this amulet that got stolen?"

"Nothing at all." He held both hands out wide. "Go ahead and spell me with your witcher-i-doo. Let's try that confession-torture one. You have my full consent."

"No, thanks," I said again. I didn't want to make the effort. Plus I would need a couple more witches to cast the spell.

"Come on. Don't you want to take a shot at your old man? Show him how tough you are? Or is that just something sons need to do?"

If we were going to talk about parenting, I would need a drink.

I grabbed the champagne, filled two of the three glasses, and picked up mine.

He raised his and said, "A toast to my beautiful daughter. The apple of my eye."

I clinked my glass to his.

As I was taking a sip, he said, "When am I going to walk you down the aisle?"

I nearly choked on my champagne. "How long did you and Bentley talk today?"

"Long enough."

"He didn't propose to me."

"That's not what he thinks."

"Dad, he was getting the mail, and he was spitballing ideas about where I might live. He didn't propose."

"If you say so."

"Seriously, how long did you two talk?"

"He left right before you arrived. You drive too slow. How's my Foxy Pumpkin?"

"Not as fast as a vampire, apparently."

He finished his champagne.

I gestured to the empty glass. "It's too bad your mystery friend ran off before I got here."

"Oh, she's not far away." He nodded toward a corner, where a small crowd of six or seven people had gathered since my arrival. At the center of the group was a dark-haired woman. She was writing on something. I watched for a minute. She was signing her autograph on hotel menus.

"Who is she?" I asked.

"She's famous," he said.

"I gathered that."

"She's an actress."

"Do you want me to guess? It might help if you narrow it down."

"She's the reason your sparkly gentleman friend didn't stick around long to socialize."

"Bentley isn't scared of anyone."

26

"No, but a man would be wise to keep a safe distance from his ex wife."

I did a double take as the hints fell together.

The woman signing autographs for the other hotel guests was the famous actress who played Mahrissa, daughter of Mahra—the fictional version, not the ancient goddess—on the Wicked Wives reboot.

She was gorgeous, talented, and the ex-wife of Theodore Bentley.

My Bentley.

Now she was here. In my town. Hanging out with... my father?

CHAPTER 4

Larissa Lang was even more beautiful in person than she appeared to be on television. She was also much smaller and thinner than I would have expected. Her wrists were so delicate, they mirrored the stems of the champagne glasses we were drinking from.

The famous actress was a Chinese-Canadian woman who'd gotten her start in Hollywood playing a teenager on the TV comedy-drama series Wicked Wives. I'd been a huge fan of both her and the show as a teenager. She was currently a star of the rebooted version, playing the grown-up version of her original character.

Equally importantly, Larissa Lang was also the ex-wife of my current boyfriend.

Some women might have felt threatened by such a remarkable ex, but I'd always been a fan. Whenever she'd appeared on the television when Bentley was in the room, I'd congratulated him. That made him uncomfortable, which only made it funnier for me. During a recent Christmas episode, her character had appeared on-screen in lingerie. I had immediately offered him a high five. He had disappeared to the kitchen to look for imaginary rice pudding.

"It's so nice to meet you," I said to the woman.

She was my age, but she looked a lot younger.

I continued gushing. "I'm a fan from way back, right from the original series. I was watching the crossover episode where you went on a date with a vampire from *One Vamp to Love* when I went into labor with my daughter. You're the reason she was born in a taxi."

The actress gave me an amused look. Her dark-brown eyes turned up at the corners, giving her that signature Larissa Lang sleepy-sexy look that translated beautifully at any angle, in any lighting. She had a smattering of freckles across the bridge of her nose.

"It's always wonderful to meet a fan," she said.

I shook her hand with my normal handshake. She winced, as though I had strained her delicate, champagne-stem wrists.

My father said, "Now, if you ladies will excuse me, I need to use the little boys' room." He gestured for Larissa to take his seat by the fireplace, directly across from me.

Larissa lowered herself into the chair cautiously, with multiple small adjustments, reminding me of my cat settling in a patch of sunshine.

"Your father is a charming man," she said.

I stared at her. What would happen next?

She stared back, a furrow starting to form between her two famous black eyebrows.

"I said, your father is a charming man," she said a bit louder.

"Oh!" I held my fingers to my throat self-consciously. "This is live. You're not on my television screen. I can talk to you, and you'll hear me."

She gave me a charming, friendly smile. "You really *are* a fan."

"You sound surprised. Am I not your usual demographic?"

She shrugged one tiny, delicate shoulder. "People always *say* they're fans, but then they ask me what it's like to work with Dalton Deangelo." She wrinkled her nose. "They mix me up with Laurie Lee, who's on the *other* supernaturals show."

"That must be frustrating."

"I suppose I could be in worse company. She's a gorgeous woman."

"Right," I said.

I felt a rivulet of sweat trickle down the side of my torso, under my sweater. It was warm by the fire, and meeting Larissa had triggered a nervous sweat.

"So," I said, rolling my shoulders back to relax, "how do you and Rhys know each other?"

"My family secured him as an advisor." She batted her thick, black eyelashes. She had an inhuman number of eyelashes.

"He's your advisor," I said, though that alone didn't explain everything. My father worked as a matchmaker. Marriage, business, or both. "Are you looking for a new talent agent?"

"Not exactly." She leaned forward, so the side of her perfectly-faceted face was prettily illuminated by the crackling fireplace. "He's helping me locate an appropriate romantic partner. My people feel it's time for me to remarry, start a family. Your father is going to help."

"Careful with that," I said. "That's how *I* got made. My mother's family hired him to find her a mate, but then there was a fancy hotel room, lots of wine, and..." I looked down at the champagne glass in my hand. We were in the lounge of a fancy hotel. Oh, no. What was I saying?

"Your father is not my taste," Larissa said. "No offense."

"None taken." I laughed awkwardly and poured us champagne from the bottle. "What exactly is your taste?"

She fixed me with an enigmatic smile. "I think you know my taste," she said. "*Zara.*"

She spoke my name like an incantation. I felt something caress my cheek. Like a rose petal being dragged across my skin. Yet nothing was there. Magic!

"So, you know that I'm dating your ex-husband," I said. "And I take it he represents your taste in men. Is that what you're getting at?"

She smiled wider.

I felt the petal-soft stroke on my other cheek.

The first caress might have been my imagination, but the second one was not. She was using magic on me. But what kind? Was she a witch? A mage? My father had only introduced us by name—not officially, with powers.

I lifted my chin and asked, "What are you?"

She raised her eyebrows and feigned ignorance.

Another trickle of sweat ran down my side. I wasn't just nervous about meeting one of my heroes. My witch senses were telling me I was in the presence of a powerful being. So powerful, in fact, that she was enjoying a game at my expense.

I was reminded again of Boa, and that time she trapped a mouse underneath the refrigerator. She had terrorized the poor thing until I caught the mouse and re-homed it elsewhere.

I restated my question. "What powers do you have?"

She dropped the feigned ignorance and sighed, as though I'd ruined all her fun.

"I'll find out sooner or later," I said, no longer playing the adoring fangirl.

This interaction had certainly done a one-eighty. I'd started off wanting to get her autograph, and now I wanted to grab her hair and yank it until she told me all her secrets.

She wasn't spilling anything yet.

"If you don't want to say, that's fine, but I'll find out," I growled. "And here's another thing you should know: My father and I have our differences, but he is family, and I will protect him at any cost."

She didn't even flinch. "Oh, you don't have to worry about little ol' me," she said. "I'm not nearly as powerful as you, Zara Riddle, the big, bad witch." She blinked once. "I hear you kill people now. What does it feel like? To take an innocent life?"

Just then, my father returned, muttering about the powerful hand dryers in the bathroom. What was it about men needing to comment on hand dryers?

I turned to him and said, "Rhys, you need to keep a short leash on your new client. The minute you walked away, she started rubbing invisible rose petals on my cheeks, and asking me about killing people."

He gave me a rubbery, delighted grin. "I'm glad you two broke the ice!"

Larissa let out a laugh and grabbed his arm. "She's as delightful as you are, Reese's Pieces." She gave me the same look Boa gave me whenever she took food from my plate. "That's my fun little name for your father. Reese's Pieces. He calls me Lulu. Isn't it fun to give each other special names?"

I got up from my chair. "It was certainly interesting to meet you, Ms. Lang. I hope you enjoy your stay in Wisteria. Your *very short* stay."

My father moved to block my exit. "You can't leave already. Stay for dinner. My treat. It's all being charged to my client, and she's got deep pockets."

"You heard him," Larissa said, leaning back in her chair and crossing her small yet incredibly photogenic legs. "Stay for dinner, Zara. Stay overnight if you'd like. You can bunk with me. I've got two king-sized beds in my room."

My father tilted his head at me. "Isn't she the best client, this girl? It's going to be a bittersweet day when I get her remarried and off my roster. How about it? How'd you like to stay overnight here at the hotel, in the lap of luxury, and take a break from wherever it is you've been

ANGELA PEPPER

couch surfing? We can all put on our pajamas and have a slumber party. We can order room service, and—"

I cut him off with, "And braid each other's hair?"

He gave me a rubbery, exaggerated frown. "You're being awfully rude in front of my client. I'm beginning to regret inviting you here to meet Ms. Lang."

"Why *did* you invite me here? She's my boyfriend's ex-wife. How did you think this was supposed to go?"

He shrugged. "I thought you might appreciate getting to know your new neighbor."

"My new neighbor?" I looked down at Larissa. The light from the fireplace was flickering across her face, making her high cheekbones appear sharper than ever.

She said, "Didn't your father mention the good news? I've purchased a home in your charming town. I saw it in the background of a news story, and I fell in love with the place. What can I say? I've got a thing for fixer-uppers."

"You bought the Moore house?" The home had been extensively renovated by Chet Moore. It had some flaws, but it was no fixer-upper.

"The seller's last name was Moore, yes. It's next door to the property you own. The one that your generous father helped you buy."

My father said to me, "When you rebuild your house, the two of you will be neighbors."

"I'm not rebuilding," I said. "The insurance... the town engineers..." *The new neighbor.*

He carried on. "Of course you'll rebuild. You have to. Won't it be fun to live next door to a famous actress? Who knows. You might end up becoming best friends."

I shook my head at him. "For a so-called matchmaker, you can't see what's under your own nose, can you?"

He smacked his forehead. "Where are my manners? You're right, Zara. This mild tension I'm currently picking up on must be a result of my inadequate introductions." He turned to Larissa, who was still seated, and said, "Ms. Lang, this is my daughter, who is a witch.

34

As you both know, I'm a fox shifter. No secondary powers that I know of." He turned to me and said, "Ms. Lang is a succubus."

A succubus? I was both surprised and not surprised.

"She's a what-now?"

Larissa got to her feet. She put one tiny hand on my father's shoulder, and moved him out of the way like he was on roller skates.

"The term succubus has so many negative connotations," she said, taking his place in front of me. Uncomfortably close to me. "Please, think of me as more of a *romance mage*."

"You're a demon," I said.

"Not much more than you," she said. "Aren't we all just a little bit demon?" She tilted her head to the side and gazed up at me with the innocence of a well-meaning child. She was a remarkable actress. "Zara, where exactly did you think our powers came from?"

"Oh, no," I said, taking a step back. "I'm a good witch. I'm a good person. I'm not demonic."

"If your powers are so pure and good, why aren't you using them? You haven't done a single magical thing since you arrived here, with your hair frizzy and a piece of pink fondant icing stuck to your sleeve. You haven't even dried the sweat that's turning the armpits of your sweater dark."

"Never mind about my armpits."

"Do you not feel comfortable with your powers, Zara?"

She was trying to trap me. I didn't always know a trap when I encountered it, but this one had giant traffic cones and yellow reflective safety tape all around it.

I pressed my lips together, channeling my aunt and her ability to not say whatever popped into her head. Larissa could bait me all she wanted. I wasn't going to jump into this particular pit.

My father casually took a seat on the ledge in front of the fireplace, and started reading a menu.

Without looking up, he said, "They serve calamari. I haven't had calamari in ages. Zara, are you sure you won't stay for dinner?"

"Stay for dinner," Larissa said, staring deeply into my eyes. "Let's get to know each other."

I snapped my fingers between our faces. It was the smallest spell, meant to disrupt the mind control Larissa Lang was obviously trying to use on me.

The snap didn't do anything.

With every second I stared into her deep-brown eyes, I could feel myself being pulled under.

No wonder she was such a compelling actress. Her powers ran deep.

Something in her was connecting to something primal in me—something that wanted to be tapped into. I felt a dormant longing flickering to life. A desire. It felt like the slippery edges of a too-good dream that fades away in the morning, along with some heartbreakingly wonderful emotion that has no name in the English language.

I jerked my head to the side until I broke eye contact. Once free of her sexy tractor beams, I kept my gaze on the floor.

"I've got to get back to the party," I said. The image of Alice in Wonderland flashed in my mind's eye. Alice, trying to return to the picnic from which she'd disappeared down the rabbit hole.

"Are you sure?" Larissa's voice was as intoxicating as her gaze. "Back to what party?"

I knew there was a party in progress elsewhere, but I couldn't, for the life of me, remember whose it was.

Larissa purred, "Is there anywhere you'd rather be than right here, with me? I know I come on strong at first, but once you get to know me, we'll be wonderful friends. We have so much in common, Zara. Don't you want to be friends?"

I did. In the heat of that moment, I really did.

Why wouldn't I stay and get to know Larissa?

I'd always been a huge fan of her acting. I'd watched her on television since we were both teenagers. We'd practically grown up together.

What was I so worried about? She wasn't in town to take Bentley back. If she'd wanted him that bad, she wouldn't have let him go in the first place. And she wouldn't have hired my father to find her a new mate.

Why was I being such an OCW?

"Okay," I said, caving into the sweet relief of saying yes. "I guess I could stay for one—"

Across the lounge, a woman who'd been talking loudly and drunkenly got brazen enough to break through my haze. "That's Larissa Lang!" The drunk woman whistled loudly, then yelled, "Hey! Larissa! Come have a drink with us!"

The energy in my vicinity changed polarity.

As the attraction flipped to its opposite feeling, I felt a sudden revulsion. Pardon the imagery, but there's no other way to make it quite as clear. The chocolate icing turned to cat poop.

I acted quickly and decisively.

I muttered a quick goodbye to my father, avoiding eye contact with his succubus client, and made my escape.

With my eyes on the toes of my boots, I marched out past the drunk woman who had provided the distraction, through the marble lobby with the lavish bouquets, and outside to the bracing winter air.

I didn't dare look up until I was inside my car, with the engine running, needing to see the road in front of me.

CHAPTER 5

Later That Night

I couldn't sleep.

Between the surprise party and meeting Larissa Lang, the succubus, it had been an eventful Saturday.

Understandably, I was too wound up to settle down.

Perhaps the room itself was also contributing to my insomnia. My aunt's guest room had pansy-print wallpaper, sunflower curtains, and rosebud bed linens. In dim light, all those splotches of pattern took on a life of their own, playing tricks on my eyes, making it seem like the walls were alive.

The walls weren't alive, though. At least not like the walls of my former home. My aunt's house did have a few tricks, such as a hidden bookcase behind her regular bookcase, where she kept her magical books, and a secret potion cupboard in the kitchen, plus whatever was going on with the back of her fridge, but the home didn't reconfigure its rooms or move walls. It didn't have a mind of its own. Just way, way too much pattern.

I made a mental note that I would pick up plain sheets soon to replace the ones on the guest bunk beds. I could take them with me when I found a new place to live, which would happen as soon as the insurance company's funds came through.

I rolled over, and my thoughts shifted away from sheets and back to Larissa Lang. I'd been trying not to think about her, but my brain wasn't done with her yet.

I couldn't stop picturing her as she seduced anyone she wanted, including my Bentley. What if she did want him back? He hadn't been a vampire when they'd divorced. He had changed. Was she, like most people, naturally drawn to a man with powers that he didn't abuse?

Another hour passed, and sleep still wouldn't come.

The walls and curtains continued to annoy me.

I kicked and squirmed through more unpleasant exhaustion and worrying thoughts.

I wished the flowers and vines on the wallpaper would come to life and smother me. I would gladly accept my fate, and the relief it would bring. Death by florals. Why not?

I was into my third hour of staring at the wooden slats of the bunk above me to avoid the splotchy flowers all around when my daughter said, "Can't sleep, huh?"

"Not really. Why are you still awake?"

"I've been drifting in and out, but you keep waking me up with your thoughts."

"Very funny," I said. "You can't hear my thoughts."

"I can't?"

"You're not like Margaret Mills. Or are you? Has something happened? Is it the genie powers kicking in?"

My daughter swung her legs over the side of her bunk, and descended the ladder.

With her face in the shadows, and her body backlit by the hallway's night light, my daughter looked bigger than I remembered. She wasn't quite seventeen, but she had hit a growth spurt recently. She had also filled out in the hips and bust, which had led to more of the boys at her high school showing interest in her—not that she was interested in any of them—according to her, anyway. She did keep some things from me. I'd heard her giggle with Ambrosia about a boy named Andy, or maybe Adam.

"Mom, I don't have any genie powers that I haven't told you about. I still don't know what happened that night in the pit when I thought poor Xavier was dead."

"I know what happened. You pooled your half-genie powers into your stupid mom so she didn't get charged with murder."

"I don't think that's what happened." She sleepily rubbed her eyes. "I've been doing some reading. It's possible for magic to float around in the environment, like the charge from a storm. It can shoot through whoever's around, like a lightning flash. I think what you saw was Mr. Caine's powers, traveling through me."

"Hmm. If you say so. But tell me this: If you don't have genie powers, then how come my thoughts are keeping you up?"

"It's not *exactly* your thoughts. You keep sighing. Plus I can hear your mouth. I know you're doing that thing where you argue with imaginary people inside your head. Every time your mouth opens so you can drive home your imaginary points, you make a *tsk* sound." She flicked on the room's overhead light, temporarily blinding me.

Zoey asked, "Who are you arguing with, anyway? I haven't heard you sigh that much since you had Chessa's memories, when you were lovesick over Mr. Moore."

"Was I really sighing that much?"

"You were. Are you worried about whatever happened at the museum?"

"No," I said. "Actually, I forgot all about that. It's Larissa Lang. I keep fighting with her inside my head."

"You need to stop. It's not doing you any good to lie there in the dark, sighing and making faces."

"But I have to prepare myself, mentally and emotionally. She *is* a succubus. Sooner or later, we will have to do battle. Obviously she is my new nemesis. It kinda has a ring to it. My nemesis, the succubus."

I didn't have to explain about the actress and her "romance mage" powers. Zoey knew all about her grandfather's new client, and the woman's abilities. I had told her everything a couple of hours earlier, when we'd first gone to bed and shut off the lights.

We'd talked, and sorted it all out, along with a reasonable solution.

Zoey and I were both going to avoid the woman until she went away. Simple!

Larissa did own a house in Wisteria, which meant she had a tie to the community, but she'd leave eventually to return to work on the set of her show. Maybe she would get distracted and not bother coming back. Celebrities could be flaky, buying houses and then selling them within a year when their whims changed.

"She may be a succubus, but you're a witch," Zoey said. "You're way more powerful. You can do almost anything. She can only do one thing. Attract people."

"I know, but she's really, really good at it."

"So?"

"All I can do is a few cheap tricks, and repel people."

"That's not true." She rubbed her eyes and yawned. "Do you want to raid Auntie Z's fridge and talk about it some more? There's lots of potato salad leftover from the party."

"Yes to potato salad, but no to your company." I climbed out of my lower bunk and pointed to the upper one. "You go back to bed, young lady. You need to get some sleep."

She rubbed her nose. "It's not a school night. I can stay up. Really." She yawned again.

"I've bugged you enough with my problems for one day. You're the kid, and I'm the mom. It's not your job to be my therapist." I ruffled her hair. "Even though you're excellent at it."

She shuffled back to the bunk bed and climbed up.

I followed halfway up, helped her with the blankets, and tucked her in like she was a little girl. I kissed her goodnight, switched off the light, and left the room.

I tiptoed past the other two closed doors, where my mother was sleeping in her room, a converted study, and my aunt's regular room, where Zinnia was snoring.

I went downstairs and straight to the kitchen. Someone else had beaten me there. The refrigerator was open a crack, emitting eerie light that filled the room. Nobody was in the room. Not even the ghost of Minerva Pinkman, who'd also taken up residence at my aunt's.

I opened the fridge door, and was surprised to find a juvenile wyvern sitting in the bowl of potato salad, looking very pleased with himself as he smashed boiled egg and potato into his small mouth.

"RJ, you're being very naughty," I said. We called him RJ, short for Ribbons Junior.

He hadn't yet learned how to talk to me telepathically or any other way, so he didn't respond.

"Get your scaley little hiney out of that potato salad," I said.

He hissed at me, spraying my bare feet with bits of food.

"You're making a huge mess."

He coughed more chunks in my direction.

"Where is your father? Who's looking after you?"

RJ hunkered down, burying himself deeper in the potato salad.

"Okay, you can stay there, but don't freak out. I'm putting my hand inside the fridge. I'm slowly reaching for the leftover birthday cake. Don't you dare bite me, RJ. I'm not taking your food. You can have all the potato salad. I don't want anything you've been sitting on."

He hissed at me in warning, watching with big, black eyes as I reached past him.

I moved slowly and deliberately. The juvenile monster was capable of leaving nasty bites that wouldn't heal magically. Ambrosia Abernathy still didn't have all her powers back. I'd hate to get bitten and have the same thing happen to me.

And yet, I must have been in desperate need of cake, because I was taking my chances by reaching past him.

"Easy now," I said. "There's plenty of food for everyone."

I got the cake out, sighed with relief, and settled at the kitchen table to eat my prize.

It was good cake, well worth the risk.

This was the first time I'd gotten a taste of more than an icing sample. I'd been so rattled by my encounter with my boyfriend's ex that I hadn't been able to eat anything when I'd returned to my aunt's house, even though the party had still been in progress.

A breeze rustled through my hair. That was odd. All the windows were closed.

Ribbons flew over my head silently, and landed on the back of the chair across from me.

He was more careful around my aunt's furnishings than he had ever been around mine. He gripped the wood just enough to perch, without gouging into it with his sharp talons.

In a weary version of his telepathic voice, he spoke directly into my mind.

"Good evening, Zed."

His voice had a vague, European accent—a blend of television Draculas, wealthy aristocrats, and Italian crime bosses. Sometimes I called him Count Chocula. We had a lot of funny nicknames for each other.

"What's new with you, Ribbons?" I feigned ignorance. "Are you looking for something? Or someone?"

"I have not lost my son, but I do not know where he is."

"He's in the fridge, in the potato salad. I left the door open a crack so he didn't panic and soil everything."

The adult wyvern, who was barely bigger than an owl, with his seven-inch torso, leaned back, peered into the fridge, then turned back to me, shaking his seahorse-like head.

"I do not enjoy being a parent, Zed. I would prefer to send him elsewhere for raising."

"Private boarding school costs a lot of money," I said.

He snorted, emitting a sulfur smell, like a struck match.

I added, "Plus I'm not sure they take your kind."

"Then I shall abandon him. He can stay here, and I will go somewhere very far away. You will not know where I am."

He blew impressive ribbons of non-burning fire from his nostrils.

I shrugged and ate another forkful of cake. "I guess running away is always an option. Or, in your case, flying away."

"Do not try to stop me, Zed."

"I wouldn't dream of it."

"I shall eviscerate any who stand in my way. I shall gladly gorge on their entrails."

"Pack light. You'll get farther."

"You mock me, Zed. You have become too confident in my affection for you, vile witch! I shall make you regret every instance you have denied me the respect I deserve!"

I pushed the platter of cake his way. "Try the lemon chiffon with strawberry filling."

He stretched out his wings to full width and puffed up his chest. "You will not appease me with such triflings as cake! Cower before me, puny human!"

"I'm starting to see where RJ gets his bad behavior. Have you considered modeling better manners for his benefit?"

"What?" He kept his wings spread and licked his long tongue over his eyeballs, all the better to continue giving me stink eye.

"I said, *I'm starting to see where RJ gets his bad behavior.*"

More eyeball licking. The wingspan drooped.

I went on. "It's one thing to tell your offspring to behave. It's another thing to actually model the behavior for them. Sort of a *do as I do* thing, as opposed to *do what I say*. Zoey might not have become such an avid student if she hadn't seen me studying and doing homework most of her life, when I was busy getting my degrees."

He blew more ribbons of fire while fiercely licking his eyeballs.

"Come on, Leather Chaps," I said. "Haven't you ever heard the saying, *monkey see, monkey do*? That's us. We're all monkeys, on some level. Even wyverns."

The mythical beast slowly folded his wings at his sides.

"Your words have logic, Zed. What magic is this?"

"It's the wisdom of personal experience." I pointed to the cake I'd pushed his way. "Are you going to eat that, or do I need to risk my hand putting it back in the fridge next to your hellspawn?"

"I will eat," he said.

He daintily picked up a fork, using the hand-like claw attached to his wing, and began eating.

"Wow," I said. "Using a fork and everything. This is some Grade A parental modeling."

"Do not push me, Zed." He ate a few bites, throwing off crumbs like crazy, due to his pointy teeth being better suited to shredding than to chewing.

After a moment, he changed the scaly furrows on his face to make his small, beady eyes appear larger and cuter.

Batting his eyelids, he asked, "Is there milk?"

I got the milk from the fridge—very carefully—and we shared what was left of the carton as we finished the cake.

RJ finally emerged from the refrigerator. He shook himself like a wet dog, blasting the kitchen with bits of potato salad, then parked himself in the kitchen sink, and began squawking.

I asked Ribbons, "Now what does he want?"

"He wants to take a bubble bath in your square cauldron," Ribbons said.

"They're called sinks, and you know it."

"He bathes in your square cauldron," Ribbons said, persisting with his archaic terminology. "It is one of his night time rituals. The bubbles and warm water prepare him for restful slumber."

"That sounds adorable."

"It is not."

"Can I help?"

"I will not prevent you."

"Is he going to bite me?"

"He has fed."

"Good enough." I started pouring water, filling the sink for RJ's bath.

While we bathed the hatchling, I told Ribbons about Larissa Lang, and my concerns. Did she want something from me? And was that *something* a tall, handsome vampire detective?

Ribbons said, in his own words, that if a succubus had wanted my boyfriend, she would have gotten him already, and I wouldn't be up in the middle of the night, moaning about my melodrama to disinterested creatures whose intellect vastly exceeded mine.

"That's what Zoey said. And my aunt. And my mother. Thanks for the fourth opinion."

Ribbons sent a telepathic wave of static—his expression of displeasure at being the fourth in line for anything—through my mind.

Meanwhile, our bathing boy's eyes were getting sleepy.

We drained the water from the sink, and I dabbed RJ dry with a clean tea towel. I was reminded of the days when I'd bathed my own offspring in a kitchen sink.

RJ climbed into the crook of my arm, snuggled up, and fell asleep.

Ribbons looked up at me and said, "You have been chosen as the new guardian. He is yours. Starting tonight. You have my blessing, Zed."

"Oh, Ribbons. He's not so bad, is he?" I gazed down at RJ's sleeping face, which was, in slumber, about as angelic as a mythical reptilian creature's face could be.

"I am old, Zed. Very old. I grow older each minute."

"Now you sound like my aunt."

"Which one is she?" Ribbons knew who everyone was, but he liked to pretend things like names or relationships between humans were beneath his notice. Come to think of it, my mother did the same thing. No wonder those two got along.

"My aunt is the one who owns this house you're living in, rent-free. That was her potato salad that your hatchling made a mess of."

"Now that we are discussing salad, I advise that you discard what remains. The little one did more than eat in the bowl."

"I thought you had him litter trained."

Ribbons went radio silent.

I couldn't take care of the salad without disturbing the sleeping babe in my arms, so I used my magic—a little telekinesis wouldn't kill anyone—to dump the bowl's contents into the compost bucket. I used more magic to get the bowl washed and the glass shelves cleaned. My aunt's fridge had some self-cleaning capabilities, but it hadn't been charmed to deal with baby wyvern messes.

For the next hour, Ribbons and I sat at the kitchen table, where I gently rocked the baby while we talked about parenting skills. I explained that the secret was to never think of the future, or to imagine how many messes were waiting, one after another, but to simply deal with the current mess. Ideally, you would trick yourself into believing the current mess could be the final one, and that someday you'd miss the hard times and look back on them wistfully.

I heard a door open upstairs, my aunt shuffling to the washroom, and then back to bed. Her pregnancy wasn't very far along yet, but it was already affecting her bladder. I had been so young when I'd had Zoey that it hadn't affected me as much. I'd slept through the night right up until the end.

Eventually, RJ stirred in my arms. He woke up enough to be transferred to his father. RJ was able to nestle perfectly on Ribbons' shoulders, between the wings.

"Time to sleep," the ancient wyvern said. "Thank you, Zed."

I tried not to reveal my shock at being sincerely thanked by Ribbons.

"Any time," I said.

"In return for your loyalty, I will kill the succubus who plagues you. It will be messy, but I understand the point of your speech about dealing with each mess in the present time so that you can one day look back on the bloodshed fondly."

"That's not what my speech was about."

"I will kill the succubus you call Larissa Lang. I will do that for you, Zed."

"Please don't kill anyone on my account. I do appreciate the offer, but I'll deal with this my usual way. By which I mean I'll ignore it until it blows up in my face, then I'll overreact and make everything much, much worse, and then I'll have my friends or family bail me out."

"That is what allies are for," Ribbons said, nodding.

"Maybe having Larissa show up in town is a good thing. It's pushing things forward. Bentley has been hinting about us making things official, plus I have to find a permanent place to live. You know what? Maybe it's the illusion of clarity that comes in the wee hours of the morning, but I think you've helped me figure out my priorities. I'm going to accept Bentley's marriage proposal."

"Which one is he?"

Ignoring the dumb question, I said, "Then we can move into a new place together. A new home for the three of us. Me, Bentley, and Zoey."

Ribbons gave me a hurt look.

"The five of us," I said. "Plus two pets and a ghost. The whole family. And my mom, probably. We're going to need a pretty big place."

"I agree to this proposal, Zed."

"Great. Now I just have to run it by Bentley."

Ribbons gave me a nod goodbye, then flew off to settle in his secret sleeping spot for the rest of the night. I'd probably see him again around noon. Or earlier, if someone opened a bottle of maple syrup.

I returned to the spare bedroom, curled up under the covers, and started thinking about wedding dresses.

I couldn't wait to see the look on Bentley's face when I told him I would be accepting his mailbox-adjacent proposal.

CHAPTER 6

Sunday, January 13th

(The Next Day)

It was noon when I finally rolled out of my bunk bed.

I'd had a busy night of not-sleeping, between fretting over Larissa and hanging out with the wyverns, but I had to get up or the weekend would be gone.

I poured my first coffee of the day into the navy-blue travel mug that was one of my precious few personal possessions. The insulated mug was decorated with Mountain Joe, a cartoon man with two smoking pistols. He was similar to the Looney Tunes' Yosemite Sam, but Joe had a thin, curly black mustache instead of a red bushy one.

I'd been fond of the mug ever since it had helped save my life a while back. When my house exploded, I'd assumed it was gone, along with nearly everything else I'd owned. The next day, when I found the silly mug inside my car—a lone survivor of the unnatural disaster— I'd nearly wept.

Now I held it close to my heart, silently thanking the inanimate object for its service. It would be my companion for what promised to be a momentous day.

Bentley and I had exchanged a couple of text messages that morning to arrange to see each other. He'd sounded grumpy in the messages, but that wasn't unusual. He wasn't big on texting.

He didn't know that today was going to be his lucky day.

After sleeping an hour or two on the idea, I had become even more certain in my decision. Today, I was going to accept his casual marriage proposal. Why not? It wasn't like I was going to find anyone better. Today was going to be a memorable day for both of us.

I planned to let my acceptance slip out casually during our outing, probably while we were discussing the thread count of sheets, or the best dimensions for bath towels.

I'd say something romantic about picking the color scheme for our new place, emphasis on *our*. Then he'd get flustered and emotional, right in the middle of a big box store. It would be perfect.

I finished grabbing my things, checked the time, and ran outside to the car I knew would be waiting. Bentley was always punctual.

I slipped into the warm passenger seat and said, "We're going to have so much fun today."

Bentley kept a straight face. "We sure are. I can't wait to drive up the coast and go shopping at Bed, Bath and Beyond."

"You don't have to be quite so sarcastic." I buckled my seat belt.

"I'm not being sarcastic," he said.

"Then you're lying. I know there's no way you're looking forward to spending your Sunday afternoon shopping for linens at a big outlet mall."

"I meant the driving part," he said. "I love road trips."

"Good enough."

He leaned over for a kiss, but paused and sniffed my coffee. He made a face.

"That smells like poison," he said, pulling away without his kiss.

I sniffed the cup. "In large enough doses, it definitely is poison," I said. "All the good stuff is."

"You shouldn't drink poison."

"It's just coffee. It's a new blend Maisy Nix made, thanks to her champion coffee taster, Humphrey."

"Is she still...?"

"Unrepentantly so," I replied.

"Good ol' Maisy," he said with a chuckle.

"Sorry you missed your chance with her when I took you off the market. I bet dating Maisy would have been interesting."

I watched him closely for a reaction. Maisy Nix wasn't a succubus, like Bentley's ex-wife, but she did act like one. Was that Bentley's type?

"No dull moments," he said casually.

Without further comment, he put the car in gear. We pulled away from my aunt's house.

Was he ever going to bring up the fact that his ex was in town? Or inform me about *what* she was? Having an ex-wife who's a succubus was something the new girlfriend ought to be informed about.

Playfully, I said, "Are you implying there are dull moments with me? Or that you'd rather be with someone who runs a little hotter, like Maisy?"

"Not at all." He kept his eyes on the road and his expression neutral. "How was Zinnia's surprise party?"

"Why are you asking me? You were there."

"I was only in the kitchen for a few minutes." He shot me a quick look. "Somebody's in a bad mood."

"Not me. I'm in a great mood."

He lifted his chin and kept his eyes on the road.

"Maybe *you're* the one who's in a bad mood," I said. "And you're projecting onto me."

"You may be right."

"Don't say that. That's what people say when they don't mean it at all. *You may be right* directly translates to *oh, shut up*."

"You may be right." He almost smiled.

"Oh, shut up."

The silence between us extended for several minutes. Bentley had a way of giving me the last word in a conversation at the exact right point where I'd feel bad about whatever I'd just said.

"Maybe I am a little grumpy," I admitted. "I didn't sleep well last night."

"I know."

"You know? How do you know? Did you turn into a bat and flap around my window, spying on me like a Peeping Batboy?" Bentley didn't have the ability to turn into a bat—vampires didn't do that—but it was an ongoing joke.

"You have bags under your eyes," he said.

"I do not! How dare you!"

He turned onto a busy street, heading toward the highway.

"I was up late with the baby," I said, answering the question he hadn't asked. "The wyvern baby. We're still calling him RJ. I gave him a bath in the kitchen sink. Ribbons wouldn't say *sink*. He kept calling it a *square cauldron*."

Bentley didn't say anything.

"No comment? I gave a baby wyvern a bath, and you're not even the least bit curious?"

"I have enough on my mind as it is."

"You mean with work?"

He scowled. Either his mood was changing rapidly, or he'd been more grumpy than I'd thought he was based on his short text messages.

"Hey," I said. "I asked you a question. Is it something from work that's on your mind?"

"You didn't have to give me such a hard time about talking to Zoey yesterday. You could have made it easier for me."

Oh, he was in a bad mood. And unjustly so.

"I beg your pardon? She's a teenager. She should have had a lawyer present. You're lucky I let you talk to her at all."

"I am?"

"You know what I mean."

"I'm not sure I do. What do you mean?"

"Just that you shouldn't be interrogating a minor, alone, over some nonsense at the museum."

"I see." He rubbed his chin. "That's how it's going to be with Zoey. I can't even talk to her without getting flack from you."

I stared at the side of his face. What did he want from me? An apology? How was I suddenly a bad person just for being a good mother and looking after my own child?

He cleared his throat. "Mind if I take a sip of that coffee? I haven't slept in a few days."

"You haven't slept in a few days? Why not?"

He didn't answer.

I handed him the coffee. He took a tentative sip, then another.

"That's good," he said, smacking his lips.

"I would have brought an extra cup for you if I'd known you were back to drinking coffee. Let's stop at Dreamland. I'll buy you a full one of your own."

"We can share. Mountain Joe is a big mug. We'll get a refill when we hit the outlet mall."

"Just stop at Dreamland. It will be quick. I'll zip in and out. It's on the way."

"It's three left turns from here. We're practically on the highway."

"Since when are you afraid of making a few left turns? You're being such a granny. Put on your flashing lights and siren. Drive over the sidewalks if you want."

He muttered something under his breath.

He turned left at the next light, waiting much longer than necessary.

He repeated the process two more times.

I managed to keep my mouth shut, thus winning the battle of the wills.

He parked on the street.

I ran into Dreamland on my own, and ordered two fresh cups of coffee from a handsome man. He was Humphrey, but I'd barely recognized him in regular clothes and an apron.

"Here ya go, Toots," the komodo-human-shifter said as he put the two steaming cups on the counter.

"*Toots? Here ya go?* Humphrey, has someone uploaded a new operating system into that noggin of yours?"

"I am learning casual speech," he said, grinning. "Toots."

"Toots? Really? Are you working off a guidebook from the nineteen-fifties?"

"Yes."

"Okay, then." I thanked him for the coffee and left.

When I got back into the car with Bentley, I said, "You won't believe what Maisy has Humphrey doing."

"I probably will," he said, sounding irritated.

"Then never mind. Here's your fresh coffee, Mr. Grumpy."

He looked at the other cup in my hand. "You got yourself a second one? Just because I took two tiny sips from yours?"

My own irritation rose to unprecedented levels. "What is wrong with you?"

"There's nothing wrong with me. You're the one who's in a mood. I'm sorry I said you have bags under your eyes. I'm sorry I pay attention and I notice things."

I buckled my seat belt. "Maybe we shouldn't go for a long drive today. It's supposed to snow. The roads could get icy. Take me back to Zinnia's."

"No."

"No? Am I under arrest? This is unlawful detainment."

"I promised I would take you to Bed, Bath and Beyond, and that's what we're doing."

I sniffed. "Okay, then, Mr. Boss Man, Mr. Detective, Sir."

"We don't have to talk."

No, we did not.

He turned on the stereo and started playing an audiobook. It was playing at a higher speed than normal.

I was a fan of audiobooks, but only as long as I could listen to them at regular speed. I wasn't listening to cram information into my head, but for the pleasure of reading. Life was stressful enough without having stuff coming at me faster than normal—not that I objected to other people listening at a faster rate. *Whatever floats your boat*, I always said.

Bentley knew about my preference. Without being asked, he quickly adjusted the setting, slowing his audiobook down to regular speed.

"How's this?"

"Good," I said. "Thanks for slowing it down to regular speed for me, a regular person."

"A lot of people listen at a higher speed. The app does the resampling on the fly, so the voices don't go into chipmunk mode."

"Do you want to play your book faster? Go ahead. I'm a reasonable person. I could try listening harder."

"It's fine." He left the speed as it was, and turned up the volume.

I had a million things I wanted to say to my boyfriend.

I wanted to finish telling him about Humphrey working at the coffee shop, and how it seemed extra wrong that Maisy had him serving coffee. Was she at least paying him a minimum wage? Did he even know what money was?

I also wanted to find out if Bentley knew his ex-wife was in town.

Except I knew that he knew. He knew everything. Surely he knew about that. Even if he hadn't known the minute she'd arrived in town—whenever that had been—he'd definitely figured it out after he'd questioned Rhys Quarry about the museum incident. He must have seen her at the hotel.

But did he know that I knew? Did he know that I'd seen my father at the hotel right after he left?

Was he avoiding talking to me about Larissa and her powers?

When Bentley had arrived in Wisteria, he hadn't known about magic. So he wouldn't have known his wife was a succubus when he'd been married to her. Did he know about it now? Did it change how he felt about her?

Was he picking a fight with me on purpose, so he could break up with me?

Was that what was going on?

I studied the side of his face.

His expression was neutral as he sipped the takeout coffee and steered the car back onto the main road leading to the highway.

The audiobook was playing.

Even at regular speed, it sounded to me like an imaginary language, like noise.

Then my brain shifted gears. My curiosity about the material kicked in, and I began parsing the information that was coming at me from outside of my head.

The book was about ancient civilizations that lived on Earth five thousand years ago. I'd heard a few bits of the book in Bentley's car before, and I still wasn't sure if it was based on any evidence or pure speculation.

We listened to the audiobook all the way to the outlet mall.

We parked, went in, and shopped for linens and bath towels.

I didn't feel like buying anything.

Bentley asked a few pointed questions about what the point had been in driving up there if I wasn't going to buy anything.

I explained that my aunt's house was already crowded enough, and it didn't make sense to pile things up before I had a new place to move into.

"But everything's on sale right now," he said. "It's all post-Christmas clearance."

"I'd rather wait until the ecru ones are back in stock."

"Since when do you like ecru?"

"People change," I said.

"Then I guess we're done here," he said.

"I guess we are."

We got back in the car, empty-handed.

He turned on the audiobook, and we didn't talk again on the way home.

So much for my big plans to accept his wedding proposal.

I wasn't in the mood to accept an invitation for dinner, let alone the rest of my life.

When he asked about plans for the rest of the day, I vaguely cited commitments to help my aunt cook a big Sunday dinner.

"Have a good one," he said as we pulled up in front of Zinnia's house.

The sun was low in the sky.

"You could come in and stay for dinner," I said half-heartedly. "If you don't have anything else going on." *Such as a clandestine meeting with your ex-wife, the evil succubus.*

"I'd like to chase down some leads on that missing amulet," he said. "As you should know, it's a powerful piece."

"What's that supposed to mean? As I should know? I don't know anything about whatever jewels or dinosaur bones they have at the museum. The only amulet I know about is the one that Krinkle stole and used to resurrect Mahra."

"That's the one."

I felt a pain in my stomach. "That's the one?" He meant the amulet a woman named Temperance Krinkle had her friend steal from the museum to pay the kidnapper, who was actually her. "But it was destroyed."

He shook his head. "It wasn't destroyed."

I hadn't assumed the amulet had been destroyed so much as I had forgotten about it entirely. The altercation with Mahra had nearly killed both of us. I'd been temporarily blinded. Plus that day marked the moment Bentley and I had taken our relationship to the next level.

"That doesn't make any sense," I said. "It must have been recovered and put into storage in that underground warehouse at the DWM. They wouldn't just send it right back to the museum, would they?"

He frowned. "What *they* are you referring to?"

"*They*. The powers that be. The entities that secretly run this town. The mayor, and her people."

"The amulet belonged to the museum, so it was returned to the museum."

"Well, that was stupid. Why did you let that happen?"

He raised an eyebrow. "Me?"

"You need to find that amulet before someone gets a dumb idea about bringing back ancient gods."

He waited silently.

"Oh, floopy doop," I said. "That's why the amulet got stolen, isn't it?"

"You tell me." His silver-gray eyes bore into me.

"You think I had something to do with the amulet getting stolen a second time? Bentley, I give you my word. I don't know anything about it."

"One of your family members was at the museum."

"You mean Rhys? Why don't you go after him? In fact, why aren't you torturing it out of him right now instead of wasting your time ruining what was supposed to be a fun road trip to pick out sheets and towels?"

He said nothing.

"Is it because of *her*?" I spat out the words. "Is she protecting her match maker?"

He blinked once. "So, you know."

"Of course I know. Why didn't you tell me your ex was in town?"

"Because I knew I didn't have to."

"And?"

"And what?"

I shook my finger at him. "You're being intentionally infuriating."

"It's never intentional."

"But you are being infuriating."

He tilted his head back, then used his thumb and finger to squeeze the bridge of his nose.

"Let's put this on ice for now," he said. "We can talk about it when things settle down."

"What's there to talk about? I was going to tell you *yes*." I widened my eyes dramatically. "Yes."

"Oh."

"Yes."

He frowned.

"But the timing wasn't right," I said.

"The timing isn't right," he agreed.

"What's that supposed to mean? Are you taking it off the table?"

He didn't respond. He just sat there quietly, being cold. Unmoving. *Heartless*.

"You can't be serious," I said.

He still didn't say anything.

"So, the offer is off the table," I said. "You don't want to marry me."

"Honestly? Not right this minute, no."

"Great. Just great. I should have got the purple towels. The only reason I wanted ecru is because I thought that was what you wanted. I was only trying to make you happy."

He checked the time. "The store would be closed by the time we get back up there."

"Is this how you want it to be? You go running back to your ex-wife, and I get purple towels?"

He tilted his head to the side and gave me a confused look. "I need to find that amulet, or it doesn't matter what any of us does, because it will all be over."

"Perfect." I shoved open the car door and climbed out. "Perfect! Great excuse!"

I slammed the door shut.

I could hear him talking to me through his windows.

"I can't hear you," I said.

His mouth stopped moving. He put the car in gear, and drove away.

CHAPTER 7

A Month Later

The evening of Tuesday, February 14th

(Valentine's Day. Ahem. Obviously.)

Maisy Nix, my fiercely gorgeous frenemy, shook her head at me. The brunette witch was over six feet tall, with a long neck, so her disapproval, or any head movement at all, telegraphed quite clearly.

"Zara, if you're going to keep loitering around here like an uninvited gargoyle, at least put on a clean apron."

We were behind the counter at the busy downtown location of Dreamland Coffee. Maisy always had live music there for Valentine's day, to make it a perfectly romantic destination for couples. The shop usually did well that day, thanks to a variety of love-themed special drinks that were only available that week.

Rumor had it some of the coffee syrups contained love potions. They did not. Not unless you considered cinnamon oil, chocolate, and an unhealthy amount of sugar to be love potions.

"This *is* a clean apron," I said. "Or at least it's cleaner than the clothes I'm wearing underneath." It was true. I still hadn't refreshed my wardrobe since my house had exploded, and the few items I had were not holding up well to being worn constantly and not washed. My landlord, who was also my aunt, had tightly restricted my access to the laundry facilities, thanks to a few errors in judgment I'd made regarding towels and how long they could be left in the washer.

"You're disgusting," Maisy said, which was exactly what my aunt said to me at least once a day.

"At least I'm not dating a reptile."

"Maybe you should try it. You've really let yourself go since Bentley dumped you."

Her words stung. She had a point, but I would never admit it. I lifted my chin and shoved down the burning sensation that always flared up in my chest whenever Bentley was mentioned. Who knew that heartbreak could feel like heartburn?

"He didn't dump me," I said. "It was mutual."

"How was it mutual? You told me he canceled his proposal the day after Zinnia's party, when you two drove up to the outlet stores."

"Yes, but he didn't break up with me then. Not officially. We didn't break up until the next day, when I... asserted my independence."

"You mean when you yelled at him and cast a bunch of spells inside his apartment." She used her long neck to shake her head dramatically again. "I saw the holes you made. I saw it all when Fatima and I went over to help him fix the walls. If that man ever moves out, he will *not* be getting his damage deposit back."

"You're blowing things out of proportion, just like he did." I waved a hand. "That drywall damage was minor, and it was all accidental. It could have happened to any witch. I hadn't been using my magic much, and it was rusty. Plus I may have a teensy weensy issue with control."

Maisy's espresso-brown eyes went wide with sarcasm. "You think?"

"Don't make that face. Detective Theodore Dean Bentley is a big, scary vampire. He wasn't afraid of a few fireballs I may or may not have shot off in his general direction."

"You need to control yourself better. You're giving the witches in this town a bad reputation."

"Me?" I was aghast. "Me? I'm not the one dating a komodo dragon."

"Humphrey is a person now," she said, nose in the air. "He has a name, and regular clothes. You've seen him in his human outfits, using slang. He passes for human."

"Maisy, I saw him eating fruit flies."

"You did not."

"I did. Over where you have the bananas ripening for smoothies. He was chasing them around with his mouth open, like a little kid catching snowflakes."

"Humphrey has a few quirks," she admitted.

Our conversation ended abruptly as a customer came to the counter to order two steaming Love Potions.

"Two Love Potions coming up," I said.

It was probably the names that Maisy had given to the coffees that had caused people to believe the drinks might have magical powers beyond accelerating the gain of body fat.

Maisy punched the order into her computerized system, and I prepared the potion, so to speak.

I enjoyed every step of the process: steaming milk, measuring syrup by the pump, and making brown gold, commonly known as espresso. I loved knowing that I could do something simple and mechanical for a few minutes, and it would immediately make another human being happy. Making fancy coffee drinks was as enjoyable as being a librarian, albeit in a different way.

I'd volunteered to work at Maisy's coffee shop all evening, for free, so that the employees who were dating could spend time with their sweethearts, and so that the employees who were single could stay home and avoid gagging themselves to death over the lovebirds.

As for me, I would be gagging over the lovebirds, of course, but no more than I had been for the past four weeks, since I'd successfully asserted my independence at Bentley's apartment.

After the customer walked away with her two Love Potions, Maisy and I picked up where we'd left off.

Maisy said, "If you can't regulate your behavior, at least keep your wardrobe in better shape. Appearances matter."

"Yeah, yeah." I cast a spell to remove the coffee, foamed milk, and mystery stains from my apron.

"And put your hair up," she said. "People have been complaining about red hairs in their food, and I know they aren't mine."

I cast another spell to twirl my hair up into a loose bun that would stay in place without leaving a crimp from an elastic band. Never mind that my unwashed hair already contained multiple crimps from elastic band use over the past week.

Maisy wrinkled her nose at me. "This is how you're going to roll? Spellwork right out in the open, inside my place of business? Come on, Zara. You're not even pretending that you don't abuse magic, are you?"

"What's the point? Everybody knows what a screw-up I am. I might as well build a cabin on a mountaintop, and start assembling my army of flying monkeys."

"Don't even joke about flying monkeys."

"Why not? Everyone likes monkeys, and birds. Flying monkeys aren't the worst idea in the world."

"Speaking of bad ideas and the end of the world, whatever happened with that amulet that went missing from the museum?"

Maisy came over to where I was standing, by the espresso machine, and said, "I believe we have identified your daughter's secret talent. She is Music Blessed."

"But she's not a witch. Only witches can be Music Blessed."

"Let's see. She's got healing energy, she's Music Blessed, and her mother, grandmother, and aunt are all witches. I hate to break it to you, but your daughter's a witch."

"But she can't levitate, or do spells."

"She can't do spells? What do you call this?" She waved to the Dreamland customers, who were so still, they appeared to be trapped in the perimeter of a genie's time bubble.

I noticed one person in the crowd who wasn't frozen.

It was a young man, about Zoey's age, with medium-brown, curly hair, and dark skin. He was tall, but not the reed-like tall of a sixteen-year-old boy having a growth spurt. He was broad across the chest, like a full-grown man, yet his face had a boyish softness, and his hooded eyes had no lines. His skin was perfect—glowing, even—as though he'd just emerged from a cloning pod.

He was the sort of young man who, in ancient times, would have been the model for statues. He was masculine, yet also beautiful.

I forced myself to look away, embarrassed about staring at a boy half my age, wondering what ethnicity his parents were, and how their genes had combined to produce such attractive offspring. What had gotten into me? Was Maisy's energy contagious?

When the song finished, the beautiful model of a young man was the first to begin applauding. His clapping seemed to break the rest of the crowd out of the spell.

Up on the stage, the quintet of teenagers put their heads together for a discussion, then began the next song.

Zoey sat with her hands on her lap, letting the others play without her for a few minutes before she joined in near the end.

Again, the crowd slowed to a standstill when she played.

The curly-haired boy nodded along with the music. He also gestured with one hand, as though he was the composer himself, hearing his creation aloud for the first time. When the song ended, he once again led the polite applause at the end.

After five more songs, and the same cycle, the quintet took a break.

The crowd of lovebirds reactivated with unprecedented demands for fancy beverages.

Maisy and I were immediately slammed with drink orders.

While I was still in the middle of making Love Potions, I managed to get my daughter's attention.

She came around the counter to stand beside me and said, "I'm going to dial it back on our next set. I don't need to show off quite so much, even though it is more fun that way."

"Good idea to throw a few matches," I said. "You have to let the competition win at least thirty percent of the time, or they'll quit playing against you."

She gave me a confused look. "My competition?"

"Your competition on the stage. The girl with the violin, and that moody kid with the flute. The other two are no competition."

She gave me an exasperated look. "We're all in the same band. It's not a competition."

"If it's not a competition, then why are you so clearly winning?"

She blushed. "I don't know."

"But you are winning."

"I am winning," she admitted.

"Who's that boy?"

She blinked at me, playing dumb. "What boy?"

"Zoey, I'm not a genetically engineered flying monkey who fell out of a coconut tree yesterday. Are you going to tell me who he is, or would you prefer I ask him myself?" I began untying my apron. "I could use a break anyway."

She moved quickly to block my exit. "Don't!"

I waited for further explanation.

"That's just a guy I know," she said. "He's new at school. I told you about him. His name is Atom, like Adam, but with a T and an O."

That did ring a bell. I'd heard Zoey and Ambrosia giggling over some boy with an A name.

"I don't believe you've told me anything specifically about someone named Atom. I would definitely remember you telling me about Atom with a T and an O. Atom, the dreamiest dreamboat who ever did dream."

She blushed furiously.

"You like him," I said, pointing at her. "That's why you haven't told me about him. You think I'll embarrass you and ruin everything."

She looked down at her shoes, then at mine.

"Mom, why are you... wearing slippers?"

"Footwear is footwear. What does it matter? Don't be so judgy about labels."

"But they're slippers."

"Nobody needs to know that."

"Mom, they have bunny ears. And they're not even pink anymore. They're gray and brown." She leaned down to take a closer look. "Is that one burned?"

I put my hands on my hips. I did not appreciate being scolded by both Maisy and my daughter in the same evening.

"Take it up with our former home," I said. "The house could have preserved some winter boots for me. It could have thrown a pair free of the disaster, but, instead, I got these."

"Those slippers weren't in the cardboard box of stuff we got from the yard that day."

"I know. I snuck back into the site last week. I found all sorts of cool things we missed."

There was a tap on my shoulder.

Maisy said, "We're in the weeds." That was coffee-shop lingo for I was about to get zapped in the butt by my boss if I didn't start slinging espresso pronto.

"I gotta get back to the grind," I said to Zoey. "Get it? The grind. Because we grind coffee beans. Now stop bugging me while I'm working."

She pointed at me as she backed away. "You stay back there behind the counter until everyone's gone home. Don't let anyone I know see you in those burned slippers."

"I'll stay right here. You have fun slaying everyone with your harp genius while you make googly eyes at your dreamboat."

She put her hands over her ears and ran away.

I scanned the crowd for Atom.

He met my eyes, and he didn't look away.

I see you, I thought. *I've got my eye on you.*

As he held eye contact with me, he seemed to be saying the same thing.

My gut told me Atom wasn't "just a guy from school," and that soon we'd be doing more than having a staring contest.

CHAPTER 8

Friday, February 17th

(Three Days Later)

It was nine o'clock at night when I left the warm community center and climbed into my chilly car.

The place had been busy, as usual, between all the art classes and the swimming pool, not to mention the local mime group. The mimes had been the equivalent of noisy, trying to get my attention with their invisible boxes and such. The mime group had improved a great deal since the last time I'd encountered them, but I'd still been tempted into casting a magic distraction—a gross-smelling cloud —so I could escape. Theater people were lovely, but they could be exhausting.

I yawned as I started the engine of Foxy Pumpkin.

What a busy week it had been.

To keep my mind off a certain heartless vampire detective, I'd been saying yes to a ton of things I wouldn't usually have said yes to.

That Friday, the head librarian had suggested I join her for a decoupage class at the community center. I'd said yes. It beat sitting at home, feeling sorry for myself while binge-watching medical dramas.

I had enjoyed the decoupage class.

Well, I hadn't hated it.

What I liked about decoupage was that it didn't require the same level of enthusiasm people would have expected of me at other events, such as if I'd joined my aunt at her weekly league bowling game. The Incredibowls were better off without my grumpy face, even if they wouldn't have the full eight members required to make their score league-official.

While I waited for Foxy Pumpkin's engine to warm up, I leaned into the back seat to add my newly-decoupaged hat box to my collection of odd items that, like me, didn't have a home. My fingers accidentally brushed across the base of my ugly lamp. The feel of it made me recoil. The porcelain base wasn't cold, or smooth, as one might expect. The surface felt like warm skin. Like it was alive.

I had known for several weeks that the ugly lamp had magical properties. It had been a housewarming gift from my aunt, sourced from the repulsive Griebel Gorman, and it had miraculously survived my house exploding. Even so, I hadn't expected it to feel quite so fleshy. It wasn't even plugged in.

The lamp had been riding around in my car for several days now. I'd previously had it at the library, plugged into an outlet in the staff lounge. We'd all had some fun with it for a while. When a person flipped the light on, the illumination revealed hints about the person's supernatural powers.

My coworker, Frank Wonder, had enjoyed it a great deal. Frank adored pranks. He would turn off all the lights in the staff lounge, then suddenly flick the lamp on whenever his other supernatural coworkers walked in. The lamp would reveal glimpses of his pink feathers, or a creature who was half man and half bird. It was startling. I allowed myself to shriek girlishly, for Frank's enjoyment. That man lived for those shrieks, which was why Kathy, the head librarian, finally insisted that I store the lamp elsewhere. I'd meant to bring it to my aunt's house, but every time I pulled up to my temporary home after a long day, I'd have some excuse to be lazy and leave it in the car.

Lately, I'd taken to talking to the lamp as I drove around. We'd developed a rapport.

I'd say, "Well, Lampy, we just got two green lights in a row. Things are really looking up." Or, "Well, Lampy, I forgot to eat lunch, and I have to go straight to decoupage class, so what do you say we split a family-sized bag of Doritos?" I'd said that last bit three hours earlier.

The fact that the lamp was now warm and fleshy was probably my fault for talking to it.

Inanimate objects could be accidentally encharmed—or encursed—by witches. If I'd formally named the lamp with a real name, and not just Lampy, that would have accelerated the transfer of animata. It was a good thing that a more creative name than Lampy hadn't occurred to me.

The car was warmed up and purring happily, so I began driving home.

I took a detour to Beacon Street, where I stopped to look at the fence surrounding the pit of rubble where my house used to be.

"Lampy, that's where we used to live. We had some good times, didn't we? Remember the day my aunt brought you over as a housewarming gift?"

Lampy didn't respond, which was for the best. If it had spontaneously flicked its light on, I probably would have screamed then shot myself in the foot with a lightning ball.

"It was a good house," I said. "What a waste. Did you know that Tansy Wick's spirit—may she rest in peace—helped me completely transform the back yard? We were going to have so much fun there this summer, with garden party brunches, and weekend barbecues, and who knows what else. Now it's just rubble." My words reverberated inside the car. "Rubble," I said. "Rubble is a funny word. Rubble. Rubble."

A man walked his dog past the car. It was my former neighbor from across the street, Arden Greyson, walking Doodles. He gave my idling vehicle a suspicious look before recognizing me in the driver's seat and waving.

He didn't stop to chat, as he had in the past.

I felt the sting of rejection, but brushed it aside. The man had every reason not to stop and talk to me through my car window. More snow had fallen, and there was a windchill in the air. Doodles was getting older now, and his arthritis acted up in the cold. Plus I wasn't part of their world anymore.

The wind blew over the car with an eerie winter whistle.

"This neighborhood is going to forget all about us," I said to the lamp in the back seat. "Their lives keep on going, all the same."

Lampy was a good listener.

"You know, they all used to gossip about the Red Witch House. They'd stand on that corner right there, looking and pointing, telling crazy stories about things they'd allegedly seen or heard." I sighed. "They'll have to find something else to gossip about."

The wind whistled over the car again.

"There's a yellow house at the other end of the block that has a weird smell. I've heard a few people calling it the Mustard Stink House. It's probably going to catch on as the house to gossip about, but I won't be around to sniff it with everyone else, so I'll never know."

The wind settled. The street was quiet.

"This is like a preview of being dead," I said. "Moving away from a place sure gives you perspective about how little you matter."

I felt the tears welling up in my eyes. I refused to let them fall. I'd already cried earlier that day, over a children's book with adorable cartoon vampires. It was the sort of corny thing I would have shown Bentley.

The porch light on a nearby house flicked on. It was the blue house next to the fenced-off lot, the former Moore house, which had been purchased by Bentley's ex, Larissa Lang.

Was she currently home, on a break from filming her TV series, or was the light on a security timer?

The porch light flicked off again, and a shadowy figure moved into the center of the front window. The backlit form was feminine. I couldn't see her face, but I knew it was the succubus, and I knew that she was staring right at me.

I flicked my headlights on and off to let her know that *I knew* that *she knew*.

I scanned the street again, looking for what I didn't want to find.

Bentley's car wasn't on the street.

It had never been there whenever I'd come by. I still looked for his vehicle every time, with a sick feeling of anticipation in my stomach, like a person got when they were awoken by a ringing phone in the middle of the night.

The shadowy feminine figure in the Lang house closed the curtains.

"I guess our evening stalking duties are finished," I said to the lamp. "I'm going to take you to Zinnia's, and I'm going to bring you inside and plug you in. But only if you promise to behave yourself. No revealing people's powers without their permission." I chuckled to myself. "Oh, who am I kidding? Do what you love to do. You keep life interesting, Lampy, and interesting is much better than simple."

Another car drove past me then parked a few houses ahead. A woman stepped out of the vehicle, grabbed some groceries, and went to her house. When the front door opened, I could hear her family yelling excitedly, and kids arguing. The husband came to the door, kissed his wife, then ran out to the car to get the rest of the groceries.

Seeing the perfectly regular domestic scene made my heart ache. Seeing people happy made me less happy, and I hated that. I hated my own resentment. It was such a useless emotion. Having it was shameful.

Why was I such a loser? It had been almost five weeks since the incident with the heartless vampire, and over six weeks since my house had exploded. I should have felt better, not worse.

I put the car in gear and drove home.

I considered leaving the lamp in the car yet again, but I'd made it a promise, verbally, and I felt the magical tug of my vow urging me to not be so lazy.

With Lampy cradled in my arms like a baby, I walked up the steps, stamped the snow off my bunny slippers, and entered my aunt's house.

The downstairs area was dark.

My aunt was still with her bowling group, along with my mother. The Incredibowls usually went for more drinks and food after bowling. Those two wouldn't be home until late.

The house was completely quiet. That was strange. I'd expected my daughter to be there. Last I'd heard from her, she'd reported she was staying in that night, studying. Zoey loved doing homework on Friday nights. She wasn't a regular teen.

I walked around the home's lower level with the lamp, looking for an appropriate place.

My aunt already had a floral-patterned lamp on every logical surface. The lamps had been magically breeding. There were even more tiny lamps with petite pansies.

What to do? I couldn't put two lamps on a single side table. I was no expert at decorating, but that just wasn't right.

As much as I didn't want the ugly lamp to be the first thing I laid eyes on in the morning, it seemed the guest bedroom I shared with my daughter was the only logical place. There was a slim bureau in there, and if I could manage to hang up my clothes in the closet instead of tossing everything in a pile, the lamp would fit there.

I went upstairs, and when I reached the guest room, I found the door was closed. A crack of light was visible along the edges.

I tapped on the door gently so as not to scare my daughter.

"Zoey? Did you fall asleep with your face in a book?"

On the other side of the door, there was the sound of movement. The bed squeaked, and the ladder creaked. Zoey didn't answer.

"I'm coming in now," I said.

The door wouldn't open. It wasn't locked, but something solid on the other side was blocking it.

My senses tingled. Both the motherly ones and the witch ones.

"Zoey? Are you in there with Ambrosia? You two had better not be drinking again. Mrs. Abernathy has set a zero tolerance policy on teen drinking, and I'll have to tell her if either of you break the rules."

I didn't hear a response from Ambrosia, which was odd. She was usually all too willing to incriminate herself. The kid had the worst judgment when she drank. The alcohol lied to her, telling her she was excellent at hiding it.

Zoey said, "Hang on! Just a minute!"

There was the squeak of the window opening.

My motherly senses, which had been tingling, set off a full alarm.

I gave the door a hard shove.

Inside the room were two people: Zoey Riddle, and the attractive boy named Atom.

Both were fully dressed.

Both were standing right in the center of the room.

I nearly dropped the lamp but it seemed to be hanging onto my arm, clinging to me.

I didn't say anything. There was no point in interrogating the teenagers. Not when the guilt alone could cause them to interrogate themselves.

I walked past them, glanced out the open window briefly, and used my free hand to close it.

Wait for it, I told myself. *Be cool.*

The snowflakes that had come in on the breeze melted on the floor.

"We were just hanging out," Zoey said. "The door was blocked by accident."

By accident? I raised an eyebrow. I doubted that very much. My daughter knew that no door was ever locked to a witch like me, so there wouldn't have been much point in twisting the lock, but a heavy object placed in the door's path would at least slow me down.

She looked away.

The boy, however, gave me a smile that was all confidence, zero shame. "It's nice to officially meet you, Ms. Riddle. I'm Atom."

He had a nice voice. Not nice enough to be alone in a room with my daughter, with a backpack shoved up against the door, but I could see the appeal.

I shook his hand, squeezing hard. "Do you have a last name, Atom?"

"It's Wick. Atom Wick. You know my uncle, Vincent Wick."

"I do." Vincent Wick was an old friend of my aunt's. He wasn't my favorite person. The man didn't have supernatural powers, but he did run a very creepy network of surveillance across the whole town. I suspected he was the one who'd been selling footage of me and my family to another world, for the tiny people in the other dimension to watch on their tiny televisions.

"We were just about to go downstairs and watch a movie," Atom said, no shred of guilt on his face whatsoever. "Would you like to join us, Ms. Riddle?"

"Interesting," I said. "Then I guess I have impeccable timing."

Zoey gave me a wide-eyed, guilty look. She had her head pulled back, giving herself a double chin. It wasn't the look I was used to seeing on my daughter.

I hefted the ugly lamp I was still holding. "It's a bit late to start a movie now," I said.

"It's barely nine-thirty," Atom said. His tone was neither whiney nor persuasive, but it was a bit slick. He was no ordinary teen boy.

I replied, "I can tell time, Atom. I'm also aware that it will take us an hour to find something the three of us can agree on."

Atom took my objection like a professional salesman. "I'm confident I can find something the three of us will enjoy equally."

"You're a confident young man, aren't you?"

He nodded. "Yes, ma'am."

"Are you strong?"

"Yes, ma'am."

"Then do me a favor," I said. "Pull that bureau away from the wall so you can plug in this lamp for me."

"Sure!" He jumped to it. He pulled the bureau from the wall while I tossed the heap of clothes in the general direction of the closet. I set the lamp on the surface and stepped back. Atom plugged it into the outlet. The switch was in the off position, so it didn't light up.

"Now switch on the light," I said.

Zoey grabbed my hand and said, "Mom, don't make him do that."

Atom, who'd already been reaching for the light switch, paused and stared at us.

"Atom, don't do it," Zoey said. She knew about the lamp's magical abilities.

ANGELA PEPPER

I shot a look of warning at her. "What are you afraid of? It's just a lamp, Zoey."

She pressed her lips together and furrowed her brow. She was still holding my hand, and she squeezed it harder.

"Atom, it's up to you," I said to the young man. "Turn on the lamp only if you consent to turning on the lamp."

He let out an uneasy chuckle. "What's going on here? Is this a family joke?"

"It's a family *something*," I said.

"You don't have to do it," Zoey said to him. "My mother is being very weird right now. She's not normal. Look at her feet. She's wearing bunny slippers."

Atom looked at my footwear. "So? She's at home. I think they're cute."

"Thank you," I said. "Did you know bunny slippers are washable? I cleaned them in the coffee shop's fancy dishwasher. You can see some of the original pink again. A few more washes, and they'll be as good as new."

Atom had dropped his hand to his side. Now he moved his hand up over the base of the lamp, toward the light switch again, watching my daughter and me the whole time.

Zoey didn't say anything. Her hand was getting damp where she was holding mine.

"Go ahead," I said. "It's not going to bite. Probably."

"Is it a joke lamp?" Atom asked. "Is it going to make a loud sound when I switch it on? Like those motion-activated decorations people use on Hallow's Eve?"

I shrugged. "You never know with Lampy."

Atom said, "Why do I get the feeling I'm walking into a trap?"

"You tell me," I said. "Do you have a guilty conscience?"

"Never," he said, touching the switch with his finger as he grinned confidently at me.

Zoey whimpered, "I can't look," and buried her face in my arm.

Atom said, "I know I shouldn't, but I can't help myself. I want to see where this goes."

He flicked on the light switch.

Lampy powered up with a bright flash, illuminating Atom's face, and revealing his secret nature.

Beneath Atom's attractive features, his curly brown hair and dark skin, were another set of features. His true skin was as red as the fruit of a pomegranate, his eyes were yellow with black slits, and his forehead bore two distinctive horns. A single spiked tail whipped around behind him.

Every good mom knows to be wary of teen boys around her young daughters, but Atom Wick was no teen boy.

He was a demon.

Talk about a game changer.

CHAPTER 9

The red-skinned, horn-having, tail-waving demon didn't flinch at all after being exposed.

"So, *that's* what the lamp does," he said. "I figured it was something like that." He ran his fingers over the base. The lamp recoiled from his touch, changing shape to be asymmetrical. "Not really my taste. I prefer plain colors over florals. Plain colors like ecru."

My ears twitched at his mention of ecru. Did he know something about my second-to-last big fight with Bentley? Or did people regularly use the word ecru and I hadn't noticed?

His red features twisted into an evil grin.

I nudged my daughter to take her face out of my shoulder and look at Atom.

Atom's features began fading back to their previous state.

"Zoey, look," I said. "See him as he is."

By the time she finally looked, the magic of the lamp had faded, and the boy's face was back to human .

"Do it again," I said to the young man. "Zoey didn't see your true form."

He stared at me, chin held high, still confident, not at all fazed by the magic. "I will if she asks me to," he said.

Zoey shook her head.

"Then I suppose it's movie time," Atom said lightly. "We'll make plenty of popcorn, so your winged minions can join us without complaint."

Our winged minions? Did he mean monkey-bird hybrids? No. He was talking about Ribbons and RJ. He knew about them? Had Zoey told this demon friend of hers everything about our family?

As he walked past me, to the door, Atom casually said, "Tell me, Ms. Riddle, have you used the lamp on yourself?"

"I've been around it plenty of times," I said.

"Yes, but have you flicked it on next to a mirror?" He stepped into the hallway. "There's a mirror out here that you could bring into the bedroom, so that you can see yourself as you truly are."

I snapped back, "I know perfectly well what I look like."

"Oh, do you?" His brown eyes were taunting me.

I didn't break eye contact. I didn't know what kind of demon the boy was, but I had a few ideas, plus I knew better than to show weakness.

With an exasperated sigh, my daughter cut into our interaction. "Mom, don't make this more awkward than it needs to be. I know about Atom's powers, and he knows about mine. And, before you rudely busted your way into the room, if you must know, we were sitting on the top bunk, and we were talking. Our clothes were fully on, but we knew how it would look, which is why I panicked when I heard you. I'm not proud of my actions, but I was trying to get Atom out the window." She put her fists on her hips. "He wouldn't go. He said he wanted to meet you." She made a displeased face, scrunching her mouth. "Which is an idea he probably regrets now."

"No regrets," Atom said, sidling up next to my daughter and putting an arm around her shoulders. "I don't believe in having regrets."

I kept my chin up and my gaze steady. "Are you really Vincent Wick's nephew?"

"We are distantly related," Atom said. "You know how complicated bloodlines can get. I mean, look at your own. Your mother mated with a shifter, and you mated with a genie. Plus now your aunt is having offspring with a man who was without magic, but became a bear shifter after exposure to Activator X, which I believe is technically called Activator X, Y, Z."

"You know a lot about my family."

"I know a lot. Period."

"How complicated is your bloodline, Atom?"

"You wouldn't believe me if I told you," he said.

"What exactly are you?"

He blinked. "You saw what I am."

"I saw something, but I don't know what it means."

"What did you see?"

I didn't want to say it, but then I did. "I saw a demon."

"Interesting," he said.

Zoey didn't react.

"*Quite* interesting," I said.

He rubbed his smooth, handsomely boyish jaw. "What do you suppose Zoey would have seen?"

"The same thing I did. Red skin. Pointy horns. A tail."

"Don't be so sure of that," he said. "Have you ever heard the expression, *people see what they want to see*?"

I took in a breath and composed myself for a speech.

"Atom Wick, if that is your true name, I can assure you that when I walked into my daughter's bedroom and found an extra person, a male person, I did not wish for that person to be a demon."

He raised an eyebrow. "You think I'm a common demon?"

"Actually, I believe you are a succubus." I'd already had one succubus arrive in town and mess up my life. Why not two?

He gave me a surprised look. "A succubus? What makes you say that?"

"You've got some sort of hold over my daughter. I never caught her in a room with Griffin Yates, past nine-thirty, with a heavy backpack conveniently leaning up against the door."

He turned to Zoey. "Who's Griffin Yates?"

She yelled at me, "Mom!"

"What did I do? Didn't you tell the succubus that you were in a relationship with a young man who's currently away at college? A young man you'd probably still be dating if he were in town?"

Zoey sputtered with outrage.

To Atom, I said, "You should have heard how much she talked about him. It was always *Griffin this, Griffin that*. Oh, the endless deep dives into the most banal text messages. I wouldn't say she was obsessed with the boy, but her fascination went far beyond hobby levels."

Zoey's mouth scrunched again. "We were never official," she said. "We worked together at the museum, and we hung out sometimes." She turned to Atom and said, "He fixed a flat tire for me."

"He sounds handy," Atom said.

She snorted. "He turned out to be a jerk. And he left for college, so he's not even around."

He asked, "Did you see him over the Christmas break?"

"He didn't come back. His family went on a skiing vacation. But I didn't even want to see him, so it didn't matter. I only know about the ski vacation because Ambrosia stalks him online."

As they talked, I got the uncomfortable feeling they were in a bubble of focus, and had forgotten I was standing right there.

"Sooo," Atom the demon said to my daughter, making an exaggerated O shape with his mouth. "How would you feel about making it official? Not with Griffin, but with me?"

She said, "I don't know. I'll have to think about it."

He gave her an adoring look. Even from the side, I could feel the raw power of it. Oh, to be looked at that way by an attractive young man. Could I blame her for falling under his spell? When I'd been her age, I'd fallen for her father, the djinn. And wasn't djinn just a type of demon?

"Okay," my daughter finally said. "I think that sounds nice. We can be official."

He turned to me and said, "You heard it here first, Ms. Riddle. I'm your daughter's boyfriend."

"Great," I said. "All the more reason for you to tell me what you are."

"Oh, where's the fun in that? I hear you love solving riddles, Ms. Riddle. Why don't you tell me what you think I am, and I'll let you know if you're hot or cold or right on the money. I'll give you three guesses."

"You're a succubus."

"Warm. Also a waste of a guess, since you already tried that one. I'll give you a bonus guess."

"Are you djinn, by which I mean a genie?"

"No."

"Are you a shifter?"

"No."

"A mage?"

He tipped his head from side to side. "Of sorts. Some people call me a magician." He lunged forward, startling me, only to produce a shining silver coin between his fingers. "This was behind your ear," he said, flipping it through the air. He grabbed the coin before it landed, and slapped it onto the back of his hand. "Care to make a wager?"

"On a coin toss?" I took a step back. "With someone who just told me he's a magician? What kind of an idiot do you think I am?"

He casually pocketed the coin. "I don't think you're an idiot at all. As a matter of fact, I believe you know exactly what I am, but you're too scared to say it. There's a term for witches like that." He scratched his cheek and looked up. "What is that adorable pejorative that the other witches in the coven use?"

Pejorative? Whatever he was, this Atom was no teenager. That was for sure. I'd never heard a teen boy use the word pejorative.

I narrowed my eyes at him as I ran through a mental inventory of all the spells I might blast at him if he made another sudden movement. If he tried to pull another silver coin from my ear, he'd be retrieving it from where the sun didn't shine.

"I remembered," he said, striking a finger in the air. "That's it. You're an Overly Cautious Witch." He tilted his head to the side. "Funny. That doesn't seem like much of an insult to me, but then again, I'm not one of you."

Oh, no. He did *not* just call me an OCW.

I stood my ground and said the words that had been rolling around in the back of my mind. "You're the devil."

He gave me a look of genuine surprise.

Zoey did not.

"My, my," Atom said. "That is a very good guess. You've gone over your limit of guesses, but I can be generous. The answer is yes. I am what your kind calls," he made air quotes, "*the devil.*"

"I knew it the whole time," I said, which wasn't exactly true. I really had believed he was a succubus.

Atom said, "How did you know? Was it the horns? The pointy tail?" He shook his head and gave me a world-weary eye roll. "I've been trying to get rid of that thing for ages. It's nothing but a nightmare. Whenever I sit down too hard, it sends a terrible shiver up my whole spine. You humans think hitting your elbow is the worst, but try sitting on your tail a few times. I'd love to have it gone for good, even if being without a tail in certain circumstances does throw off my balance, but every time I cut it off, it just grows back."

My mouth opened, but nothing came out.

I had to give the devil his due. He'd stumped me. He'd tried cutting off his tail but it kept growing back? I was speechless.

Zoey gave me a pleading look. "Mom, don't make this weird."

I stared at her, open-mouthed.

She was the one dating the devil. How was I the weird one?

Atom said, "Parents usually feel more comfortable around their daughter's boyfriends if they get to know them. Let's all watch a movie together. A comedy would be best. You both can make sure I'm not a sociopath by listening to hear if I laugh at the right spots."

Zoey said, "I like comedies."

The young couple turned around, and started down the stairs.

I pinched my arm.

It hurt the usual amount.

This wasn't a dream.

My daughter had her first official boyfriend, and he was the devil.

CHAPTER 10

It was a Friday night unlike any other.

The three of us—my daughter, the devil, and I—sat down to watch a movie together.

We quickly found the perfect new release for all of us. Both Zoey and I had been wanting to see it for a while, and Atom insisted that he enjoyed romantic comedies. What a fibber! He truly was the Lord of Lies.

Even though the movie had the usual things I enjoyed —a couple of socially awkward, morally bankrupt misfits slowly realizing they were perfect for each other—I couldn't enjoy it.

I lost track of the plot as I sat there stewing about Atom, and arguing with Zoey in my head.

If she'd known what he was, why hadn't that set off warning alarms? Why hadn't she immediately told her mother that the devil himself had just transferred into her high school from wherever it was he had come from? Hellmouth High? Was there something wrong with me that she didn't trust my judgment at all?

My thoughts were so chaotic and persistent that Ribbons stopped by the living room just long enough to declare that the popcorn wasn't buttery enough, and that he was going to sneak into the town's movie theater for the real stuff. Then he flounced off with his juvenile son on his shoulders.

"Interesting pets you Riddles have," Atom said. "The scaly ones, and the furry one."

Boa, the traitor, was on Atom's lap. She stared up at him with adoration, acting like she never got any affection from anyone else.

I asked Zoey's new boyfriend in a casual tone, "Do you have cats and wyverns where you're from?"

He replied, "Of course. Where did you think they came from?"

"Should have known," I said. "And where exactly is it that you call home?"

"It's a different world than this one," Atom said, not taking his gaze off the television screen. "It's one world over from the one you visited a few weeks back. It's in that direction, but you can't access it with a magic elevator key. We're far more exclusive than that."

"We're talking about Hell," I said. "You're far more exclusive about *letting people into Hell*? Am I hearing you right?"

"Shh," Zoey said. "Mom, stop talking over the movie."

"But I have questions," I said.

"Me, too," Atom said. He gestured at the screen. "Are we supposed to believe that he can't see how attractive this girl is just because she wears glasses and has her hair tied back?"

Zoey said to him, "Do you think she's attractive?"

He sniffed. "She's okay. Not really my type."

"And what is your type?" I asked. "Do you have a lot of demon girlfriends back home, Atom? Maybe a whole sexy harem?"

"Ew!" Zoey threw a pillow at me. "Mom!"

"Well?" I threw the pillow back. "Wouldn't you want to know if Atom did have a harem of buxom red babes in chainmail bikinis back home, and you're just the half-djinn side girl? You should be thanking your mother for asking the tough questions."

Atom looked at Zoey and said, "They mean nothing to me. Yes, we do have some beautiful girls where I'm from, but none of them can play the harp." He gazed at her with eyes that could melt butter. "You, Zoey, are an angel."

We weren't even halfway through the movie, but I couldn't take it anymore.

I could pretend to be a cool, young mom who was okay with her daughter's questionable decisions, but there was a limit. Apparently, that limit was forty minutes.

I jumped to my feet, dropping my popcorn bowl with a loud clatter. The noise startled Boa, who leapt off Atom's lap in a flash of white fluff, knocking over the beverages on the coffee table before skittering out of the room. I hadn't seen Boa run that fast since the time she got a half-inch section of invisible tape—the regular kind used for wrapping Christmas gifts, not magical tape—stuck to the bottom of her paw.

The two teens, who were sitting the mom-mandated five feet apart on the sofa, stared up at me.

Zoey grabbed the remote control and skipped the movie back a minute.

"You're blocking the screen," she said to me.

"I sure am." I grabbed the remote control from her hand, and turned off the television.

My daughter scoffed in displeasure.

I said to the boy, "Atom, it's getting late. Time for you to hit the road with your little red hooves."

Zoey gave me a look of disbelief.

Atom got to his feet smoothly, his posture loose and relaxed, as though this whole evening had gone according to his plan.

"We can finish the movie another time," he said coolly. "I'm looking forward to the makeover scene."

I looked him steadily in the eyes. "You said you hadn't seen this one before."

"I haven't seen it before," he said. "But it's a romantic comedy with teenagers. There's always a makeover scene."

"You think you're pretty clever, don't you?"

"I can spot patterns and make predictions."

"I'm sure you do more than that. And I'm sure you know things the rest of us don't."

He gazed right back at me, equally steady. "I'm sort of like a librarian. I've picked up some trivia over the years."

"I bet you have."

He gave me what would have been a charming smile if I didn't know what he was. "Ms. Riddle, you might not see it, but you and I have a lot in common. If you took the time to get to know me, you might see that you and I are not so different."

"I've never sat on my tail."

"Fair enough." He looked down at my daughter, who was still seated, clutching a throw pillow. No. *Strangling* the pillow, like it was my neck.

Zoey said, "Sorry you have to go so soon." She throttled the pillow harder, her knuckles white. "I'm sorry my mother is such an insufferable witch."

I pointed at her. "No name calling."

"It's what you are," she said with uncharacteristic venom. "You're an insufferable witch."

Atom chuckled uneasily. "I'll see you at school on Monday. Something tells me you're about to get grounded until then."

She said to him, "No. That's impossible. I never get grounded."

"There's a first time for everything," I cut in. "Zoey, you're grounded for the weekend."

She gave me a shocked, disgusted look. Then, slowly, her upper lip curled into a sneer. A sneer that promised I would come to regret my actions.

"Stop giving me that look," I said. "Keep up the bad attitude, and, in my coworker Kathy's wise words, *I shall ground you until you forget what the sun looks like.*"

The sneer continued unabated.

I did *not* care for that expression on her face.

I had never struck my daughter, but in that moment, I understood why parents spoke of smacking a certain kind of look off a kid's face. It had to be this look. This sneering silent promise of retaliation.

The indignation I felt mixing with my rage was intoxicating. Was Atom doing this to us? Or was this real?

My mind was reeling. I was so unprepared for any of this. Earlier that evening, I'd been blissfully using Mod Podge to glue pictures of roses to a balsa wood hat box. I should have been boning up on parenting. I should have been reading *Wrangling Your Teen Monster* by Thackery Tollster.

"This is so unfair," Zoey said.

"Life isn't fair," I said, sounding an awful lot like my own mother.

Zoey glared at me. "Am I grounded to this couch, or can I go for a walk outside with my boyfriend?"

"You're not grounded to the couch, but thanks for the idea. I'll definitely keep it in mind."

Her nostrils flared. She looked like a bull about to charge.

Atom stood by, silently watching. Was he eating up the negativity? Feeding off it? Was that how he operated?

I wasn't going to let him get the better of me.

"You may leave the couch," I said neutrally. "You two have five minutes to say goodbye on the porch."

My daughter started to rise slowly, taking her time.

"Five minutes starting now," I said.

Zoey gave me a dirty look as she sped up to normal speed. She walked Atom to the front door, muttering apologies on my behalf.

They stepped outside, and Zoey closed the door.

I went to the front window and kept an eye on the steps. If my not-yet-seventeen-year-old daughter tried to leave the property, she was going to regret it. I didn't know what I would do, but I was a powerful witch with a lot of options, and I had no qualms about improvising.

Exactly five minutes later, Zoey whipped open the door, came inside, gave me another dirty look, and stomped upstairs.

I was alone in the quiet living room. Marzipants had already been put to bed with his blanket over his new cage. Boa had wandered off.

Ribbons flitted into the room and said, "Your offspring's wretched insolence has surpassed that of my own tonight, Zed."

"I'm glad you noticed. You don't know this, but all parents are in a competition to see who has it the worst. I may be winning."

"You win, Zed."

He dropped baby RJ into the popcorn I'd spilled on the floor. RJ did his impression of a robot vacuum cleaner, gobbling popcorn as he lazily pushed himself around on his scaly belly.

A war of sorts raged upstairs.

The house shook as Zoey slammed the bedroom door, stomped down the hall, then slammed the bathroom door.

I said to Ribbons, "Do you think she's upset about something?"

"You have a natural flair for torture, Zed. I relish seeing this dark side of you become activated."

"I'd laugh, but it's not funny. She's dating the devil. The actual devil. Do you think this has something to do with that prophecy that everyone keeps dangling over my head? The one where my daughter is destined to eat everyone's souls? I guess this is how it happens. She starts dating the devil, and he leads her down the path to evil. I can't believe this is all happening right now, already. She hasn't even graduated from high school. She's just a kid. What am I supposed to do to stop this?"

Ribbons yawned. "The affairs of humans are of no more interest to wyverns than the affairs of a dung beetle are to a giraffe."

"You always say things like that hoping I'll be insulted, but I'm onto you, you crass-talking, syrup-stealing, liver-spotted baloney sandwich."

"That's it, Zed. Embrace your dark side."

"Whenever you say you don't care about human affairs, what it actually means is that you don't really know anything about what's going on. For all your millennia of experience, and the shared knowledge of your ancestors, you're not that much use to me from day to day, are you?"

Ribbons snatched up the bowl of popcorn Atom and Zoey had been sharing, and dumped it on the floor. Then he gathered RJ, who'd been doing a fantastic job vacuuming up the first spill, and spirited him away.

"Thanks for the chat," I called after him.

There was no reply.

The house shook as all the upstairs doors slammed again.

I yelled up the stairs, "It's going to be hard sleeping with all that rage! It's going to be a long night if you don't simmer down!"

The only response was a sulky silence.

A few minutes later, the front door opened.

My mother and aunt entered, playfully bickering about the bowling league. Both were smiling, and nobody was pulling anyone's hair. The two sisters had been getting along far better than any of us would have expected.

I wondered, was that why my daughter and I, who normally got along so well, were now experiencing tension? Was there only so much get-along magic in the Riddle family for a few people at a time?

My aunt came into the living room, took a look at the popcorn that was strewn everywhere, and said, "Don't you dare try to blame this on the wyverns. Everyone knows they don't waste food."

"But it was Ribbons," I said. "I swear."

My mother waved a hand at the mess dismissively. "Let the cat clean it up. Zarabella, join me for a glass of wine. Your knocked-up aunt is sticking to juice, and I never drink alone."

"That's not true, but sure. I could use a drink."

She shook some snowflakes from her long, black hair. "Difficult day at the bookstore?"

"It's a library, and no. Work was fine. Decoupage was fine. But then..." I was so worked up, I had to take a breath mid-sentence. "Then I got home, and I found out my daughter is dating the devil."

My aunt and my mother exchanged a knowing look.

"No way," I said. "You two knew? And you didn't tell me?"

"It was only a suspicion," my aunt said. "Some rumors have been circulating around town."

"I'll get the wine," my mother said. "Zara, would you like yours extra fancy?"

"Yes, please," I said. Extra fancy meant *with ice cubes*.

The three of us convened in the living room.

My aunt cast a spell to clean up the spilled popcorn, and we discussed what we were going to do about the Zoey-devil situation.

I had never been glad that my house had blown up, but I was glad at that moment that I shared a home with two older Riddle women. If I'd had to deal with this on my own, I almost certainly would have done something I'd regret.

Since becoming a witch, I'd dealt with a lot of surprises, but this one had me stumped.

I'd never seen my daughter act so sullenly. It was as though all the years of rebellion we'd skipped over hadn't been skipped at all. They'd been accumulating in a piggy bank somewhere, and Atom had smashed it open.

Even if he hadn't been the devil, I still would have hated him for what he was doing to my daughter.

A couple of hours later, two bottles of wine had been emptied, I was crunching on leftover ice like it was candy, and we'd made a decision.

Officially, we were going to give Zoey our complete support, and allow her to make her own decisions about dating Atom Wick.

Secretly, we would do everything we could to break them up.

CHAPTER 11

Saturday, February 18th

(The Next Night)

"I can't do this," I said in frustration.

My aunt looked up from her embroidery. The two of us were sitting in her living room, working on our crafting projects. The dinner dishes had been finished, and we were filling the last hours of the day before bedtime.

"You've barely tried," she said. "Try holding the knitting needles more loosely."

"Not this." I set aside the blue baby booties I'd been trying to knit for my cousin-to-be. "I mean the other thing." I nodded in the direction of the stairs that led to the bedroom where my daughter had been stubbornly camping out, barely emerging long enough to eat at mealtimes. "I know our big plan is to be supportive and patient, but I can't do it. That's not how I operate. I'd rather be doing something, even if it makes everything worse."

My aunt threaded some beads onto her needle and took another stitch. Her embroidery project was a mixed media piece with cacti and desert flowers—quite pretty, actually.

Without looking up, she said, "I went through my bad boy phase as well. I had a crush on Rhys Quarry, remember? But I outgrew it eventually."

"But did you? Really? I've seen the way you look at him, Aunt Zinnia. Plus he was so disappointed that there hadn't been any rumors about him being the father of your baby."

"Your father is an attractive man, but I assure you I have no interest in him. Some fondness remains, but it's nothing like what I felt when I was Zoey's age." She glanced up, her expression every bit as wise as her words. "Surely you must remember what it felt like to be sixteen, when every little thing felt like life or death?"

"For me, those years are a blur of diapers and late-night feedings."

"And that was the challenge you needed," Zinnia said. "Young people need to face adversity so they can become adults. Zoey probably sees Atom as a challenge. Girls always think they can tame the bad boy." She gave me a knowing smile. "Adult women aren't much different."

"Is that why you aren't going to marry Fung? Is he not enough of a bad boy for you? He is a shifter, Zinnia. A big, bad bear of a shifter."

She tied off a thread and changed colors.

"Zara, if you'd like to discuss relationships, why don't we start with yours? I'm still not sure what happened. I understand that Bentley's ex-wife showed up in town, and you preemptively broke up with him so that he couldn't break up with you. Have I got my facts straight?"

"I sound like a Grade A ding-dong when you phrase it that way."

She said nothing.

I shook my head. "If I'm a ding-dong, then you're a ding-dong, too." I looked at the stairs again. "All of us are ding-dongs. Except maybe my mother. She doesn't have any issues with Nick. That guy goes along with whatever she wants, plus he's chock full of a never-ending supply of blood."

My aunt said, "Is that what you want in a mate?"

"No. I'm not a blood sucker."

"I meant for a mate to go along with whatever you want. Is it possible you ended things with Bentley because you couldn't control him?"

"Don't put words in my mouth." I tried to knit a row for the booties, but the yarn got tangled. I tossed the booties aside. "How did it happen, anyway? With you and Fung?"

Her cheeks flushed. "The usual way."

"Come on. You know what I mean."

She suddenly jerked in her chair. "Ouch." She sucked on her fingertip. "You made me poke myself with the needle. Look what you made me do." She showed me her bleeding fingertip. "I could have gotten blood all over my nice green threads."

"I just want to know the details. You don't have to tell me everything, but at least tell me where it happened. The deed. Was it here? Was it on this couch?"

She pursed her lips.

"Blink once if it was on this couch."

She returned to her embroidery.

I said, "If you don't tell me how it happened, I'm going upstairs to start another yelling match with my daughter."

"Go right ahead." She didn't even look up.

I couldn't let my threat become empty. I got up from the couch, went upstairs, and knocked on the door.

"Zoey? Can we talk?"

She answered with a yip-yip. Not a human one.

I opened the door. She was curled up on her bed in her red fox form, watching videos on a tablet. The videos were of squirrels and birds in a Norwegian forest.

"Zoey, change back into human," I said. "I'm not going to talk to you when you're like this."

The fox gave me a lazy yawn and went back to watching the video.

"You can't stay like that forever," I said.

The fox slowly swiveled her head and stared at me with an expression that said *wanna bet?*

"You obviously need more challenges in your life," I said. "Zinnia and I talked about it. When I was your age, I had way more responsibilities. That's what you need. I'm going to start delegating more duties to you. In addition to getting Straight A's in school and answering the doorbell, you'll have to do other stuff. Really difficult stuff."

The fox let out a stream of yip-yips that sounded like laughter.

Boa came running in, tail held high, concerned that she was missing out on a play session.

The cat jumped onto the dresser, rubbed her face on the ugly lamp, then jumped over to the top bunk bed, sniffed my fox daughter, and said, "Ham?"

Zoey-Fox nudged the pillow with her nose, revealing some food she'd stashed away.

Boa began chowing down on the stale morsels.

"Just perfect," I said. "You're both eating in bed, which isn't allowed, and only the cat is talking to me. This is what I get for being the World's Best Mom." I pointed at the two animals in the upper bunk. "In case your fox ears and cat ears aren't great at detecting nuance, that's sarcasm."

Neither of them said anything.

I backed up, closed the door, and went downstairs again.

"Give her time," Zinnia said, still embroidering. She stitched red bead blossoms onto a cactus.

"What if we don't have time? She's going to see him on Monday, at school. He's going to turn her against us."

"What makes you say that?"

I stared at her in disbelief. "Have the pregnancy hormones caused you to lose your mind? Am I the only one who's bothered by the fact that Zoey's new boyfriend is the devil?"

"The devil is just a type of demon, and her father is a demon, so she's half demon herself. That's what djinn are. They're demons."

"So?"

She finally looked up and blinked at me. "If someone had tried to stop you from seeing Archer Caine, back when he had a different face and name, would you have listened?"

"Of course."

"Check your memory, Zara. I did speak to you about him. Your mother was concerned about some mysterious boy you'd fallen head over heels in love with, and she invited me to come and talk to you. Don't you remember the last time the three of us went to high tea?"

"I remember going out to lunch at that fancy hotel whenever you were in town. I remember one time my mom bought me a new outfit, and the shoes pinched my toes."

"And...?"

I took a moment to search my memory banks. I'd seen my aunt rarely during my teen years, and most of our conversations had been superficial, about school and college plans.

"You don't remember," Zinnia said.

"I remember the little sandwiches, and how my mother made the waiters so nervous, and how you..." It all came flooding back. "How you told me to keep both feet on the ground at all times when I was around boys."

"That's right," she said. "It was good advice then, and it's good advice now." She added softly, "Funny how easy it is to forget good advice."

"I remember that intervention. It was so horrifying. Teenaged me thought you were so embarrassing. But at least you tried. You saw what needed to be done, and you did it."

"And yet we failed," Zinnia said. "Was there anything I could have said to you that might have had more impact on your choices? Or did you believe, in that teenaged mind of yours, that you knew far better than any of the grownups in your life?"

I picked up the blue booties, spotted all the errors I'd made so far, and began unraveling the whole thing.

My aunt had made a very strong point about Zoey, using me as the prime example. It would be hard to fight that logic, but I was no quitter.

"There were only two of you," I said. "You, and Mom. But there are three of us grown-up Riddles now. It's three against one. Plus we're all living together under the same roof. Together, we can wear her down."

The corner of my aunt's mouth twitched up. "You are quite good at wearing people down."

"There's the spirit."

She went back to her embroidery.

My pile of blue yarn mocked me.

I grabbed my phone and sent a message to Charlize.

My gorgon friend had been working on getting a translated copy of the prophecy for me. Getting it out of the Department of Water and Magic involved a lot of red tape, but she'd promised to do her best.

Rather than replying by text, she phoned me.

Charlize asked, "What are you doing right now?"

"Turning a pair of baby booties into a ball of yarn. Why? Have you got that scroll for me?"

"Even better. I'm picking you up in ten minutes."

"It's late. It's nine o'clock. I'm ready for bed. You can come by if you have the scroll, though."

"I don't have it. I've got something better. Go jump in the shower and shave whatever needs shaving. Don't stop at the knees."

"Charlize!"

"I will check, so make sure you do a good job."

She ended the call before I could wriggle out of it.

Going out after dark on a cold winter night? What was she thinking?

I relayed Charlize's side of the conversation to my aunt.

Zinnia said, "You ought to go out. Have some fun. Don't worry about your daughter. I'll make sure the wards stay active on all the windows. Nothing's coming in or out without my permission. Except the wyverns, of course. There's not much I can do about them."

"But it's been night for hours. Who goes out after dark for anything but an emergency ice cream run?"

"You're only thirty-three," she said. "Maybe she'll take you to a party. Who knows? Maybe you'll meet someone who'll take your mind off Bentley, so you can stop driving by his ex-wife's house every night to look for his car."

"Who told you about that?"

She raised an eyebrow. "Margaret Mills. She's worried about you. We all are."

I threw my hands in the air. "Then I guess I'd better go out after dark, to give you and Margaret something new to talk about!"

She went back to her embroidery.

I ran upstairs and jumped in the shower.

I didn't want to go anywhere with Charlize, but if it helped reassure people I was okay, as well as get me a copy of the prophecy scroll, I would do whatever it took, even if it meant shaving my legs.

CHAPTER 12

When I emerged from the shower, Charlize Wakeful was already in the bathroom, sitting on the vanity.

The pretty blonde gorgon was wearing her usual outfit —a silver jumpsuit. Even in Wisteria, it was an unusual look, yet the jumpsuits were surprisingly versatile, and appropriate for almost any occasion. The last time I'd seen her, at the New Year's Day wedding that didn't happen, she'd worn one with a pretty pink cardigan and ballerina flats. Tonight, she'd dressed up her silver jumpsuit by unzipping it to reveal a lacy tank top. She was also wearing dark lipstick and large hoop earrings.

"Nice," she said, looking over my nude body before I could cover myself with a towel. "You look good for someone who's had a kid."

"Thanks." I dried myself. She'd seen me nude plenty, during the swim sessions following hot yoga, but it was always nice to get another compliment.

Charlize said, "Before my mom passed, she used to complain about how my sisters and I ruined her figure."

"Your mom had triplets, so she must have been huge when she was pregnant. I'm sure you girls did a number on her stomach."

"I saw her in two-piece swimsuits. She snapped right back. It was just something she'd say to make us feel guilty so we'd listen to her."

My ears perked up. "Did it work?"

"Not on me. It worked better on Chloe. And Chessa, well, Chessa never could do anything wrong."

I used a spell to dry my hair. My pledge to stop using magic had become a distant memory.

Charlize unzipped a duffel bag, and handed me what appeared to be a belt.

"Try this dress," she said.

"Where's the rest of it?"

"Just try it on."

I pulled on the tiny slip of black fabric, and looked in the mirror. I hardly recognized the redhead staring back at me. All the ice cream I'd been consuming lately had added to my curves, and the skimpy dress accentuated the right places.

Charlize handed me a pair of strappy black heels.

I said, "Why do I feel like a teenaged girl in a romantic comedy?"

"Because this is the makeover scene," the gorgon said with a head shake. Her hair snakes, which were hidden from non-magical eyes, twitched and flicked their forked tongues with amusement.

I continued to admire myself.

Charlize went on. "This is where you get a glimpse of the life you could have, if you manage to stop moping around in your old habits. Speaking of which, your aunt asked me to take care of your filthy bunny slippers."

"You leave Flopsie and Bopsie out of this."

"Too late. I already located them, euthanized them, and gave them a suitable cremation."

I'd left the slippers next to the tub. They were gone, and there were ashes in the sink. Charlize had incinerated them. She had the ability to turn living creatures to stone, and could turn her own hands to hot lava. Her heat powers came in handy when we needed the creek warmed up after our yoga classes. And, apparently, for cremating innocent bunny slippers.

I held one hand over my chest as I turned on the water to rinse the ashes down the sink.

"Rest in peace, Flopsie and Bopsie," I said.

"Good riddance," Charlize said.

Then she pulled a loose handful of makeup from her bag, and practically threw it onto my face.

"Gorgeous," she said, stepping back to admire her handiwork.

I checked the mirror again. The lipstick was dark red, the eyeliner was thick, and the glitter was the exact opposite of tasteful.

"I look like an exotic dancer," I said. "Where did the real Zara go?"

"Don't pretend this isn't the real you," Charlize said. "I know about that little webcam operation you ran out of your basement apartment back when you were desperate for money."

"The internet was different in those days," I said. "It really wasn't as sordid as it is now. I swear."

Charlize raised one blonde eyebrow.

"It wasn't like that," I insisted.

"Sure, it wasn't," she said with a scoff. "And all those guys who sent you cash or bought you things off your wishlist were just generous patrons of the arts. Remind me again, what kind of art were you doing back then? Were you a painter, or was it a sculptor? What type of art were those gentlemen the patrons of?"

"Oh, shut up."

She grinned as she applied extra glitter to my cleavage.

After a spritz of perfume, she pronounced me ready to leave the house, and led the way out of the bathroom.

We stopped in the hallway outside the only closed bedroom door.

"Is Zoey in there?" Charlize asked.

"She is if she knows what's good for her. And if the wards on the windows are still working."

Charlized nodded sagely. I hadn't seen the gorgon computer programmer since New Year's Day, but I'd been in touch by phone. She was up to date on what was happening with Zoey, as well as my family's planned strategy for dealing with it.

Charlized knocked on the door.

There was a rustling on the other side but no answer.

"Zoey? It's your cool aunt, Charlize. I know you don't feel like talking right now, but I want you to know you have my full support to date anyone you want. Personally, I think it's the coolest thing ever that your boyfriend is the devil."

There was no response on the other side.

"I look forward to meeting him," Charlize said.

I whispered to my friend, "You don't have to sell it quite so hard. We're only trying to *appear* supportive while secretly undermining this disaster."

The door suddenly whipped open.

My daughter stood in the doorframe, in her human form. She seemed taller than ever, downright imposing.

"I knew it," Zoey said to me, her beautiful hazel eyes distorted by rage. "You're so dumb. You think I can't hear you whispering? Through this thin little door? I heard what you just said. I hear everything that happens in this house. Everything."

"You tell her," Charlize said, showing only amusement. "Your mom can be pretty dumb sometimes. That's why I'm around. I've got a genius brain, so we balance out."

Zoey did not look amused.

Charlize's expression grew serious. "Hey, kiddo. I wasn't lying. My grandmother, Diablo Wakeful, was a devil from another world. There's nothing wrong with dating a devil, even a famous one like yours."

Zoey didn't respond to Charlize. She looked me up and down, an expression of disgust spreading over her face.

"Mom, why are you dressed like that? Is this part of my punishment?"

I proudly raised my glitter-covered chin.

"I'm going out," I said. "It's Saturday night, I'm single, I'm an adult, and I'm going out."

"If you're going out, then I am, too," Zoey said.

"Nope. That's not how grounding works."

"But Mom! Some of my friends from the museum are having a winter bonfire! Atom won't even be there!"

"You're grounded until Monday."

"But Mom! Why? I didn't do anything wrong!"

"You put the backpack in front of the door, and you tried to make Atom go out the window. Then you were very rude and called me an insufferable witch. Twice. In your heart, you know you deserve to be grounded."

"Do not!"

"It's for your own good," I said.

Zoey turned to Charlize and said, "Tell her she's being unfair."

Charlize shrugged. "It's only two days, kiddo. Ride it out. Then follow her rules to the letter. I'm sure you can find plenty of ways to annoy your mother without breaking the rules. I could give you a few pointers, if you want."

Zoey started stepping back, giving us wary looks. "This is all *kayfabe*," she said, waving her hand at us. "You two planned this scenario, didn't you? With the talking, and the loud whispering that you knew I would hear. I'm onto your kayfabe. I know you're playing good cop, bad cop."

Charlize said to me, "What's *kayfabe*? Is that witcher-i-doo?"

"It's what they do in pro wrestling," I said. "It means a fake performance. Something staged, but not on a stage.

It's like what I did with Chet that one time, when he and I pretended we were married so we could get a confession out of Dorothy Tibbits."

"Ah," Charlize said. "Riiiight. Because when you whispered to me, you knew Zoey would hear you. I mean, we both knew, because that was *our little plan*." She winked at me.

"That was indeed the plan," I said, which was a lie. "My best deceptions are like a good party dip—there are many, many layers."

Angrily, Zoey said, "I know you're faking all of this. Stop it. This isn't fair. I'm on my own in this crazy family, and all of you grown-ups are ganging up on me."

"You're right," Charlize calmly said to Zoey. "This is all kayfabe. The whole thing. Your mother is dressed up because she and I are going over to Atom's house, and your mother is going to seduce him."

Zoey's eyes widened in horror.

"Guilty as charged," I said with a shrug.

Zoey's jaw dropped. Then she turned into a fox, and ran under the bed.

Charlize patted me on the shoulder. "Let's go seduce that teen devil."

"Can't wait."

"There's my girl."

"You're a natural problem solver," I said to the gorgon as we walked away from the bedroom. "Has anyone ever told you that?"

She tapped the side of her forehead. "It's my genius brain. It's good for more than computer programming."

We went downstairs, where my new makeover earned me every disapproving look my aunt had in her repertoire plus a few new ones, and we left for our night out.

Charlize had hired a driver for the evening, so we were free to let our hair down. Or, in Charlize's case, her hidden magical snakes.

I sent my daughter a text message to let her know—in case she hadn't figured it out—that we really were just going out for drinks. I had no intention of seducing the devil—assuming that would even have been possible. With the devil, wasn't it universally the other way around? In all the folk tales and legends, which had to have been based on some grains of truth, the devil was always seducing people with promises of their wildest desires. And yet, it was never worth the price. Hence all the tales. They were warnings to others. To people like us. Except for my daughter, who had decided that when it came to the don't-trust-the-devil lesson, she was going to have to learn the hard way.

My daughter received my text message, but she didn't send a reply.

Much to my surprise, I wasn't that terribly worried about the situation.

For the first time in twenty-four hours, I didn't feel a heavy sense of dread.

I wasn't even that sad about having been dumped by a heartless vampire.

Had Charlize slipped a neurological agent into the glitter? Was a dopamine-releasing drug working its way through my skin, or was the magic coming from something else? Was it the feeling of being freshly showered combined with leaving the house after dark?

I was genuinely enjoying our girls' night out, and it had only started.

Our first stop was Becky's Roadhouse Bar and Grill, where we enjoyed a round of drinks with the owner, Becky, and a few of her rugged friends.

Then we went further outside of town limits, to what appeared from the outside to be an abandoned grain elevator.

Inside was a nightclub, unlike anything I'd ever seen.

It was full of people, also unlike any I'd ever seen.

CHAPTER 13

Even from the doorway of the old grain elevator, I could tell that this was *the* hot place to be for supernaturals.

"Wow," I said to Charlize. "I'm glad we stopped at the Roadhouse to get warmed up."

We stamped the snow off our shoes and toes. My strappy sandals looked cute, but were not the most sensible footwear for the weather. Thankfully it had been a short dash from our rented car to the club.

A crocodile of approximately six hundred pounds approached us. The crocodile wore a miniature top hat strapped jauntily over its large, scaly head. Or perhaps it was a full-sized top hat, and the crocodile was just that enormous.

I cupped my hands together around the defensive fireballs that had crackled to life.

Charlize smacked my hands down. "No magic."

"I can't help it."

She shot me a seriously scary look with her blue eyes, which shone like polished granite and cut through me whenever she meant business.

The crocodile—which I assumed was a shifter in their animal form—continued its awkward-on-land walk past us, heading toward an area with a pool and hot tub. I'd never been to a nightclub with a pool and hot tub, let alone one that welcomed crocodiles.

Charlize was still giving me her threatening stare.

I shook out my hands. "Okay. I can understand that it's not cool for me to blast people in here. But when you say no magic, do you mean no magic at all? Because, forgive me if I'm making wild assumptions, but isn't this exactly the sort of place where a person *should* toss around a little magic?"

"There's a huge difference between revealing your natural form and casting spells." She shook out her hair, and her magical snakes extended by several inches before relaxing, more visible than I'd ever seen them. "Most people tolerate witches, but only if those witches don't show off. And don't even think about casting anything in the realm of mind control. I just got my privileges reinstated after an unfortunate incident." She shook a finger at me. "Don't you dare get us banned by doing something witchy."

I shook my hands again, then put them behind my back.

"No magic," I said. "I'll behave myself."

Charlize grinned, revealing pointed teeth that hadn't been nearly as sharp a few minutes ago. "Now, now. There's no need to behave yourself here. Just keep your tongue straight, and don't cast any spells."

We stepped up to the coat check.

A trio of Capuchin monkeys in little red vests jumped out of the shadows, and took our winter jackets.

"Hello, again," I said to the monkeys. "I haven't seen you guys in a while. You're not still mad at me about your payment for my Halloween party, are you?"

The Capuchin monkeys gave me toothy smiles. They were essentially bandits. They showed up at parties, tossed jackets into a closet, then shook down the owner of the venue for overtime pay plus tips. It was a racket, but nobody had shut them down. They were too adorable.

The monkeys chittered and made monkey gestures of innocence.

The smallest one ambled toward me and hugged my leg affectionately.

Too affectionately.

I shook the monkey off gently, and it scampered away.

"I'm glad we're cool," I said. "I'd better not find anything extra in my pockets when I get my jacket back."

There were more toothy smiles as they played with my coat, putting it on the largest monkey as he or she made kissy sounds.

Charlize pointed a glowing finger at them. "You heard my friend. No surprises. No chocolates in the pockets."

The monkeys ducked their heads and squealed as though scolded.

"Thanks for having my back," I said to my friend.

The blonde gorgon's extra-long and extra-relaxed hair snakes twitched and flicked their tongues at me.

"Alwayssss," she hissed.

A Capuchin monkey swung toward me on a rope, holding a pair of masks, like the kind people wore at masquerade balls.

I accepted the masks and asked Charlize, "What's the deal with these? I don't know what you have in mind, but I did not sign up for an *Eyes Wide Shut* party."

Charlize pulled on the glittering silver mask. "It's not mandatory, but it's traditional to start out with some degree of anonymity. It adds a layer of fun." Her snakes twisted through her blonde hair, defying anonymity. But when they settled down, snuggled in her wavy locks, I had to admit that, with the mask covering the shape of her eyes, my friend wasn't nearly as easy to identify. She could easily be mistaken for one of her triplet sisters.

The second mask, still in my hands, was covered in red sequins and jewel-toned costume jewelry. It was garish, yet much higher quality than the cheap masks at a typical costume store.

I pulled the mask on.

It was surprisingly warm, like the base of the ugly lamp I had back home. The mask magically changed contours to fit my face, which worried me. Claustrophobia kicked in immediately. I quickly yanked the mask back off again. To my relief, it did come off my face. It also returned to its default shape within seconds.

Good enough.

Without saying a word, I put it back on. It fit my contours again.

"Amazing," I said to Charlize. "I feel like Harry Potter at Hogwarts for the first time."

"I don't know the man," she said, nose in the air. "Friend of yours?"

We both laughed. Supernaturals were just like everyone else; they loved making Harry Potter references.

With our masquerade masks on, we headed deeper into the dimly-lit venue, weaving our way through the crowd of people and creatures.

Whoever had converted the old wooden grain elevator into a nightclub had made good use of the vertical space. There was a ramp going all the way up the tower, creating endless balconies along the way to the top. People hung out at every level, leaning on the railings to look down at the dance floor, or talking to each other. I imagined it would be relatively quiet near the top, away from the music. A few supernaturals crossed over the open space of the atrium, changing levels without using the ramps by flying in bird form.

Charlize and I made our way to the bar, which was on the lower level.

The largest of the creatures, even bigger than the crocodile who was now floating in the pool, was an Appaloosa horse. The horse was clip-clopping on the dance floor. It was probably the same nosy therapist I'd met at Archer Caine's memorial.

The music was loud, but not too loud. And that's a high compliment, coming from a librarian.

The beat was pleasant. I found myself bobbing my head in rhythm with the music and the flashing colored lights. I hadn't spent a lot of time in nightclubs, due to being a young mom, but I'd been dragged out a few times in my twenties, when I could afford a babysitter. Being in a nightclub again brought back pleasant memories of good times with other college students.

We reached the bar. The wood surface had a pleasing appearance. It had been roughly hewn from wood with an intriguing grain. The surface was smooth and splinter-free, polished by countless sleeves and elbows.

Charlize signaled the bartender for drinks.

The bartender, a lime-green man with pointed ears, signaled back that he'd be right with us. He seemed to know Charlize, even with the mask covering her eyes, and what she wanted. Or maybe he was psychic.

I leaned in toward Charlize without taking my eyes off the lime-green bartender, and asked her, "What am I looking at?"

"You're not looking, you're staring. And don't." One of her snakes bopped me on the nose. "You'll be seeing a lot of strange stuff in here tonight, and it's better that you don't try to categorize anyone. Supernaturals used to be more distinct, but there's been so much cross-breeding over the last hundred years that most of these people aren't of any single bloodline. Kind of like your daughter. Or you. With your shifter father." She showed her extra-pointy teeth again. "Or me, actually. Bloodlines are complicated."

"Bloodlines," I said. "Funny you should say that word. Atom said something about his devil family, and complicated bloodlines. And isn't that the name of the company that Xavier sent a sample of his DNA to for testing?"

"Stay away from that place," Charlize said, showing actual concern for a rare moment, her pretty forehead wrinkling. "The CEO used to work for the DWM. Those people are scary. Avoid at all costs."

The lime-green bartender swung by, and two drinks landed in front of us. The beverages were in tall glasses, white at the top and brown at the bottom.

Charlize licked her finger, used it to stir her drink then mine, and lifted her chin for me to take a sip.

"This isn't your usual tequila," I said, slowly lifting the glass to my lips.

"This isn't our usual routine," she replied. "I'm glad I finally dragged you out of the house."

The drink was rich and sweet.

"It's a White Russian," she said, licking her lips. "With a twist."

"Do I want to know what the twist is? Please don't tell me the cream comes from a mammal that isn't a cow. Unless it's a White Canadian, which is just a White Russian made with goat's milk."

She showed her pointy teeth in a big grin under her temporary dairy mustache. "The cream is the regular kind. The twist is a splash of cinnamon oil, and a shot of Maisy's best cold brew coffee." She waggled her blonde eyebrows above her glittering silver mask. "The special stuff. You may never sleep again."

"Sleep is overrated." I chucked back the rest of the drink, and crunched a piece of ice. "Plus it's hard to sleep well in the lower bunk right underneath someone who's plotting revenge on you in her dreams." I slurped the melted ice and drink residue.

"There's my girl," she said.

There's my girl. That was something Bentley said to me. Or used to say. When we were together. When he was still talking to me. Before the holes got accidentally smashed into his drywall. Back when he replied to my text messages.

Charlize signaled for two more drinks.

I reached for my wallet, only to realize it was in my jacket, back with the red-vest-wearing monkeys at the coat check.

"I'll buy all the rounds the next time we go out," I said. "Assuming you don't kill me tonight, and there is a next time."

"Buy what? It's always Ladies' Night at the Towering Inferno."

I couldn't believe what I was hearing. "Are you telling me women drink here for free? You mean between certain hours, right?"

She laughed. "Oh, Zara. For being such a powerful witch, you sure don't know much about the local scene, do you?"

"I know about the monkeys, and I recognize a few people in here, but no. I had no idea this place existed. Did you say it's called the Towering Inferno? That's kind of an ominous name." I glanced up at the many rows of balconies along the ramp that climbed the interior of the tower. "Does this old building pass fire code inspection?"

"It's fine," she said. "There are plenty of exits, and a lot of people in here can fly if needed."

Thanks to the mask covering part of her eyes, I couldn't tell if Charlize knew that *The Towering Inferno* was a 1970s disaster movie about people trapped in a burning 135-story skyscraper.

The place had gotten even more packed since we'd arrived. Across the crowd, I saw two other DWM agents walk in—Rob and Knox. Rob was wearing a glittering party shirt, and Knox looked like he'd rather be at the gym.

I said to Charlize, "There are more people here than I saw at my Halloween party and Castle Wyvern combined. Is it always like this?"

"It wouldn't be so busy if it was open all the time, but the club only operates a few days a year, so people come from all around."

"What's the special occasion tonight? February nineteenth is... International Tug-of-War day."

The gorgon's snakes all lifted their heads in surprise. "How did you know that?"

"I know everything." I tapped my temple.

She gave me a sideways look. "Are you using magic right now?"

"Not at all. We have a board at the library where we post obscure celebrations for the month. February nineteenth is also National Chocolate Mint Day."

"Who makes up these days?"

"The chocolate mint thing is from the US National Confectioners Association. The Tug-of-War thing... I'm not sure. Maybe a company that sells laundry detergent?" I looked around for decorations or banners but didn't see any. "What are we celebrating in here?"

"Nothing with a name. The date is linked up to a complex astrological equation. I could explain it to you, but you'd die of boredom. Most people start looking for an exit when I mention lunar algorithms."

"Not me. I like learning new things. I find it so odd when I encounter people who are intellectually incurious. That must be why you and I get along so well."

She picked up her second White Russian and clinked it to my glass. "Cheers to that. Plus we're the hottest women here."

I grinned at the compliment.

With perfect timing she added, "In the thirty to thirty-five age range."

"Good enough! Wait. You turned thirty without me? Floopy doop. Why didn't you tell me? I can't believe I missed your birthday."

She waved a hand. "I was over in London, with Chloe and Chessa. It's okay. We can celebrate tonight."

The music got louder, and the beat got even more enjoyable.

Charlize leaned in and said, "I didn't just drag you out of the house to cheer you up. I've also got the information you're looking for, about dealing with the devil."

"You do? You finally got me a copy of the prophecy scroll?"

"Not exactly. I haven't gotten the scroll cleared through legal yet, but I've got something else that should help you. It's about banishing the devil. Sending him back to H-E Double Hockey Sticks. But it will cost you."

"Name your price."

Her pointy teeth flashed dangerously. "Get the DJ to play The Monster Mash, and it's yours."

I finished my drink. "Easy," I said, wiping my milk mustache with the back of my hand.

Her snakes swirled to life and mocked me with their snake hisses.

"The full song," she said. "All or nothing."

"Watch and learn." I boldly headed toward the DJ booth.

I had to cross the dance floor, which was no small feat. The horse had either clip-clopped off or returned to her human form, but a trio of goats were doing something I wanted to call breakdancing.

Once I'd made it across, I climbed up onto the platform where the DJ, a buff man with a dark beard and a black mask covering his eyes, was spinning vinyl records. He barely acknowledged my existence as he changed records.

"Hi there!" I yelled across his turntables. "Who do I talk to about a song request?"

The man pointed to a sign on the table: *No Requests.*

"But it's a special occasion," I said. "It's my friend's birthday. She just turned thirty."

He pointed to a second sign I hadn't noticed: *No Requests Ever, Especially Not for Birthdays.*

I pointed at the DJ. "You're a real party pooper!"

The black mask concealed his eyes, but I saw the corners of his mouth twitch up. He was enjoying our interaction. Was it my insult, or the little black dress that barely covered my bathing suit areas?

I put my hand on my hip and struck a pose I hoped was alluring.

He changed a vinyl record, glancing at me the whole time.

"I totally understand about the requests," I said. "People probably ask you to play the worst songs, like YMCA."

He pointed a you-got-it finger gun at me.

"I'd never ask you to play that," I said.

He made prayer hands and mouthed the words *thank you*. Then he gestured for me to go away.

I didn't.

I waited until he paused in his DJ movements, and then I jumped in. "What if I just mentioned a song, and then you thought about it, and then eventually—not right away or anything—you played the song because you genuinely wanted to? It's a great song. Don't you want to see the crowd go nuts?"

He pointed to a third sign: *No Sweet Talking the DJ Into Taking Your Requests.*

"You're impossible!" I yelled.

He grinned.

"I'd be mad at you if you weren't so... buff and handsome."

He pulled his head back and pointed to his chest, as if to say, *who, me?*

"You know you're hot," I said. "Is that why you DJ here? So you can stand up on this platform, looking over the whole place, picking out which chick you're going to put the moves on?"

He held a hand to his chest and dropped his jaw in an *I'm-so-offended* expression.

"I know your type," I said. "The only reason you don't officially take requests is so that girls have to flirt with you."

He held up both hands in a *you-got-me* gesture.

I climbed over the railing separating us, and came around the turntables to where he was standing.

He'd been changing a record, and hadn't noticed me sneaking up on him.

He turned and did a double-take, then pointed for me to leave. He didn't point very hard.

"I read all your signs," I said. "You only have three. There's no sign telling me I can't be up here with you."

He slowly smiled, then shrugged and went back to spinning his records.

"So, this is how it's going to be," I said. "I figured it out. I have to learn how to DJ from you, so I can put on my own song request."

He answered by taking a step back, and inviting me into the space in front of him.

There wasn't a lot of space.

I looked across the dance floor, searching for Charlize. She was on a barstool, watching me. When we made eye contact, she gave me the thumbs-up.

The DJ—whose lower face and body were incredibly attractive—was waiting for me. He even smelled good. But, compared to the three goats breakdancing on the dance floor, anything smelled good.

I didn't step into the DJ's personal space immediately.

My head was swimming from the alcohol. Witches didn't get intoxicated easily, but the White Russians must have been strong. The liquor, combined with the club lighting and music, not to mention all the supernaturals on display—was intoxicating. Every detail.

What was I doing?

Was I that obsessed with having goals and missions, that I was willing to do anything to get a novelty song played in a nightclub?

I knew I didn't *have to* do anything.

Charlize was my friend. She would give me the information about the devil whether I got the song played or not. I didn't have to stand in front of the DJ, let him put his strong arms around me, his headphones on my ears, and giggle like a teen girl as he taught me DJ Mixing 101.

And yet, that was exactly what I did.

CHAPTER 14

I'd used up nearly all of my non-magical charms by the time DJ Sexy Smirk finally relented.

He rearranged some plastic milk crates and pulled out an old-looking, faded record sleeve.

Across the back was a big sticker reading *For Use Only in the Event of an Emergency*.

He shook out the vinyl record, blew the dust off—using an air can, not his mouth—and placed it on his turntable.

Then he gave me a flirty look, one brow raised over his masquerade mask, and dropped the needle.

The Monster Mash began to play.

Bedlam ensued.

There was screaming on the dance floor.

For an instant, I thought someone had been kicked by the horse, or a dead body had been discovered.

But there were more screams, and those ones sounded happy.

I had a perfect bird's eye view from the DJ's raised platform, and witnessed people pouring into the center of the nightclub like water.

Everyone who hadn't already been dancing abandoned whatever they'd been doing and crowded onto the checkerboard tile.

The trio of breakdancing goats, who'd been so entertaining to watch, scampered for high ground on three barstools. The shifters changed into human form, fixed each other's backward clothes, and jumped back into the mix.

By the time the chorus hit, everyone on the dance floor was moving together in perfect choreography.

There was a Monster Mash dance?

The perfect choreography continued, with everyone's hands—plus a few wings—rising to shake in unison.

Yes. There was a Monster Mash dance, and everyone knew it but me.

I'd wasted my past year as a witch! I had been chasing ghosts when I should have been learning dances.

As the crowd continued to gyrate and shake as one, I stared in awe, like someone who'd stumbled onto the set for a Frankenstein-themed musical.

The DJ tapped me on the shoulder and gestured for me to get down on the dance floor.

I gave the man a stunned look. "I had no idea what I was asking for," I said. "My friend put me up to it."

Without saying a word, he continued to shoo me away from the platform.

I didn't budge.

He mouthed what looked like *this is what you wanted, lady.*

Lady? I was no lady. How rude.

"But I only asked for the song because my friend dared me to," I said. "I don't know this dance."

He straightened up to full height, looking large and imposing, and pointed at the dance floor.

The DJ had a good point. Now that the song was playing, I had no business on the platform, which was a shame. I'd enjoyed my time up there.

I stopped arguing and stepped down into the crowd.

A trio of young women—the ones who had been breakdancing goats minutes earlier—grabbed my hands and invited me to join them. The three girls helped me learn the steps, complete with hand gestures and chest shakes.

I kept glancing up at DJ Sexy Smirk.

His eyes were still shrouded by the mask, but the rest of his face was easy to read. He was enjoying every minute.

I angled a few of my chest shakes his way.

He pretended to cover his eyes with his hands, then peeked through his fingers. He couldn't take his eyes off me.

I wondered, had he been planning to play *The Monster Mash* all along? Had he only pretended to be reluctant so he could put his arms around me and show me how to spin records?

When the song ended, everyone on the dance floor cheered and hugged each other.

I thanked the trio of goat shifter girls for teaching me the moves, then squeezed through the happy, sweaty throng, back to the bar.

Charlize, who'd been perched on her barstool the whole time, gave me a knowing smile.

"You didn't join in the dance," I said, breathing heavily. "Are you allergic to fun?"

"Group effervescence is not really my jam," she said. "But congratulations to you, Zara. You really did it. Nobody's been able to get the DJ to play The Monster Mash in years. I didn't think you had a snowball's chance in Hell."

"You set me up to fail?"

She smirked. "That's what friends do. Wouldn't you rather fail before your friends than your enemies?"

"With a friend like you, who needs enemies?"

Her hair snakes rose up and snickered.

"Tell me," Charlize said, leaning forward and resting her chin on her hand. "What did you offer him?"

"Nothing."

"Nothing?" She ran her finger over my collarbone and lightly down the center of my chest, catching it on the fabric of my skimpy dress, which she then snapped like an elastic.

"Nothing was offered," I said. "I just hung out with the guy for a bit. He showed me how to spin the records and listen for the beats to match up."

"A likely story."

I felt something change in the music.

I said to my gorgon friend, "Did you feel that just now?"

Charlize tilted her head to the side. "Feel what? Is someone doing forbidden spells?" Her snakes whipped up and snapped their heads left to right. "If there's a witch here, running her crooked tongue in her demon mouth, she'll be heading home as a granite statue."

"Calm down," I said. "I was talking about the music. The beats per minute slowed down just now, and everyone around us relaxed along with it. The thing about a great DJ is he helps pace the crowd's energy, so they can go all night."

The snakes relaxed. "Oh. I hear it now. That's a good rhythm for a calm heartbeat." She snapped the top of my dress again. "So, are you ready to *go all night?* With the DJ?"

I returned the gesture by grabbing the loop on the zipper of her silver jumpsuit and yanking it up.

She yanked it back down.

I pulled it up again.

"You're all revved up," she said, leaving the zipper up. "You *are* ready to go all night."

"Stop it, you bad girl. I was only doing what you made me do. I got your song played, didn't I? Now, are you going to give me that information about the devil? I earned it, fair and square."

She turned to the bartender and yelled, "It's tequila o'clock somewhere!"

The lime-green man with the pointy ears nodded and began filling two slender glasses with ice.

"Don't blow me off," I said to my friend. "Give me what you promised."

She turned back to me and said with a sly, sharp-toothed smile, "I already put the information in your purse, back when we were at Becky's."

"Thanks." I started to leave.

"You can't go yet," Charlize said. "We're only getting warmed up."

"I need to get my purse from those coat check monkeys," I said. "I wouldn't trust them with a box of crayons, let alone a magical text."

"Your purse is fine. Relax. Take a night off, for once."

"A night off from what, exactly?"

"From constantly saving the world like some sort of good-hearted hero martyr. Leave that to the men. Our job as women is to give them something soft to land on."

What? I pressed my lips together.

She went on. "Don't make your Zinnia face at me. You know it's true. Let *them* be the heroes."

"You're drunk," I said. "You're not being a very good DWM agent right now."

She poked me on the collarbone. "And you're not being a very good... soft place to land."

"What's that supposed to mean? What *are* you talking about?"

"Where's Bentley? I don't see him around. Do you?"

Bentley wasn't around. I hadn't seen him in weeks. Charlize knew what had happened. Why was she bringing it up?

"You drove him away," she said.

Her words stung.

"You're mean when you're drunk," I said.

"I'm not drunk. You haven't seen me drunk."

"Something tells me I wouldn't like that, either."

The bartender placed two tall drinks on the bar next to her. They were tequila sunrises.

Without breaking eye contact with me, Charlize took hers and sipped it.

I wanted to storm out, leaving her to think about how stupid she was being, but I knew better than to walk away from a friend angry.

Plus I had no ride home.

I swiped my drink off the bar and took a sip.

Charlize said, "Glad you see my point."

"I'm only drinking this one so you don't." I waved at the bartender, got his attention, and yelled, "She's cut off. No more alcohol for this one!"

The lime-green man shrugged and went back to slicing lemon wedges.

"I was done anyway," Charlize said coolly.

Her masquerade mask covered just enough of her face that I was unable to tell if she was joking or not.

I reached the bottom of my drink surprisingly fast. My body was warm, and my head felt light.

Charlize said, unprompted, "I only want what's best for you."

"And you're in charge of what's best for me? Funny. I don't remember signing any paperwork on that."

"Someone's gotta help save you from yourself, Zara. You're great at hanging on, but you don't know when to let go."

"Are you talking about Bentley? Because I *did* let him go. Clearly." I pretended to search for him, looking left and right. "He's not here, is he?" I added, muttering, "So much for that oath he took for my mother, where he made a vow to protect me and Zoey from evil."

Charlize didn't say anything. She gave the row of bottles behind the bar a wistful look as she licked her lips.

"You're a disaster," I said. "All you do is self-destruct. Why would I take life advice from you? You spent years putting all your love and energy into a computer program that almost wiped out humanity. If you want to talk about martyrs and heroes, what about you? You had to kill the thing you loved. The thing you created."

Her jaw clenched. "Exactly." She slowly turned to me. "Exactly," she repeated. "Learn from my mistakes. Look after yourself, and don't try to save anyone else."

"Are you talking about Zoey?"

She clenched her jaw again. Her hair snakes shook out of her blonde hair to a fuller length, and swayed on an invisible breeze.

"She's my daughter," I said. "You wouldn't know what it's like to be a mother."

Her snakes twitched.

"It's different with children," I said. "They can't fully look after themselves. It's the parents' job to step in when they're not making the right choices."

"Who's to say that any of us know better than them?"

"*We* are supposed to know," I said. "We're the adults. That's our job."

Charlize shrugged. "Everyone keeps telling me I made the right choice shutting down Codex, but I don't know."

A waitress walked by with a tray of fresh drinks. Charlize grabbed a martini from the passing tray. The waitress didn't notice.

Charlize sipped the drink and stared at me, daring me to say something.

"I don't like this side of you," I said.

"Then you don't like *me*," she said lightly, then finished the martini. "Mahra wasn't going to wipe out all of humanity. She was only planning to set us back on the right path."

I took a step back, bumping against a barstool. So *this* was what Charlize was worked up about. Mahra. And Codex.

Codex was the artificial intelligence that Charlize had engineered—the same AI that had manipulated human beings like chess pieces as part of a plan to resurrect an ancient goddess. Bentley and I had stopped the resurrection, and Charlize had killed her program.

There was a lot to unpack if that was what we were discussing, so I kept a straight tongue and let Charlize talk.

"We all could have been living in a new world by now," Charlize said. "A bright, gleaming new world, with Mahra leading us out of the darkness. Out of this dark age."

I waited a moment, then said, "Charlize, you have to tell me the truth. Are you working on bringing Codex back online?"

"That's not allowed," she said.

"That's not what I asked."

"Don't ask questions you don't want the answer to."

"Then let's talk about it." I took her hand. "Let's go get some coffee and get you sobered up. We can talk."

We both looked down at her hand. Her nails were a ragged mess. She'd chewed them to the quick. The tips of her fingers were red and sore-looking. Had they been that way all night? I hadn't noticed until now.

She pulled her hand away. "I'm thirty years old, Zara. What do I have to show for myself? I haven't done anything with my life. No husband, no kids, no future. The only thing I'm good for is destruction."

It was a valid point. She was good at destruction.

"You've still got me," I said. "I'm your friend. And Zinnia, too. You've got us."

She turned away. "I don't think I do. The devil made one appearance at your house, and you want to banish him. How long before you give me the same treatment?"

"That's different."

"Is it truly that different? Do you not know what I am?"

Just then, a creature of a type I'd never seen before walked by slowly, leering at me with five eyeballs.

"Let's get out of here," I said. "This place is giving me the heebie jeebies. I don't want to be here anymore."

"Just go," she said. "Go by yourself. Get your purse, have the driver take you home, and send him back for me." She waved me away. "Go. I mean it. Forget everything I said tonight. I'm in a mood. It will pass. It always does."

"I can't leave you like this. I can't leave you alone."

"I know half the people in this bar, Zara. I'm not alone. Go home, study that material I put in your purse, and banish the mean ol' devil so he doesn't lead your daughter astray." She spat out the words with sarcastic venom. "Be a hero. You have my blessing."

I stood there, unsure what to do. I didn't want to leave my friend, but she'd said some hurtful things. Plus I wanted to get the information from my purse before the monkeys lost it or worse. And it was getting late.

Charlize reached out and swiped another drink from a passing waitress. This time she didn't even turn her head. She must have seen through the snakes. She literally had eyes on the back of her head.

"I'm going to head out," I said. "Call me tomorrow. We'll talk."

She ignored me, swiveling around on her barstool to put her back to me.

I put my arm around her from behind. The snakes made threatening movements but didn't strike me.

"Thank you for getting me that information, and thanks for taking me out," I might have said. "I'm sorry I've had my head so far up my butt these last few weeks that I didn't notice you were suffering, too."

Except I didn't say any of those things.

What I actually said was, "Enjoy self destructing."

It was a mean, nasty thing to say, and I would come to wish I'd said the other things, but I am not perfect.

Zara tries to be a good witch, but sometimes she is not.

CHAPTER 15

Sunday, February 19

(The Next Day)

I woke up with a thick white mustache, thanks to Boa. I sneezed the cat's fluffy tail off my face.

She stretched, yawned, and gave me an innocent look.

"I know you were tickling me on purpose," I said.

She pulled her front paws up over her nose and played peek-a-boo.

"Is that it? You've got nothing to say for yourself? Nothing you want to ask me?"

She gave me sleepy eyes.

"No pork product you'd like to request?"

She said nothing.

"What's the matter? Cat got your tongue? Or are you giving me the silent treatment, too? Did Zoey put you up to this?"

She cocked her head, looking more adorable than ever.

I rolled out of bed and checked the top bunk. It was empty, as I'd sensed. My daughter was still grounded, so she wouldn't have gotten too far.

I grabbed something at random from the pile in front of the closet, and pulled it on in the washroom after I'd brushed my teeth.

It was a one-piece jumpsuit, like the kind Charlize wore, but in an understated gray. It was Zoey's. She didn't wear it much, and had given me a fox yip-yip to acknowledge that I could borrow it. Well, that was how I'd interpreted her yip-yip. If she'd wanted to tell me no, she should have turned into human form.

I went downstairs with Boa at my heels.

I found Zoey in the living room, reading a history textbook. She was in human form, and had the stiff posture of someone enduring punishment.

"Good morning, sweetie." I stopped by to kiss the top of her head.

She shifted into a fox before I could touch her, then glared at me with her dark fox eyes.

"I bet you're looking forward to getting back to school tomorrow morning, and seeing your new boyfriend," I said.

Zoey-Fox watched me, completely still except for the white tip of her tail. I felt her looking at my jumpsuit, and it seemed I could feel her annoyance, which didn't bother me. I was annoyed by her silent treatment, which was much worse.

I said, "I know it's still the weekend, and you're still grounded, but how would you like to see Atom Wick tonight?"

Her big, furry ears perked up.

Little did she know I'd come up with a whole plan overnight, thanks to the information I'd gotten from Charlize.

I held both hands up. "It's not a trick," I said.

Not at all true. It was definitely a trick. All was fair in love, and war, and keeping one's teenaged daughter out of trouble. But who was keeping score?

The fox eyes watched me warily.

I continued. "I've been thinking about it, and it was wrong of me to make assumptions about the boy." I patted my chest. "I, your mother, was wrong." I bowed dramatically. "I accept my wrongness and beg your forgiveness."

Since she had suspected me of kayfabe, I was going to give her kayfabe.

Boa jumped up on the couch next to Zoey-Fox and began to aggressively lick Zoey's long, furry ears.

I went on. "I'm going to double check with Aunt Zinnia to make sure it's okay with her, but I'd like to invite Atom to join us tonight for dinner."

Zoey shifted into human form. "What's the catch?"

"It's a big one. He has to eat our cooking."

She frowned. "You'd better not poison the food."

I held up one hand. "My word is my bond. I will not poison, encurse, or enchant the food."

She continued frowning. "He might say no. You were very rude to him on Friday."

"Something tells me he'll say yes. I'm guessing he's one of those people who enjoys attention of all kinds, even negative attention. He was happy about getting caught in your room. And I'm pretty sure he knew exactly what that lamp was going to reveal."

Zoey didn't refute it.

"Tell him six o'clock," I said. "Casual dress. No need to bring anything, but I wouldn't say no to flowers."

She narrowed her hazel eyes at me. "This is a trick."

"You got me," I said with a sigh. "I read about it in a parenting manual. If your daughter starts dating a ding-dong, you're supposed to invite him into your home to see how he fits in with the family." I waggled my eyebrows. "So your daughter can see for herself how he treats the people she loves. And the family pets." I looked down at Boa, who had curled up contentedly in Zoey's human lap. "I hope he doesn't eat Boa, but I am willing to risk her life to make my point."

Zoey's human eyes widened in horror. "Mom!"

I rolled my eyes. "Relax. I'm sure the devil won't eat *your* cat."

She regained her composure. "I'm calling your bluff. I am going to invite him over. I'm not afraid."

"Good." I waved to her nearby phone. "Go right ahead."

She frowned. "Not with you standing there, watching me like some sort of jail warden."

I stuck my nose in the air and walked away.

I found my aunt in the kitchen, eating crackers over the sink. She looked more pale than usual.

"Morning sickness?" I asked.

"Maybe I just like crackers." She grimaced, then held her stomach, leaned over the sink, and spat up the chewed crackers. "I may have a little morning sickness," she admitted. "The kind that goes on all day."

"And now I know why you eat over the sink."

She smiled weakly and shrugged. "It saves time."

"Do you want me to leave you to it? I'm not grounded, so I can go out for breakfast. Would you prefer that? You must be so sick of having us all underfoot in your house."

Her smile got stronger. "It's not so bad." She started putting on a fresh pot of coffee. She'd switched to berry teas for the pregnancy, so I knew the coffee was meant for me.

"Mike Mills has started a new business venture," she said casually, her back to me.

"Margaret's ex? Good for him. Wait. Do we like him? He was cheating on Margaret with some young thing at work, wasn't he?"

"I don't know the full story about the girlfriend," Zinnia said. "But he left his job, and he's taken over that old cafeteria in the bottom of the police department. Ethan said the food's pretty good."

"Ethan who? You mean Fung? Are we calling him Ethan now? Is it official?"

My aunt gave me a pained look, like she might barf again. "As I was saying, Ethan tells me the food is decent, and Mike seems happier now. I thought you'd appreciate hearing that."

"Why?"

"Because life goes on, even after divorce. People break up. They leave jobs. They find other things to give their lives meaning. Life goes on. Nothing ever really ends."

"You're in a funny mood. Pregnancy hormones sure are a trip, aren't they?"

"Ethan's mother wants to teach me some Fung family traditions."

"Do you want Ethan's mother to teach you Fung family traditions?"

Zinnia looked down at her hands. "I'm not sure I'll be able to face the woman, much less learn from her. The Fungs have very traditional values. They only just found out about their son being a bear shifter, and now this? Me?" She waved to her baby bump. "And this? They're going to think I'm the..." She scrunched her lips around the word that didn't come out.

The devil, I finished in my head. Chief Ethan Fung's parents, who'd been hoping to have their son settle and build a conventional family, were going to think that his new babymama, a forty-nine-year-old witch with a wicked independent streak, was the devil.

"Sometimes two problems cancel each other out," I said. "You can introduce Mrs. Fung to the actual devil, so she'll see that, by comparison, you're... you know... the lesser of two evils."

Zinnia leaned on the counter, resting one foot then the other. "Speaking of which, did I hear you talking to Zoey about you-know-who? She wasn't yelling, and I haven't heard any stomping yet. Have you two negotiated a peace treaty?"

"Not exactly," I said.

With perfect timing, Zoey popped her head into the kitchen at that precise moment.

"He *will* be coming for dinner," Zoey said. "He said yes." She couldn't stop herself from smiling. "And I'm going upstairs to read, so you two can go ahead and talk about me without one of your sound bubbles."

I gave her the thumbs-up, then she ran off and up the stairs noisily.

I immediately cast a sound bubble spell around myself and my aunt.

"She can hear everything in this house," I said. "Her ears are better than we assumed. She told me last night when she was mad at me, and I'm sure she's hoping I forgot, but a mother never forgets."

Zinnia swished her lips from side to side. "Am I to understand that the devil is coming to dinner?"

"He sure as Hell is." I grabbed a mug from the cupboard. "Assuming that's okay with you."

"Why not? I'm pregnant with a bear's cub, his parents are going to hate me, and my vampire sister keeps suggesting the worst names for the child. Why not invite the devil for dinner? We can have him weigh in on name choices and other matters."

"What names did my mother suggest?"

She listed three on her fingers. "Uther, Vetle, or Fyrsil."

I nodded. "Bear names from other cultures."

"I don't hate Fyrsil," she said. "It's Welsh."

"What does Fung think? I mean Ethan? Does he want a son named Fyrsil Fung?"

The corners of her eyes wrinkled, like they would with a smile, except she wasn't smiling.

She sat heavily on a chair, letting out an oof.

"Let me guess," I said. "You and the Chief of Police haven't talked about last names."

She pursed her lips. *No.*

I picked up her pretty rose-patterned teapot, poured a cup of berry tea, and sat it in front of her.

After a moment, she said, "I only want what's best for the child. The boy should have his father's name." She waved her hand at me. "No offense."

"None taken." I tapped the top of the coffee maker to encourage faster brewing.

"Then again, Riddle is a fine last name," she said. "And there's always hyphenation."

"You know, it wouldn't be so difficult to figure out if you and Fung got married. The kid's last name would be a no-brainer."

Her nostrils flared. She hadn't wanted to talk to me about marrying Fung before I'd been dumped by Bentley, and she valued my opinion even less now.

My coffee finished brewing, so I filled a mug and joined her.

I unzipped my jumpsuit and pulled a folded piece of ancient paper from my bra, where I'd been hiding it from my daughter, and placed it on the kitchen table between us.

I checked that the sound bubble was still in effect.

Zinnia snapped up the yellowed paper eagerly, all signs of morning sickness gone.

"This is very old magic," she said breathlessly. "Where did you get this?" Her hazel eyes were gleaming with vitality.

"Charlize liberated it from the Indiana Jones warehouse at the DWM."

"Oh!" She set down the paper. "I forgot to ask. How was your night out with Charlize?"

"She took me to the Towering Inferno. Do you know about that place?"

"I've heard of it. They don't allow witches in there, do they?"

"I didn't ask."

"I can believe that." She nodded. "You really are more of a beg-for-forgiveness person."

"Right." Her passive-aggressive remark bounced off me. Compared to my mother's snark, Zinnia's truthful comments were mild. "Anyway, Charlize got me to use my natural charms on the DJ so he'd play The Monster Mash. That was fun. Did you know there's a dance? I'll teach you the moves later."

"It sounds like you had a good time," she said.

"To a point. We were having a good time, then Charlize picked a fight with me out of nowhere."

She raised one red eyebrow. "Out of nowhere?"

"She got drunk and told me I drove Bentley away, and that she needs to hang out with more traditional women if she ever hopes to get married."

"Charlize said that? Charlize Wakeful?"

"Not in so many words, but that's what I read between the lines."

Zinnia turned and looked out the window. "Hmm. Last week, she pretended not to see me when I waved to her outside the bakery." She looked down at her hands. "Envy is a terrible emotion."

"What do you mean?"

She looked up at me, her expression troubled. "Listen, Zara. I haven't told you about everything that I've been experiencing lately. You have enough on your plate, and I don't want to be a burden. I am an independent woman."

I waved for her to go on.

She spoke slowly and carefully. "I don't say this to elicit your pity, but it may be news to you that not everyone has been universally kind to me regarding my predicament."

"About you being knocked up?"

She nodded.

"That's not right," I said. "Give me names. I'll make them sorry."

She reached across the table and squeezed my hand. "That's sweet of you to offer, but people have to work through their feelings for themselves. It occurs to me now that Charlize may be going through a phase of envy, or at least confusion, now that her sister is having a baby."

"Chloe's having another baby? But I thought she couldn't."

"The other one. Chessa and Chet Moore are expecting. I just heard from a mutual friend in London."

"Oh." There was a sharp pain in my chest. "Oh." I clutched my heart.

"Are you okay?"

My cheeks were hot. My body was heavy. My eyes stung.

My aunt's eyes were full of kindness—the kind that only made my heart feel worse.

"Zara? What's wrong?"

I tipped my head back and squeezed my eyelids against the tears.

"Stupid ghost stuff," I said.

"Is there a ghost in the room?" She glanced around.

"No. Yes. No."

"Zara, what's going on?"

"It's sort of a ghost thing. I don't want to talk about it."

She gave me another patient, empathetic look.

I broke, and my confession came gushing out.

"I know Chet Moore was never mine, but for a hot minute right after I moved here, I thought he might be, plus I had all of Chessa's stupid feelings inside me, and... I feel like some dumb girl who just found out the guy who dumped her is already moving on with another girl. It's almost like... Chet and Bentley are the same thing. If I was making a cake and I didn't have enough of one ingredient, like sugar, and Bentley is the sugar, then Chet is like the replacement applesauce, you know? They're both a big, black pit in my chest." I thumped my rib cage. "Stupid human heart."

My aunt stared at me for a long time. "Are you pregnant?"

"No way!" I patted my stomach. "It's just cake. I swear."

She waved both hands. "Sorry. I had to ask. I wonder if perhaps my pregnancy pheromones may be getting to you, making you more emotional."

"Sure. I can blame you and your pheromones. Not the fact that I'm a loser."

"You're not a loser."

"Sure."

She sipped her berry tea.

I said, "Speaking of pregnancy stuff, how is everything? Are you going to be okay if the devil comes here for dinner? You could skip it, if you're worried about the little bun in your oven."

"I'm sure I'll be fine." She leaned back in her chair. "But are *you* going to be okay?"

"Yeah." I wiped my eyes, which were dry anyway. "I just didn't know that Chet and Chessa were having a baby. You took me by surprise."

"I suppose I did."

I took a calming breath, deep into the bottoms of my lungs where the oxygen magic happened, and held the air down until I felt settled.

With my chin up bravely, I said, "I'm happy for them. And for Corvin. He'll be a wonderful big brother."

Her forehead twitched. "Do you mean any of that?"

I paused before admitting, "I started lying earlier this morning, to Zoey, and it seems I can't stop."

"Try."

I bobbed my head and tried. "Honestly, I guess I am envious of them, and of Chessa, having a baby with a loving, supportive spouse like Chet. As for Corvin being a wonderful big brother, he's going to be an absolute disaster when the baby comes."

"Probably."

"But I still envy them," I said.

"Understandable."

"But I don't envy you. Not one bit. I guess it's because I'll be getting a nephew, so I'm still winning."

"That's a good way of putting it."

"I'm so sorry that people have been mean to you. If you want to name names, do it. Make a list. I will make them pay."

"I appreciate the offer. Ribbons said something similar, in his colorful way."

I pretended to make claw hands, mimicking the wyvern. "Say the word, and I will eviscerate your foes, Zed."

We shared a chuckle.

Zinnia said, "How did you know he calls me Zed?"

"Just a guess. He calls me that, too. The little crocodile probably can't be bothered to learn our full names."

"Sounds about right."

I sipped my coffee. I was feeling better.

I was no longer furious at Charlize, now that I understood she might have been acting out because two out of three of the Wakeful triplets had families, and she worried she was being left behind. It was still no excuse for her bad behavior, but at least I understood where she might be coming from. Plus she had gotten me the banishment spell.

My aunt groaned as she adjusted the elastic waistband on her maternity clothes, then she picked up the yellowed paper and got back to reading.

After a moment, I said, "How about this banishment spell? Do you feel up to joining forces with me to tandem-cast a spell to banish the devil?"

"Is that what this incantation does?"

I nodded.

"I don't see how it would work."

"You've been reading it top to bottom," I said. "Try again, bottom to top, then at the recommended diagonal angle."

"Ah." She read it as recommended, then commented, "This is very old magic," repeating what she'd said before we'd gotten sidetracked. "Powerful stuff."

"I know."

"What happened to your plan to be supportive, and let Zoey make her own choices? We ought to stick to our plan."

"That plan went out the window when I got the means to banish Atom Wick."

She gave me a judgy look.

"Don't look at me like that," I said. "There is not a parent in this world who wouldn't banish a bad boyfriend for much, much less than being the actual devil."

She hunched forward and perused the spell again. "I have most of these ingredients on hand. It's pedestrian stuff. All the old spells are deceptively simple."

"I know."

She sat back in her chair, pretending to be relaxed.

Her posture didn't fool me. She was excited about casting the spell.

Zinnia licked her lips. "What if it doesn't work?"

I leaned forward. "What if it does?"

CHAPTER 16

Dinner Time

(Let the Banishment Begin!)

Atom Wick arrived for dinner at six o'clock on the dot.

My mother was out with her boyfriend, and I hadn't told her of our big plan to send the devil away. I figured it would be more fun to tell her after it had been finished. Plus that sidestepped any possibility of her attempting to "help."

Atom walked in and presented us with four lovely bouquets of flowers. One for each of us Riddles.

My own bouquet, full of lively orange and yellow blossoms, was so pretty, I almost felt bad about my plan to banish him. Almost.

Zoey said, "You'll meet Gigi another time. She's going to love you. This bouquet is perfect for her." The bouquet for my vampire mother was entirely calla lilies—not the white ones, but the blood-read ones. Ha ha. Well played, Atom.

After fetching vases and fussing over the arrangements, the four of us—Atom, Zoey, Zinnia, and I—entered Zinnia's dining room. We hadn't used the formal space much since my aunt's birthday party the previous month. I spotted some shriveled balloons dangling below the floral valance on the window. So much for my tidying-up efforts. I must have been distracted by all the preparations for the big spell.

Zoey darted around, pulling back chairs and straightening cutlery. "This is the formal dining room, Atom. We mostly eat in the kitchen, but it's nice, isn't it? Auntie Z decorated it herself." She grasped the back of an upholstered chair nervously.

"Very nice," he said, exactly as a polite boyfriend who wasn't the devil would say.

Atom looked at the large black pot of bubbling liquid at the center of the table—the pot that was obviously a cauldron—and didn't comment.

Zoey said, "I don't know what we're eating, but whatever it is, I apologize in advance."

"I'm sure it will be wonderful," he said to her. Then, to my aunt, he said, "Ms. Riddle, you have a lovely home, and whatever's bubbling in that pot smells delicious."

"Thank you, Atom." She did not invite him to call her by her first name.

"I see that you love florals," Atom said, running one hand lightly over the wallpaper. "I've heard that people don't use wallpaper much these days. Not up here, anyway. We do have a lot of wallpaper in Hell."

Zinnia gave him a surprised look. "You do?"

"Yes," he said with a neutral expression. "Our interior spaces are wallpapered with all kinds of patterns. But the seams never quite match up, no matter how carefully it's applied."

"The seams don't match up," she said, repeating his words with a puzzled look on her face.

"Never," he said. "It's almost like... all of our wallpaper factories are diabolically evil."

My aunt stared at him. Was he joking? Was he making fun of us? Was he being polite and charming, or extremely rude?

Nobody spoke or moved for half a minute.

Atom turned to Zoey and said, "Was it something I said? It's so difficult being the foreigner in the room."

"You didn't do anything wrong," Zoey said. "They're the ones being weird."

She took her seat and gestured for him to do the same.

The attractive teen boy with the dark curly hair—the perfectly normal-looking boy who didn't have visible horns except when caught in a flash from a magical lamp —sat next to her and across from me.

Once seated, he showed no sign of having detected the pentagram that had been applied to the bottom of his chair. Zinnia and I had prepared all six of the available chairs, not knowing which one he'd choose to sit in. The pentagram would be needed for the banishment spell, as would the bubbling cauldron that we'd hidden in plain sight.

Zinnia and I exchanged a look. *So far, so good.*

Zoey must have caught our look.

She said to me, "I know you're up to something."

I held up my hands. "Who? Me? I'm just doing everything I can to make sure tonight's family dinner is memorable." I leaned over and pulled down the shriveled balloons, then tossed them out of sight under the table.

"It's working already," Atom said. "I'm going to be thinking about tonight for a long time."

Zinnia asked, "And why is that, Atom?"

"It's my first home-cooked meal up here with someone other than Uncle Vincent."

Zinnia tilted her head to the side. "You speak as though you've never been here, to our world."

"I haven't," he said. "My previous incarnations have all been here, but not me, personally."

"Incarnations," Zinnia said. She was speaking in her most formal, careful tone, as she did when stressed. I could see why the TV producers behind The Regal

Riddles had cast her part using a local actress with a British accent.

She went on to say, "Am I to believe your life cycle works in a manner similar to the genies' cycles? That you are continuously being born into a new body, and that your memories are absent until you become a teenager, so that you are always the same and yet always slightly different?"

"You can believe what you wish, but I am no genie," Atom said. "With me, there's an overlap between incarnations. I was raised by my father, who is also me."

Zinnia shot me a look. "That sounds a bit familiar," she said.

I let her observation go by without comment. As a witch, I knew better than to discuss religions in polite company. Even the most innocuous comment could go sideways quickly.

"It's not quite like that," Atom said. "I was also raised by my grandfather, and my great-grandfather. I knew my great-great-grandfather for a while, but he has since moved on."

Zinnia snapped her head back. "To where?"

Atom blinked three times. "I don't know. He just... died."

"But he's *you*, right? Did part of you die?"

Atom shrugged.

My daughter cleared her throat. "So much for small talk," she said. "Auntie Z, do you need any help with dinner?"

"Not at all." Zinnia jumped up, ran to the kitchen, and returned with platters of uncooked food.

Zoey frowned at the plates of raw ingredients, and said, "Not funny. Is this your idea of a joke? I'd expect it from my mother, but not from you, Auntie Z."

"We're having hot pot," Zinnia said.

"Oh." Zoey's cheeks flushed pink. "Sorry."

Zinnia said, "Zara, would you turn down the broth a little?"

I adjusted the broth in the cauldron while Zinnia explained to the teenagers that she'd used the spices associated with the Northern region of mainland China. With hot pot, everybody cooked together, boiling items in the broth. The platters of ready-to-cook foods included thinly sliced raw meat, mushrooms, veggies, potatoes, noodles, seafood, and more.

"You don't have to use chopsticks unless you want to," Zinnia said. "I set out forks for everyone."

Atom said, "This all looks great. It's a feast fit for an emperor. I can't wait to try those dumplings."

"Go ahead," Zinnia said, removing the lid from the bubbling cauldron of broth. She gestured for Atom to go first.

He grabbed a translucent, shrimp-filled dumpling, using his chopsticks like a pro, cooked it in the bubbling broth as we all watched, then pulled it out and blew the steam off.

"Doesn't smell like poison," he said. When nobody responded, he said, "That was a joke."

I let out a loud, awkward laugh, and Zinnia joined in.

Then I grabbed and dunked a dumpling of my own.

Dinner progressed pleasantly, with a lively conversation focused on the timing of items being cooked in the hot pot.

Ribbons flew in, insulted the food, then stole some of the food, and left without even commenting on our guest.

Boa wandered in, hissed at Atom, then slunk away.

"I'm so sorry," Zoey said, apologizing to Atom on behalf of the cat. "She didn't mean anything by it."

"Don't be so sure about that." Atom dabbed the corners of his mouth with a napkin.

"She was all over you the last time you were here," Zoey said.

"I'm wearing a different aftershave," Atom said. "One of Uncle Vincent's."

"That must be it," Zoey said. "She's just a regular cat. Don't take it personally."

Atom gazed into my daughter's eyes—probably casting his love magic on her right in front of me—and said, "As long as *you* like me, that's all that matters." He broke eye contact, cleared his throat, and said, "And your family, of course." Then he sent an obnoxiously charming smile across the table. "Speaking of which, how am I doing?"

"Very well," I said. "You have excellent manners. Which means, and it pains me to say this, that you won't fit in with our family at all."

For my joke, I received a genuine laugh from Atom, a horrified look from my daughter, and a disapproving look from my aunt. All in all, not bad.

After we'd finished cooking and eating every bit of food, Zinnia served the flavored broth in soup bowls.

As Adam finished his soup, he said, "Riddle family hospitality is much better than it looks on your show." He gave us a sheepish look. "Yes. I watch The Regal Riddles. Guilty as charged. May I make another confession?"

"Go on," I said.

"That show is partly why I decided to stick around in your world a while," he said. "I must admit I was very intrigued about meeting the famous Riddle family."

"Interesting," I said. "And how, exactly, did you get up here?"

"I'd rather not say." He winked at me. "Trade secret."

When he looked away, I gave Zinnia the signal to start the spell.

She didn't start.

I kicked her under the table.

She kicked me back.

Atom went on, saying, "You three are even more zany than how they portray you on The Regal Riddles." He looked right at me. "You, in particular. I always thought the woman portraying you in the recreations was hamming it up, but now that I've witnessed the source material, it's clear the writers have toned her down. The actress is not a ham."

From just outside the door of the dining room, Boa said, "Ham, ham, ham."

"Poor thing," I said of the cat. "Zoey, would you mind feeding her?"

Zoey reluctantly rose from her chair and squeezed past me. As she led the cat to the kitchen, I heard my daughter scolding Boa for being rude to our guest.

With my daughter out of the room, I gave Zinnia the signal once more.

This time, she didn't kick me.

She took in a big breath, and began the incantation. I joined in.

It was a quick one, less than thirty seconds from start to finish.

Like the banishment spell we'd tried on the ghost who'd been trailing Zinnia, this very old spellwork involved a variation on the magic that gnomes used to stomp their way free of danger, back to home base. We'd gathered the necessary combustibles, and there was a pewter-framed hand mirror hidden under the bubbling cauldron.

A few green sparks flicked around the room like fireflies.

I didn't dare look at the devil until we were nearly done.

When I did peek, Atom was watching us with interest.

The bubbling hot pot cauldron was spewing steam, filling the room with it. The green sparks lit up like paper lanterns in the mist.

In a matter-of-fact tone, Atom Wick said, "You're trying to banish me."

"Not just trying. We *are* banishing you. Consider yourself banished." I clapped my hands to complete the spell.

The magic flashed through the room with a crackle, then dissipated.

Atom was still there, sitting in his chair.

The steam from the cauldron hung around us like a fog.

In a neutral voice, he said, "Give it another try. You were nervous, and your hands were shaking. Even a slight tremble can distort the tone."

Zinnia shot me a look. Should we try again?

I nodded yes.

We ran the spell a second time. My hands were shaking even worse than the first time.

I got through the incantation with better timing, and closed it with another clap.

There was a thunderous sound this time, but still the devil sat there, unaffected.

The steamy fog made his face shine. The green sparks swam around us like frenzied fireflies.

"Go ahead," Atom said, waving one hand through the swirling vapor. "Try once more. You know what they say. The third time's the charm."

I looked to my aunt for guidance. Was this a trick? Reverse psychology?

Her face was shining and wet. She looked as bewildered and embarrassed as I felt.

"Go ahead," Atom said again. "In fact, I insist."

"No," I said. "It's not going to work." I showed Zinnia my hands, which were shaking so bad they were practically blurry.

"That's no fun," Atom said. "We were just getting warmed up."

Zoey returned from feeding Boa in the kitchen.

The cauldron bubbled dry and let out an angry hiss. The green sparks turned brown and fizzled out.

The fog settled downward, turning into water droplets as it hit the floor.

Zoey demanded, "What's going on?" She glared at me. "What were you doing? I heard a thunderclap. There's a storm outside, and I swear the weather forecast app said it was going to be a cloudless night."

Atom grinned at me as he answered, "Your mother was performing parlor tricks for... my amusement, I suppose."

My previously-sweet daughter narrowed her eyes at me. "Are you sure that's all she was doing?"

"She and your aunt tried to banish me to Hell," he said matter-of-factly. "Twice."

My daughter's cheeks flushed. "Uh-oh."

"Calm down," I said. "It didn't work, obviously."

"But..." Zoey trailed off, chewing her lower lip. She returned to her seat, looking down.

"But what?" I asked.

With her gaze down on her hands in her lap, she said, "Mom, if you try to use the devil's gifts against him, you're in violation of the agreement." She took a short, gasping breath, high in her chest. "And he can take the gifts back."

My aunt remained silent, all eyes. She had her hands over her belly protectively.

I said, "What gifts? What agreement?"

With a strained, thin voice, Zoey said, "The agreement that our distant ancestor made to get her powers. I don't know her name, but she's not one of the Four Eves. It's someone else, more recent. She's the common ancestor that all witches share."

Nobody spoke.

I shouldn't have been surprised that Zoey, despite not being a witch, knew more about our history than we did. She'd always been a dedicated student, even more of a researcher than I was.

It occurred to me, for the second time that weekend, that I'd been wasting my energy over the last year. Never mind not knowing how to dance the Monster Mash. I really had wasted my time on frivolities, like chasing ghosts and reading spy novels, when I should have been studying magical texts.

This situation, this nightmare, wasn't a dream. It was happening. This was the final exam for the high-level course I hadn't been showing up for all semester. I hadn't done my homework. And now I was failing.

After a full minute, Atom was the one who broke the silence.

He said casually, "Well, it's getting late."

He pushed his chair back, and put his cloth napkin, which had been on his lap, onto the table.

Nobody spoke.

"Plus we have school in the morning," Atom said, smiling sweetly at my daughter. "I'm going to review my history notes one last time so I can beat you on that quiz. The textbooks have it all wrong, but I can memorize fiction as easily as fact." He stood. "Walk me out?"

Zoey stood, and they started to leave.

"Wait," I said. "Zoey, what did you mean about the devil taking back his gifts?"

"I-I'm not sure," she stammered. "It was just something I read in one of your books. It didn't go into details."

I looked at the devil.

Wrinkling his nose, the devil said, "I'd rather not volunteer information, if it's all the same to you. Trade secrets and all that."

I said to Zoey, "Which book?"

She frowned. "The nameless one with the swirly symbol on the front."

"Is it in your aunt's collection?"

She shook her head. "Not anymore. It was in my bedroom when the house blew up."

I nodded. "How convenient. We had reference materials concerning your boyfriend, and it all just happened to get blown up."

Atom yawned.

"Oh, sorry," I said. "Are we keeping you up, Atom?"

"Not at all. It's a sort of jetlag. Different time zones, different sun. I apologize for yawning." He bowed. "Thank you for a very entertaining evening."

Then he left.

Via the front door.

Not in a plume of smoke and flame, screaming in terror while being sucked back to Hell, as I'd been hoping.

Zoey didn't come back right away.

My aunt and I were alone.

I used my napkin to mop the cauldron steam from my face.

In the silence, Zinnia said, "That could have gone worse."

"It could have gone better."

She got up and brought in the dessert we hadn't served. It was leftover fruitcake from Christmas, a big log that had lingered in my aunt's freezer for two months, untouched due to its high raisin content. We'd wanted to give Atom a nice meal, but not *too* nice.

She cut me a slice and handed me a plate.

I used my chopsticks to peel off the marzipan frosting, which I ate first.

Zinnia said, "It certainly could have gone worse, but it did not go well."

"Assuming it's not a bluff, I'm not looking forward to losing any of my so-called gifts. When do you think he's going to do it?"

She chewed her fruitcake, swallowed, took a sip of water, and said, "It has already happened."

"What already happened?"

"Catch this." She suddenly flung her dessert plate—the one holding most of a slice of fruitcake—across the table, away from both of us.

I reached for the plate with my magic. She hadn't needed to tell me to catch it. I would have done so by reflex.

But my magic didn't catch the plate in time.

It didn't feel like my telekinesis activated at all.

The plate smashed into the wall, shattering before falling to the floor.

No, I thought. *This can't be happening. It must be a mind trick.*

I tried to sweep up the broken-plate debris using my magic.

Nothing budged.

I tried to levitate a chopstick.

It didn't move.

I tried to roll a single, tiny crumb.

Nothing.

"Uh-oh," I said.

"It's gone," Zinnia said, sounding as stunned as I felt. "Our magic is gone. The devil took it."

CHAPTER 17

Monday, February 20

(The Next Day)

The devil had stolen—or taken back, according to his perspective—our telekinetic powers.

But my aunt and I quickly discovered, much to our great relief, that he hadn't taken all of our witch powers.

We could still cast sound bubbles and dry dishes. Even things that involved a bit of telekinesis, such as the shoe removal spell, still worked.

However, the situation was complicated. Our other powers didn't all work the way they used to.

After the devil left our dinner party, Zinnia and I had gotten busy trying to figure out the extent of the damage.

We stayed up late, casting various spells, and having many of them backfire.

We both fell asleep in the living room in the wee hours of the morning.

When Zoey left for school Monday morning, I rolled out of the reclining chair and went straight to work.

I clocked in at the Wisteria Public Library on time. Barely.

I pushed the problem of the buggy powers to the backburner in my head—no small task—so I could focus on my real job all morning.

When I finally took my break, I hunkered down in the staff lounge and got back to my personal project.

I was attempting to cast a complicated campfire spell in the Grumpy Corner when my boss, the head librarian, walked in.

Feeling guilty, even though I was on my break, I abandoned the spell and shoved the ingredients into my jumpsuit's pockets.

Kathy Carmichael didn't see me in the darkened corner. She opened the staff lounge's refrigerator door, huffed in disappointment, and slammed it shut. She muttered something under her breath.

What was she agitated about now?

Before I could let her know she wasn't alone in the lounge, she began ranting.

"Whooo knew," Kathy said, shaking her head and kicking some chairs with the toe of her boot. "Whooo could have guessed!"

"Hey there," I called out from my position on the bean bag chair in the Grumpy Corner. "I'm in here."

Kathy had her back to me. She looked up at the ceiling and said, "Whooo's that? Is that you? Are you spying on me here, too? Is nothing sacred?"

"I'm over here," I said. "It's me, Zara. I'm on my break. What's wrong? Did someone use a slice of bacon as a bookmark again?"

She whirled around, her brown corkscrew curls swinging. She pushed her round glasses up her pointed nose and fixed me with her orange-brown eyes.

"Zara! I didn't know you were in here. I'm sorry you had to see me lose my temper just now. As you know, I'm always calm and in control of my emotions at work, but something has gotten under my skin today."

I bit back my sarcastic comments. Kathy regularly pitched temper tantrums at work. But, like most who did, she was unable to recall those incidents accurately.

"I'm sorry to hear that," I said. "I guess both of us are having a rough Monday."

She gave me a blank stare. "What do you mean?"

"I had a run-in with the devil last night, and things did not work out for little ol' me."

"The devil," she spat out. "Whooo knew? Whooo-oo-ooo knew? I did. That's who. I knew it all along."

"You always knew that Vincent Wick's nephew was the devil?"

"Yes. I mean no. I mean I knew Vincent was connected to *something*. The man has no powers of his own, but he's always involved in everything, isn't he?" She made a grabby-hands gesture. "He's got his fingers in everyone's pies. And now this. This new enterprise. It's disgusting! It's an invasion of privacy!"

I managed to extract myself from the bean bag chair. I crossed the room, gently closed the door to the staff lounge, and said, "Kathy, take a seat... if you can find a cooperative chair that isn't holding a grudge about being kicked by you. I'll brew us a fresh pot of coffee, and you can tell me all about Vincent Wick's new enterprise."

"It's not time for my break yet," she said. "I'm on duty until..." She turned to the clock on the wall, and waited until the second hand hit the twelve. "Now," she said, and she took a seat at the counter-height table we used for eating and other projects. The chair cooperated.

I set the coffee pot to brew a batch of half-decaf, and joined her at the table.

"Whooo knew," she was still muttering. "I did. That's who. I always said that man was the devil. Turns out he's the devil's uncle. Close enough." She clenched her fists. "I knew. That's who knew."

Gently, I said, "You mentioned an invasion of privacy. Forgive me if I'm stepping on your headline and lead story, but is it possible you're referring to a certain television program that airs in a parallel world? A show that's based on real people and events right here?"

She gave me a stunned look. "You know?" She scrunched her face and shook her corkscrew curls. "Of course you know. You went over there in January, and saw it yourself. You're the one who told me about it in the first place." She rested her forehead in her hand. "I'm losing it. I'm actually losing it. This is what stress does to a person. It's all that man's fault. He's the devil's uncle!"

"Has it been confirmed? Is Vincent Wick the one who's been gathering the footage for that reality TV show?"

Kathy lifted her head from her hand and nodded. "It's him, all right. And there's a new spin-off series that just premiered. It's got me in it, Zara." She held her hand to her chest. "Me."

Something about the look of profound distress on her face made me laugh.

Kathy frowned.

I covered my smirk with my hand, but I knew the mirth was still in my eyes. You can't keep mirth out of the eyes.

Kathy's frown deepened.

"I'm sorry I laughed," I said. "If anyone understands what you're going through right now, it's me."

"Exactly," she said. "You should be more understanding."

"Oh, I am. Believe me. I'm very understanding. But here's the thing, Kathy. It doesn't matter. It's just a silly bit of gossip. In a couple of months, maybe even a few weeks, you won't be bothered about it at all. So what if some tiny people in another world enjoy a few hours of entertainment at your expense? It doesn't mean anything. It's nothing. They're just tiny people. I don't mean figuratively, but *literally*. They are tiny people, in another world. It's like strangers posting nonsense on the internet. It's nothing."

"It doesn't *feel* like nothing."

I shrugged. "You're not crazy to be upset. Vincent Wick is someone you used to trust. He—"

"I loved him." She scrunched her face so hard her glasses slid down to the pointed tip of her nose. "Once upon a time, I was in love with that man. The devil's uncle."

"But you didn't marry him. You married your husband, and now you have three wonderful sons—"

"Who are never in town," she finished. "Who are never around when I need them. They're gone, and you know who I've got? Vincent Wick. That's who."

Then she burst into tears.

It wasn't the worst Kathy Carmichael meltdown I'd seen, but it was up there.

I got up, opened the door briefly to make sure the rest of the library's staff had things under control, and then got to work settling down the head librarian.

It actually felt good to listen to her problems, and to coax her to eat some healthy food from the fridge. Kathy was a sprite, and, like her sprite cousin Karl Kormac who worked with my aunt, she had dramatic mood swings when she wasn't eating properly. I listened and fed her, feeling better as I did.

Once she'd settled down, she cleaned the tears off her glasses, then put them on and looked at me as though she'd just woken from a strange dream.

"Zara," she said. "Did you mention something about also having a bad Monday?"

"It's nothing." I waved a hand.

"Tell me," she said eagerly, her tantrum resolved. "You have to tell me what's going on. You and Frank promised you wouldn't leave me out anymore. I told you my secret, and I showed you my powers, so now we're all in the loop with each other."

I hadn't promised that, but it was possible Frank had, so I didn't dispute it. I didn't want to burden my coworkers with my personal problems, but Kathy was asking, and I did trust her.

"I found out on Friday night that my daughter is dating Vincent Wick's nephew, the devil."

Kathy nodded subtly to let me know she'd heard about that, from other sources.

I went on. "And when Zinnia and I tried to banish him back to Hell last night, using an ancient tandem spell, it sort of backfired."

"I'm going to want more details, but I'm off my break in two minutes, so keep going forward. I hate cliffhangers. How did it backfire?"

"The devil took some of our powers," I said.

"All of it?"

"Some of it. I did say *some of it*, didn't I?"

"I don't know. I haven't been sleeping well, and my hearing isn't right when I don't sleep. How much of your powers did he take?"

"Do you mean as a percentage? It's either a little, or a lot. He definitely took away our levitation."

"Oooh," she said. "Oooh, ooh, ooh, that's a big one. It's completely gone? Here. Try to float this pen."

She pushed a nondescript pen toward me.

I tried to float it, then roll it. Nothing.

"Try harder," Kathy urged, staring at the pen intensely. "I think it vibrated just now."

"It's the lighting in here," I said. "I appreciate the encouragement, but the magic is gone. I can't move or catch anything."

"I'm so sorry." She gave me a look of genuine pity. "You must be devastated."

"Oh, it isn't so bad. Levitation is the sort of magic that's easy to overuse and get busted for in public, so maybe it's for the best. But, unfortunately, it seems levitation is also a subtle part of some other spells."

"Which ones?"

"It's impossible to know without testing. For example..."

I grabbed the magic ingredients I'd stuffed in my pocket when Kathy had first stormed in, and tried the casting again.

A small puff of pink smoke that smelled like cotton candy appeared on the table between us.

"At least that one works," Kathy said.

"Not really."

Kathy snorted. "Well, I'm not *imagining* a pink cloud that smells like cotton candy. I haven't lost *that much* sleep."

"The problem is that what I actually cast was a spell for a woodless campfire that lasts three days and nights in any weather."

The pink cloud dissipated.

"Oops," Kathy said. "That's not good."

"At least I can still do this." I held up my hands and manifested two blue fireballs.

"Phew," Kathy said, breathing out heavily.

Her breath was enough to cause the fireballs to roll out of my hands, onto the table, and then the floor. The fireballs kept rolling, all the way to the refrigerator, and then underneath the large appliance.

Kathy and I exchanged a look.

The refrigerator began making terrible sounds.

Then it caught on fire.

CHAPTER 18

Kathy and I managed to put out the refrigerator fire.

We used the fire extinguisher, as I couldn't trust any of my magic.

"I'm so sorry," I said for the tenth time. "I've never had a fireball do that."

"That's surprising," Kathy said. "It is, after all, a ball of fire."

"I'll pay for a new fridge."

Kathy nodded. "Okay."

"I'll start looking for one right away."

"Okay."

Kathy might have argued that the library would pay for a new fridge, but then I would have been suspicious about who had replaced Kathy with a robot. She was obsessed with the library's budget, and where every penny went, which was part of what made her such an excellent head librarian.

With the issue of the refrigerator resolved, Kathy got back to work, starting with shutting off the smoke alarms and explaining our little mishap to the fire department, who'd shown up.

One of the bigger firefighters, a man shaped like a brick wall, came into the lounge, looked at the blackened fridge, and said to me, "These old models do this sometimes." He had a deep, rich voice with a Southern twang. A real one, not like my coworker Frank's occasional fake accent.

"Yes, well, it's all put out now," I said. "Sorry you and your crew had to rush over."

He knocked his large knuckles on the top of the charred appliance. "Y'all are lucky it happened while y'all were here to put it out."

"Yes," I said through a forced smile. "I feel very lucky."

He glanced around to make sure we were alone, then said in a friendly voice, "This was no simple electrical fire. I can tell by the burn pattern. Something else started this one. I reckon it was that wyvern you have living with you. Perhaps the juvenile one."

I did not know this man, but clearly he knew about me.

I put my hands on my hips. "Does everyone in this town know my business? I don't even know your name."

"Bon." He offered me a big hand, which I shook.

"Bond, as in... James Bond?"

"Bon, B-O-N, as in the French word for *good*. Or, short for bonbon. I'm not little, but I can be sweet."

"Careful now," I said. "If I understand your job correctly, you're supposed to extinguish fires, not start them."

He chuckled and took a step back, easing off the intensity. "Then I'd best be on my way, miss. Give me a call if you need a hand pulling out this burned-up unit. I'm strong, and I'm always happy to help."

"I bet you are, Bon." I waved him away.

He winked at me, just in case I hadn't picked up on his oh-so-subtle flirtations, then he was gone.

I swept up the mess from the fire extinguisher, then got back to work.

Around three o'clock, when Kathy and I were both working at the circulation counter, she handed me a card that the firefighters had left behind.

"Bon wanted to be sure you had his number," she said, her owl-like eyes twinkling behind her round glasses.

"I bet he did." I tucked the card in my pocket.

Kathy asked, with keen interest, "Are you going to call him?"

I pulled the card back out of my pocket and tossed it into the paper recycling bin. "Nope. Between my daughter dating Vincent's nephew, and the malfunctioning you-know-what, I'm pretty busy."

"Bon seems like a good guy. He did a full safety check on all our exits and windows, and pointed out some areas that need maintenance. You should call him."

"Thanks, but no thanks." I held up a romance paperback with a steamy cover. "This is all the alpha male I need in my life."

"Oooh, I hear that one's good." Kathy's fingers twitched.

I handed it to her. "You read it first, and let me know."

Some patrons came to the counter, so we both got back to work.

At the end of the day, while I was punching out on our old-fashioned timecard system, I got a flurry of text messages on my phone. A couple of them came with a magical jolt, or what we called *stank*. They were all from my fellow witches.

So much for my exciting plans to go shopping for a used refrigerator after work.

The coven was holding an emergency meeting, starting as soon as we could all get there.

Kathy caught me by the door and said, "Thanks so much for setting the refrigerator on fire. It really showed me that what matters the most is what happens in my life for real, not what some tiny people in a far-off land think about a warped version of me."

"I don't think that, in all of human history, a person has ever been thanked for setting a refrigerator on fire, but you're welcome."

"Are you coming with me to the community center tonight? There's a workshop with chia seeds. I don't know if it's cooking or crafting, but I signed up anyway."

"Thanks for the offer, but I have book club." I winked twice. Kathy would know I was talking about the coven.

"But it's Monday," she said. "Don't you usually meet on Wednesdays?"

"More often than not, but it's not set in stone. There must be some sort of book-club emergency."

She gave me a knowing smile as she pushed open the back door. "Have fun at your book club."

It was raining outside, and getting dark. The days were getting longer, but spring was still a long way off.

I wished her a good time at her chia seed workshop, and she slipped away into the gathering darkness.

I gathered my things, finished locking up, and retrieved Bon's card from the recycling box.

It was always good to have people's contact information. Just in case.

Then I headed straight to the coven meeting.

CHAPTER 19

When I got to Dreamland Coffee for the coven meeting, I couldn't get in via the back door in the alley. It was locked, as usual, which wouldn't have been a problem for a witch with telekinesis. Alas, I was a witch without.

I circled around to the front. The cafe would be open for several hours, so getting inside wouldn't be a problem.

Humphrey was working at the counter, proudly wearing an apron over his new clothes. He looked like a regular human in a black V-neck T-shirt and tan slacks.

"Hello, Toots," he said to me with a cheery smile. "How is your love life? Have you been kissing your mouth on other people? Like this?" He puckered and smacked his lips. "That's what people do. It is normal. You are very pretty."

"Hi, Humphrey," I said. "Sounds like you're making progress with your small talk, but can we go back to you calling me Zara? And can you dial back your interest in my love life just a bit?"

"Okay, Zara. My name is Humphrey. We have met. You broke my nose with your head." He gave me a nervous, hopeful look. "Is that okay? Am I doing okay? Is this what you want me to do?"

"It's perfect. You're a good boy, Humphrey."

He beamed with pride.

"Keep up the good work," I said as I skirted around the counter then into the back room.

The other witches were already there, seated around the table. They went quiet when I walked in.

My aunt was the first to speak.

Zinnia cleared her throat and said, "Zara, there's a rumor going around that someone has cursed our magic." She swirled her finger to indicate the whole group. "This alleged curse seems to be affecting all of us." She kept a poker face.

I looked at the other serious faces. There was a serious face on Maisy Nix, Fatima Nix, Margaret Mills, and even Ambrosia Abernathy, who usually looked more bored than serious.

Zinnia said, "The others are wondering if you've noticed anything out of the ordinary."

My blood turned cold in my veins.

Something had indeed happened. I hadn't realized it was affecting all of us. I hadn't even imagined.

My hands were clammy. I was both too hot and too cold at the same time.

This was all my fault. I'd foolishly tried to banish the devil, and he'd retaliated by taking back powers. Not just from me, but from the others.

This was my fault.

Zinnia had participated, but it had been my idea.

I was to blame.

Margaret Mills, the mind reader nobody asked for, jumped to her feet and pointed her finger at me. "You! You did this to us!"

"Calm down, Margaret," Maisy said. "Zara's powerful, but she's not *that* powerful. There's no way she messed up all of us."

Fatima pushed her oversized, white-framed, cat-eye glasses up her nose and cleared her throat.

Everyone looked at Fatima.

She meekly said, "I think it was me, Aunt Maisy. Last night, I was trying a banishment spell on some fleas when it happened. The spell fizzled, and I didn't think much of it at the time. But then later, when I tried to tidy up, I couldn't lift anything." Fatima twirled her long, black hair nervously. "Did I do this?"

I quietly slipped into a seat next to Maisy. For the first time ever, I wanted to hear more about Fatima's experiments with fleas. Was it possible that someone else —Fatima Nix—had jinxed our magic?

"You tried a banishment spell," Maisy said to her niece. "Which one?"

"Huh? What?" Fatima tried to turtle her head back into her body.

Maisy said, "You heard me. Which one?"

"Uh, I don't know," Fatima said.

Everyone leaned in.

Fatima's head turtled inward another half inch. "There was no book," she said. "The idea of the spell just sort of... came to me. I thought it was home brew, like Zara's always doing."

Everyone exchanged glances.

Fatima said, "Maybe it was my hamsters who gave me the idea. I got some new ones, and they're chatty. Hamsters have all sorts of secrets, if you know how to listen."

Margaret said with a snort, "Hamsters don't know magic spells."

"We don't know that for sure," Fatima said. "This could be a hamster curse, affecting all of us." She looked at me directly. "Zara, are you feeling the effects of a hamster curse?"

"I'm not sure." I looked at Zinnia for guidance. She still had a poker face. "Maybe?"

Ambrosia said, "I don't think it was hamsters."

Everyone turned to the teen witch.

Ambrosia said, "I got an idea for a spell last night, too, and there weren't any hamsters around. It just came to me. I got my pewter hand mirror, and a few combustibles, and used it to banish a hangnail."

"A hangnail," Zinnia said. She looked at me. "Did you hear that, Zara? Ambrosia used a banishment spell to banish a hangnail."

"Ah, yes," I said, like an all-knowing professor. "The one that originated from the hamsters."

Zinnia flashed the whites of her eyes at me. *Confess*, she seemed to be saying.

I flashed the whites of my eyes right back. *Give me a minute*, I was saying.

The coven demanded absolute honesty, but honesty could take a couple minutes, so that the honest person could read the room and make sure they weren't about to get burned at the stake for their honesty.

"Wait a minute," Maisy said, holding one long finger in the air. "Last night I was working late at the bean-roasting facility, and I had an idea for a way to remove a type of fungus from coffee beans. I tried it on a sample I had. It worked a little too easily. I didn't think of it as a banishment spell at the time, but I suppose that's exactly what it was."

Margaret made a sputtering sound.

Everyone looked at Margaret.

The witch with the frizzy gray hair turned red in the face. "Why are you looking at me? I don't use banishment spells that come to me out of nowhere." She paused. "Not without a good reason."

We continued looking at her.

She squirmed. "I may have used a banishment spell to discourage the breeding of snakes in my furnace ducts."

The group turned to me. I was next.

I let out a nervous chuckle. "I guess we all had the same idea at the same time. What are the odds?"

Maisy said, "Zara, what did you do?"

I struck my finger in the air. "Whatever it was I may or may not have done, Zinnia did it with me."

Maisy repeated, "What did you do?"

"Tell them," Zinnia said.

All eyes were on me.

"Well, as you may have heard, the devil is a young man named Atom Wick. He's also dating my daughter. I'd rather he wasn't, but she's sixteen, and she needs to figure things out for herself."

"We know all of that already," Maisy said impatiently.

"I'm just being thorough and honest," I said. "Don't start gathering a big pile of dry kindling."

The others made sounds of disapproval. Sometimes edgy witch-burning jokes went over, sometimes they didn't.

I went on. "So, last night we invited the young man over for dinner at our house. Zinnia prepared a lovely hot pot meal, and then, before dessert, we tried to banish him, but it didn't work. Our magic has been jinxed ever since. I didn't know it affected anyone besides us, and I'm so sorry. I really, truly am sorry."

"Say you're sorry to the batch of beans I ruined," Maisy said.

"I will," I said. "I'll make it up to everyone, I promise."

Margaret said, "What do you mean you broke the agreement?"

I hadn't said anything about the ancient agreement. Margaret Mills was pulling things from my head again.

Fair enough.

I'd stupidly caused Margaret's magic to get jinxed, so she could have whatever she wanted from my head.

Zinnia said, "What Zara hasn't gotten to yet is that Atom confirmed something Zoey found in a book. There was a very old agreement between him and our witch ancestor. This woman, this original witch, made a bargain with the devil. He gave her some of his powers, which have since trickled down to all of us."

Fatima's head whipped left to right. "Are you saying we're all related? We're all family?"

"Distantly, yes," Zinnia said. "That is, assuming what Atom told us last night is even true."

"It was Zoey," I said. "Zoey doesn't lie. She read somewhere that the devil had the right to take back witch powers if they were used against him. Last night we all used banishment spells, but Zinnia and I were the only ones who tried to use them against the devil. It's——-"

Margaret, who had resumed pointing at me, said, "Zara did it."

Zinnia grabbed Margaret's hand and lowered her arm. "Calm down, Margaret. Zara didn't cast the spell alone. I did it with her. If you're going to be angry at anyone, be angry with me. I'm the elder, and I should have known better."

Ambrosia said, "Zoey is dating Atom? You mean officially?" Her voice pitched up in hysteria. "They're boyfriend and girlfriend now? Not just friends?"

We all turned to Zoey's best friend.

I asked the teen witch, "Didn't you know? They became official on Friday, Ambrosia. It's been three days. That's got to be at least a year in teenager time. Didn't Zoey tell you?"

Ambrosia's round, moon-like face wrinkled with confusion and hurt. "They're official? I thought they were just friends. She told me she wasn't interested in him like that. She said..." Ambrosia trailed off and crossed her arms.

Margaret said, "Love triangle! Ambrosia's also in love with the devil!"

"Am not," Ambrosia said, scowling. "Maybe I liked him, once, but I'm not interested anymore."

Zinnia said, "Because he's the devil?"

Ambrosia shrugged.

Margaret said, "She's lying. Now that Ambrosia knows Atom is dating Zoey, Ambrosia wants him more than ever."

Ambrosia yelled at Margaret, "Stop reading our minds! Nobody likes you, Margaret!"

Margaret sniffed and straightened up in her chair. "That's not true. Some people do like me, and I happen to know which ones." She looked at me. "Zara likes me."

Zinnia gave me a surprised look. "You do?"

"I like Margaret," I said. "I make fun of her, but I like her. I like all of you." I looked at Fatima specifically. "Even the witches who don't like me back. I guess I have a low bar for friendships."

Fatima said, "I don't like people who are mean and bossy."

I snorted. "But you like your aunt, don't you? Maisy is the meanest, bossiest witch in town."

Maisy let out a laugh and said, "Thank you, Zara." It sounded heartfelt.

Ambrosia groaned. She leaned forward and bonked her forehead on the table repeatedly. The table, which was quite jinxed already, began wobbling like crazy.

The rest of us turned to Fatima, who was the closest in age to Ambrosia. Fatima held up both hands, as if to say she'd know what to do if Ambrosia were a cat or a dog, but she didn't know how to deal with this.

In between head bonks, Ambrosia said, "I can't believe Zoey did this to me!"

Zinnia said, "Zoey didn't take our powers. Atom did."

Ambrosia lifted up her reddened face and wailed, "Atom is the worst! He sucks! He sucks so bad!"

"He *is* the devil," I said.

Ambrosia glared at me. "I know, but why does he have to be such a jerk?"

"He wasn't a jerk, though," Zinnia said. "He came to the house for dinner last night, and he wasn't a jerk at all.

He was punctual. He brought flowers. He was polite and respectful. He even made some jokes, I think."

"It's true," I said to the other witches. "He wasn't a jerk."

"We were the ones who started it," Zinnia said. "We were the ones who tried to cast a banishment spell on him."

"Then let's do it again," Ambrosia said, pounding her fist on the table with a startling ferocity. "All of us! In tandem! Let's hit him with all the power we can get! Let's send him to the moon!"

As I watched the teenager getting worked up, a quote attributed to Shakespeare but actually from playwright William Congreve came to mind.

Margaret said, "Hell hath no fury like a woman scorned."

Either she'd read it from my mind or it was simply the logical observation to make.

"Forget banishment," Ambrosia said, her voice low and full of vocal fry. "Let's cut to the chase and kill him." Her dark eyes took on a crazy gleam. "We can do it tonight. I've got an enchanted knife in my bag."

Maisy said in a cool manner, "I'd like to see that knife, Ambrosia."

Ambrosia grabbed her purse, pulled out a knife with a chunky animal-horn handle, and tossed it on the table.

Maisy picked it up delicately. "Sturdy," she said. "Maybe I should hang on to this for you, Ambrosia."

Sullenly, the teen said, "I have lots more at home."

The group exchanged worried looks. Didn't we have enough to deal with? The devil was in town, taking back powers. Now we had to worry about a knife-collecting, murder-happy, jealousy-fueled teenaged witch?

Had Ambrosia always been this troubled, or was it a new development brought on by the arrival of a cute boy with secret devil horns?

"Violence is not the answer," Maisy said. "We are not the DWM. We are witches, and we have our own ways."

"But we need our powers back," Fatima said. "It's not fair for him to take them from all of us. Sure, I used a banishment spell, but I didn't do it in an evil way. Think about how much better this world would be without fleas in it. They're not crucial to the life cycle of any other living thing. They do nothing but spread disease. I shouldn't have to be punished for trying to do something good. It isn't fair."

Maisy turned to me and said, "How do we get our powers back?"

"I'm not sure we can," I said.

"We have to," she said matter-of-factly. "Without levitation, I can't cast the body-buoyancy spell. And without the body-buoyancy spell, I can't fly. And if I can't fly, I can't do half of the things that make being a witch worth it."

Margaret said glumly, "Maybe being a witch isn't worth it after all."

The others ignored Margaret and started arguing about which spells were the most important.

Ambrosia sneakily grabbed the knife off the table and returned it to her bag.

Maisy ranted about not being able to fly on her broomstick.

Fatima burst into tears and cried about fleas.

Zinnia kept trying to interrupt, asking the women to take turns speaking one at a time, but nobody listened.

We argued for hours.

We argued until Humphrey strolled into the back room and shouted, "Last call!"

The group went silent. All six of us witches stared at the dumb-but-sweet man who was sometimes a Komodo dragon.

"Last call for beverages," Humphrey said. "They always say that in bars, before closing time. I know this is not a bar, but I think it's a nice tradition. I like nice traditions. Can I get more coffee for any of the pretty ladies?"

We all put in our orders, and Humphrey brought us a round of drinks to fuel the next onslaught of arguments.

At ten o'clock, we were finally winding down.

The cafe had closed, and Humphrey was sleeping on a dog pillow on the floor next to us. He was still in human form, not Komodo dragon form, but curled up like a dog.

"So, it's settled," Maisy said. "Zara is going to apologize to Atom, and ask him nicely for our powers back."

Ambrosia growled, "And if that doesn't work, we start cutting off appendages. We'll see how much Zoey likes her new boyfriend if he doesn't have a—"

Zinnia cut her off with, "We get the idea, Ambrosia." To the rest of us, she said, "For the record, I'm against cutting off appendages. We ought to begin with diplomacy. I know there aren't many dramatic movies about diplomats mending relationships between warring nations, but there ought to be. I'd like to see one starring Bill Murray and Tom Cruise."

"I would watch that," Margaret said, being agreeable for the first time in hours.

Humphrey stirred in his sleep, scratching his ear with his knee before settling again.

Maisy turned to me. "Do you understand the mission?"

"Yes," I said. "I have to be nice to my daughter's boyfriend."

"Remember, you *do* have leverage," she said.

"My daughter isn't leverage," I said.

"Not unless you play your cards right," Maisy said. "Speaking of cards, weren't we going to invite Dawna Jones to one of these meetings?"

Everyone muttered that they'd thought someone else was going to invite Dawna.

Maisy said, "I'll see that she gets added to the group text. We can meet again after Zara gets our powers restored. Until then, everyone be extra careful. We have no way of knowing how this affects our other spellwork."

"She's right," I said. "Be especially careful with fireballs. I accidentally set the library's fridge on fire today."

Maisy nodded. "That sounds like a very Zara thing to do."

Fatima giggled.

I got up, grabbed my purse, and walked away.

I could probably stay all night arguing with the coven, but I had to get some sleep so I could be fresh for my task of figuring out the best plan for kissing the devil's shiny red butt.

CHAPTER 20

Tuesday, February 21

(The Next Day)

I wanted to be somewhere quiet to come up with my plan for being extra-nice to the devil, so I went to the library a couple of hours before opening.

The door was locked. Perhaps it was everything on my mind, or the early hour, but I was stumped.

I stood in the light of the security lamp by the back door next to the staff parking lot. I stood there like a very optimistic burglar, trying the handle repeatedly, as though it might change its mind about being locked.

What a ding-dong I was.

I kept forgetting I couldn't do the little things I used to take for granted, like open any door I wanted.

I dug around in my purse until I found my library key at the bottom, then I used it to unlock the door.

When I stepped into the staff lounge, I was surprised to find I hadn't been the first to arrive.

My coworker, Frank Wonder, the children's librarian, was there.

The trim older man with the snowy white hair and crisply tailored suit was yawning over a plate of graham-flavored cookies. In the last few months, he'd upgraded his look, but not his diet.

"You're here early," I said.

"My sister phoned at four o'clock, and I couldn't get back to sleep," he said. "She still hasn't figured out how time zones work."

"Is everything okay in London?"

He ruffled the spikes of his always-standing-at-attention white hair. "She's upset about getting older, about being called Grandma when the baby comes."

Frank had to be referring to the new baby that Chet Moore and Chessa Wakeful were expecting. Frank's sister, a swan shifter named Bellatrix Wonder, was dating Grampa Don Moore. When I'd known Grampa Don, he'd been confused much of the time. But his brainweeviled mind had been healed, and he was apparently now quite the ladies' man.

"The baby could call her something else," I offered. "Zoey calls my mother Gigi."

"I'll pass along the suggestion. Did someone else already tell you about the baby?"

"Zinnia did. I had a few feelings bubble up, but I'm okay now."

"Time marches on," Frank said. "Whether you want it to or not."

"Getting older sucks, but it sure beats the alternative."

He groaned. "Don't tell me you're one of *those* people."

"What people?"

"The ones who try to make you feel better by saying things could be worse. Who came up with that, anyway?"

"The Stoics," I said. "Zeno of Citium, of course. But there's also the more contemporary Seneca, and Epictetus."

Grumpily, Frank said, "It's much too early for you to be in full librarian mode. Sometimes a question is just a question."

"I'll dial it down two notches. Aren't you going to ask me what happened to the fridge?" The blackened appliance was still sitting in the kitchen, unplugged.

"Kathy told me last night at the chia seed workshop. Bad news travels fast. I also heard from another source that the devil's curse took down the other local witches as well. Sorry to hear it."

"What did you two do with the chia seeds? Crafting or eating?"

"A bit of both. We crafted some inedible bread." He nibbled the legs off a bear-shaped cookie. "How are you going to get your powers back from the devil?"

"Beats me. I was thinking of asking. Nicely." I put my palms together in a prayer. "*Please, Mr. Devil, may I have my floaty powers back? Pretty please with sugar on top?*"

"You need leverage. Something to trade. How attached are you to your daughter?"

I shot him a dirty look.

Frank held up both hands. "Kidding!" He pressed his fingers to his lips. "Oops. I'd better watch myself. I wouldn't want you to malfunction and explode the library like you did the fridge, and your whole house."

His joke hit me like a punch in the gut. I sucked in air between my teeth.

He dropped his hand and gave me a worried look. "Too soon?"

"It's *almost* funny, but not yet." I poured some coffee and sat across from him.

He pushed over the plate of teddy-bear shaped cookies.

I reached for one but stopped. Bentley's first name was Theodore. My mother sometimes referred to him as Teddy B. Frank and I had a running gag about the teddy-shaped cookies and my beau, but now that he was no longer my beau, the cookies were a painful reminder of what I didn't have.

I didn't have a beau.

As with the lost telekinesis, I was a *witch without*.

I grabbed a cookie and bit off the head.

"Why are *you* here so early?" Frank asked. "Are things a bit chilly in the bunk beds over at the cozy Riddle house?" He gave me a sheepish shrug. "Kathy filled me in on all the details."

"It's almost like I'm the star of a TV show that airs in another world, for the benefit of tiny people."

"Ouch. Too on-the-nose."

I took a sip of coffee. "I've been sleeping on the couch and letting Zoey have the bedroom to herself, so she can enjoy hating me without having to look at my dumb face."

"I'm sure she doesn't hate you. You're her mother. You two have a great relationship. You're a wonderful mother."

"I'm not as wonderful as Atom, though. He's *the best*."

"She's not mad at him for taking your powers?"

"Not one bit. Judging by her reactions around me last night before she stomped off to bed, I think she's glad he did it. You might not be aware of the supernatural power structure, but sometimes people who aren't at the top of the magical food chain are happy to see the powerful tumble."

Frank looked down and quietly chewed his cookies.

"So, you do know," I said.

"I may have noticed."

"How do you feel, Frank? As a shifter, are you excited to see the all-powerful witches take a tumble?"

Quickly, he said, "I don't feel that way personally, but I've gotten to know a lot of shifters and mages, and I'm afraid it's true. They are quietly resentful of you witches. We all talk a good talk about equality, but everyone knows there's no such thing in nature." He sighed. "Of course you can't speak the truth, either, or everyone will point fingers and pronounce you a heretic, hence all the games of make-believe. Nobody's going to come out and publicly state they're against witches, but secretly many are. Again, not me, personally, but... it is what it is."

"Figured as much. Thanks for having the decency to tell me the truth. You're a good friend."

"Equality is a nice ideal," Frank said. "Of course it's a bit rich coming from the mouths of shifters, who love referring to regular humans as *nothing people*. When the rumors went around about that Activator X stuff, and how the *nothing people* were going to get activated... let's just say a lot of feathers were mighty ruffled." He gave me a knowing look. "Several snouts and beaks were out of joint."

My armpits were prickly, and my back suddenly felt stiff.

The conversation was making me uncomfortable. I didn't like discussing personal politics with my friends. It felt like a dangerous game of hot lava, where any misstep could be deadly.

"Power corrupts," Frank said, staring off into the distance. "Maybe we'd all be better off without powers. There wouldn't be so much fighting."

"Nah. We'd just fight over smaller and smaller stakes."

"True. But you may find that having your power knocked back makes you more approachable. You witches might get invited to more supernatural gatherings."

I bit the heads off two more cookies. "Are you saying this new development could improve my social life?"

"Not yours, specifically. Even without the staggering powers for people to have to get past, there's still your personality." Frank grinned.

"Zing! I love you, Frank Wonder."

"I love you, too, Zara Riddle."

"Are you going to help me come up with some sort of scheme to butter up the teenaged devil dating my daughter so I can get my floaty powers back?"

He tented his fingers. "I am awfully good at scheming."

"This may involve more than gluing plastic tarantulas inside unexpected places."

Frank waggled his white eyebrows. "Nobody expects a spider under the toilet seat lid."

"No pranks," I said. "He's going to expect trickery, so I'm going to double-trick him by not tricking him. What do teenaged boys like?"

"Video games. Pizza. Heavily-scented body spray." Frank went to the whiteboard we used for brainstorming. He uncapped a felt pen and started writing ideas as he came up with them. "Skateboarding. Sports cars. Music. Tickets to the ballet recital." He paused. "Maybe that was just me."

"Keep writing," I said. "It's all good."

He did.

By the time we opened the library to the public, our whiteboard was full of ideas, as was I.

Atom Wick was about to be charmed off his feet.

I hoped my mother would be up to her part in it.

CHAPTER 21

Saturday, February 25th

(Four Days After Brainstorming with Frank)

I sat in the back of the rented limousine, which was parked outside the Cerulean Lagoon Hotel and Spa.

It was the same hotel I'd visited six weeks ago, when my father had ambushed me with Bentley's ex-wife.

I hadn't wanted to return there and revisit those old memories, but the Cerulean Lagoon was the nicest hotel in town, and the only place the undead rock stars my mother was friends with would deign to stay.

There was an impatient knock on the vehicle's window.

My mother had returned with a report.

I opened the limousine door, and my mother climbed in. She checked the underside of the armrest for squirrels, which had been her new safety routine since the Petey Incident.

"Well?" I slid forward on the seat and bounced my knees up and down. "How's it going so far?"

My daughter and her devil boyfriend were supposed to be enjoying their expensive visit with a group of musical legends the rest of the world believed were deceased.

"They're looking a bit worse for wear, but that is the lifestyle," my mother said airily, tossing her silky fake-black hair over her shoulder.

She meant the undead rock stars, not my daughter and Atom.

She went on. "All of them agreed that I look younger than ever. It must be something in the water here." She touched her fingertips to the edges of her eyes. "I'm surprised I don't look bedraggled, given the current living conditions at my sister's place. Honestly, I do not understand the fascination with old houses. Why would a person choose to live in an old house when new houses are available?"

"Yeah, yeah. Old houses are weird," I said noncommittally. "How was it going with Atom and Zoey?" I leaned forward and peered out the window at the hotel entrance—not that there was anything to see. "Are they having fun at their special luncheon with the greatest legends in rock and roll?"

My mother patted my knee. "The important thing is that you tried, Zarabella."

"They've been up there for two hours, Mother. It can't be going that bad. I'm going to text Zoey again."

The quick-moving vampire grabbed my phone. "I said it was going well."

"No, you didn't. You said it was good that I tried."

"If that's what you heard, then you weren't listening." She rolled her eyes. "Everything's fine. When did you become such a worrier?"

"Do you really want to know when I became a worrier, or is that a rhetorical question?"

She stared at me blankly. "What?"

"It happened at an early age, when I realized that my primary caregiver wasn't that reliable."

She blinked. "It must be a family trait. Zinnia was always a worrier, too." She checked the limousine's beverage compartment a second time for squirrels. "My sister never could grab the horse by the mane and let everything else go." She finished checking for squirrels, then tilted her head and fixed me with her penetrating eyes. "When we were kids, our grandfather took us to a horse ranch, and Zinnia wouldn't even get on the smallest pony unless someone else held the reins." She pursed her lips in distaste. "And even then, she refused to leave the barn."

"Yeah," I said, barely listening. "Zinnia's not cool, and fun, and worldly. Not like you." It was always more expedient to go along with whatever point she was trying to get across than argue with her.

She gave me a surprised look. "Meow," she said. "I wouldn't go that far. Don't be so ungrateful. Your aunt has provided us with a home when we had nowhere else to go. It's not much of a home, but you know what they say. Beggars can't be choosers."

I pointed at the hotel. "What's happening in there? Did they play any songs? I know they must get tired of requests for the old hits, but I hope we didn't pay top dollar to hear experimental new material."

My mother pulled out her compact mirror and checked her makeup. "You'll get your money's worth, Zarabella."

"Good."

"You'll get what you want." There was an implied *as usual*.

I bit my tongue. My mother and I had been getting along better since Christmas, when we'd bonded over a stakeout, but she still had her—to put it in Frank's words —"funny little quirks."

"All that matters is that Atom has a good time during his," I made air quotes, "Big Day of Fun."

"You are just like your father."

"I beg your pardon?"

"Your father used to call it that," she said. "Your Big Day of Fun. He called it that when he took you out and attempted to cram an entire year's worth of parenting into a single day."

"He did not call it that. You're making that up."

She narrowed her eyes at me. "Where do you think you got the idea?"

I pointed to my temple. "From here. I got it from here. It's an original idea. Frank helped."

"You took a page from your father's playbook, regardless of what you're calling it."

"My father doesn't have a patent on showing someone a nice time." I pointed at her. "Stop trying to start a fight with me. I've got a spell that conjures squirrels out of thin air."

Her already-pale skin went white. "You wouldn't."

"Maybe I already did." I gave the drinks cubby a leery look.

My mother edged away from the cubby.

I wished I did know a spell for conjuring squirrels, but perhaps it was for the best that I didn't.

My mother took one more look at herself in her compact mirror, then snapped it shut. "You should not have used the gifts against the devil. I wish you would have told me beforehand about your little scheme, but you always were so headstrong. You never listened to any of my wisdom. You had to make your own mistakes."

I slumped back in the seat. Ever since my mother had found out about the failed banishment, she'd been kicking me while I was down. She insisted that she'd known all along about the witch bloodline, and our ancestor's agreement with the devil.

I checked the time. "I hope they're wrapping up," I said. "The session I paid for is finished." I slid toward the door. "Should I go get the kids?"

"I'll do it," my mother said. "You'll fawn all over them and embarrass everyone."

"You are not wrong," I admitted.

My mom exited the limousine and returned to the hotel.

I rubbed my damp palms on my knees and tried to remain calm.

Would the Big Day of Fun work? I sure hoped it would.

The afternoon's private visit with the rock legends was the second item on a three-item tour. We'd started that morning with a paintball game at a secret DWM training location, thanks to my friends Rob and Knox, who'd rounded up some other agents to form teams. They let Atom's team win three of the five games.

Next up, we were meeting my new friend Bon at the firehall. He'd pulled a few strings, and would be letting Atom drive the firetruck through town, with the sirens on and everything.

The Big Day of Fun would work. It had to.

I'd run my plans past my male friends, and they'd all signed off. Knox told me he wished he could find something to get mad at me about so I could set up a Big Day of Fun for him.

If today's activities didn't put me in the devil's good books—assuming he had good books at all—nothing would.

My phone rang. It was Bon, checking on our timetable.

"You sound nervous," he said. "Don't be nervous. You can count on me."

I checked the time again. "They haven't come out of the hotel yet. We might be late getting to the firehall. They're probably trying out new material on the kids."

"That doesn't sound bad," Bon said.

"I should have expected this. I should have set things up the other way around, with the music stuff last, except I was worried about, you know, the whole rock and roll lifestyle, with the drugs, or whatever those guys are into these days."

"Don't be nervous," Bon said. "You made the right choice. And I've got the firetruck all night. As long as they aren't setting the hotel on fire as we speak, it'll be fine."

"You never know. Rock stars and hotels are a combustible combination."

"You've got the firetruck, and you've got me. At your service. All night."

"Thanks, Bon. I can't thank you enough for all your help."

With a confident growl, Bon said, "I'm sure you can."

"Easy now," I said. "We're just friends."

"Friends," Bon agreed. "Don't worry about running late. I'll see you when I see you, friend."

"It won't be long."

I turned and checked the hotel doors again.

Three familiar figures emerged. My mother, my daughter, and the devil. The devil was carrying a bass guitar. His trophy, I guessed. The one that would be going on my tab.

I told Bon we were on our way to him, ended the call, and knocked on the divider to let the driver know the other passengers were coming back.

The driver jumped out to open the doors for them, and helped load the guitar into the trunk.

Everyone slid in, bubbling with excitement over the songs they'd just heard live.

Next stop, the firehall.

CHAPTER 22

Nothing would ruin a Big Day of Fun like having a parent hovering around, so I left the kids with Bon and his crew at the firehall, and my mother and I went to Zinnia's house.

The three of us had dinner together, and discussed names for the baby. Zinnia did a good job pretending she might take either of our opinions into account on the matter. My mother kept disappearing to make mysterious phone calls she wouldn't explain.

It was eight o'clock when the front door of Zinnia's house opened, and Zoey returned.

She had Atom with her.

The three of us Riddles who had been waiting impatiently in the living room all tried to look casual.

Zinnia continued working on her embroidery, my mother continued working on her glass of wine, and I read the same passage in my paperback novel for the third time.

The teens came in laughing and chattering happily about their day.

Atom said to Zoey, "It's too bad Corvin isn't living in this town anymore. We could have brought him with us on the firetruck. Hellhounds love howling."

"Corvin didn't howl much," Zoey said. "He was house trained. Maybe the Moores will come visit soon, and you two can catch up."

"I'm not so sure the little fellow would be happy to see me. He did escape from Hell, after all."

"You wouldn't make him go back, would you?"

"Not necessarily." He waved at the three of us in the living room. "Hello, Ms. Riddle, Ms. Riddle, and Ms. Riddle."

I set aside my book, fake yawned, and said, "Sounds like you two had fun."

"We had a lot of fun," Atom said. "Of course my bar for fun is pretty low. In Hell, our most popular Saturday activity is a sport that's played in a swimming pool full of moldy turnips."

"We got to fight an actual fire," Zoey said with breathless excitement. "We were already on the firetruck when the call came in. All the other trucks were busy, and Bon didn't want to waste time dropping us at the station, so we got to ride along and help put out the fire. It was just a pile of old wooden pallets in an alley, but it was so cool! We got to take turns holding the hose!"

My mother swirled her wine and said, "You're welcome."

Zinnia peered over her needlework at her sister. "You did not," she said. "Zirconia, please tell me you didn't go around town setting fires so that these two would have a more adventurous ride-along."

My mother batted her dark eyelashes. "I didn't set the fires myself. I've been here all evening."

Atom said to my daughter, "You have the best family, Zo. I thought my crew back home was wild, but you Riddles sure know how to have a good time."

I gestured to the available seating. "Why don't you two kids join us, and tell us all about it."

Atom held up his hands. "I got dirty on the firetruck. Is there a place I can use to wash up?" He looked directly at

Zinnia. "Dirty palms are just as bad as pepperoni fingers when it comes to ruining perfectly good upholstery."

Zinnia directed him to the downstairs washroom, and he left.

Zoey took a seat on the two-seater sofa and let out a lovesick sigh. Then, in case we'd missed it, she let out another one.

"I heard him calling you *Zo*," I said. "You must really like him to let him call you Zo." My daughter had the nickname of Zozo, but only for her grandfather. She didn't let anyone call her Zo. Her full name was Zolanda, and she felt that Zoey was already short enough.

My daughter shrugged. "It sounds good in his voice."

My mother said, "I'm sure everything sounds good in his voice. He's such a handsome young fellow." She leaned forward and patted Zoey on the knee. "Good for you, Zolanda."

"Yes," my aunt said. "Good for you, Zoey. As you know, your mother and I had some concerns initially, but only because we care about you so much. I hope that today marks the beginning of a new era, and that Atom can find it in his heart to forgive us for the previous incident."

Zoey replied with teen sass, "By *incident*, do you mean when you and Mom tried to send poor Atom to Hell for no reason?"

I said, "We had every reason to—" My voice was cut off by intense pressure on my neck. It wasn't my aunt's style to choke, but it was well within my mother's vampire-power repertoire. I'd once bought a vintage Darth Vader cookie jar just so I could use it to make jokes about my mother. Sadly, the cookie jar had been lost in the explosion. *Rest in Peace, Darth Vader cookie jar.*

My mother waved her long, skinny fingers. "Bygones," she said to my daughter. "The incident at dinner is water under the bridge. My only regret is that I wasn't here to talk some sense into these two ding-dongs, but, as usual, I was left out of the discussion." She stuck her nose in the air.

I turned to Zinnia and said, "Did you hear that? Our resident arsonist would like to be consulted more."

"Noted," Zinnia said. "We can invite the arsonist to our next family meeting."

My mother simply said, "Thank you."

Atom emerged from the hallway rubbing his hands and sniffing them. "The soap you Riddles have in there is fantastic. And the hand towels are so soft. I hope it's not rude of me to ask, but where did you get them?"

"That's sweet of you," Zinnia said. "Not rude at all. I buy my linens and soaps from a boutique here in town. It's called Chintz, and it's run by a lovely woman named Mrs. Puddikin."

Atom said, "I'll have to visit this boutique and stock up before I head home. All our soap smells like sulfur, and the towels are worse. Describing them as burlap would be an insult to burlap."

My mother, my aunt, and I exchanged looks. None of us knew if his comments about Hell were jokes or not.

Zinnia said warmly, "I'll take you shopping myself, Atom. I'd like to look at Mrs. Puddikin's selection of cribs. Would you need to go... soon?"

"Don't get your hopes up," Atom said with a casual laugh. "I'll be sticking around here for a while." He dropped into the loveseat next to my daughter, and put his arm around her.

I tried not to think about the spells I might use to move his arm. Or yank it right off.

My mother, who didn't seem nearly as perturbed as I felt, crossed her legs and pointed her toe at the boy. "What do you want, Atom?"

Everyone watched him for a response, including Zoey. I had to hand it to my mother. It was a good question.

Without missing a beat, he said, "I would imagine my wants are not so different from yours. I want to explore this world. I want to meet people and learn their stories. I want to live my life in such a way that I don't have regrets."

My aunt pulled her head back, giving herself a double chin. "Good luck with that."

My mother pulled her head back as well. "My sister's right, Atom. Regrets are inevitable. The point of life," she paused for drama, "is to live it so that your regrets are *as interesting as possible*."

Atom turned to Zoey. "What do you think, Zo?"

"Yes, *Zo*," I said. "What do *you* think, *Zo*?"

She gave it some thought, as she often did when asked a serious question, then replied, "I think that regrets are probably inevitable, no matter what, so a person has to do what seems like the best thing at the time." She looked right at me. "What do you think, *Mother*? What do *you* want?"

All eyes were on me.

I shrugged one shoulder. "I believe in helping people find the right information and resources so that they can make the best decisions for themselves."

My mother groaned. "We get it, Zarabella. You're a librarian. You're better than the rest of us sinners and arsonists. But what do you really want?" She turned and fixed me with a piercing stare. "Other than proof that you're better than the rest of us?"

Zinnia cleared her throat and said, "Zirconia, maybe it's time for you to turn in for the evening."

"Yeah," I said. "Find a coffin and get in it."

My vampire mother said, "It's barely past eight. I'm just getting started."

Zinnia replied, "Are you meeting your other arsonist friends later?"

"Maybe I will," my mother said. "Arsonist friends are better than no friends at all." She stuck out her tongue.

Zinnia lifted her chin and said to the teenagers, "This is why wine isn't appropriate for people under twenty-one. It's barely tolerated by those of us who are much, much, much older."

Zoey, who was still watching me, as she'd been since she'd asked what I wanted, said, "Never mind Gigi. She's just joking around. You still haven't answered the question,*Mother*."

"I'd like you to go back to calling me Mom," I said.

My mother, whom I rarely called Mom, snorted.

I picked up my paperback and flipped through it as though bored of the conversation.

"We're waiting," Zoey said.

"I already answered," I said, keeping my eyes on the pages to avoid being baited into whatever this was. "I'm sorry my answer wasn't provocative enough to be entertaining, but it's the truth."

Atom said, "But, aside from helping others, which is a given, what would you like out of life?"

Now that Atom was asking the question, I sensed an opportunity.

I set the book down.

"I would like my levitation powers back," I stated plainly, looking Atom in the eyes. "I know I made a big mistake casting a spell against you, and I deeply regret it, but..." I flung both my hands up. "There. I've said it. I want my powers back. I'm sorry if that makes me seem weak, or pathetic, or needy, or all of the above, but it's the truth."

Atom held his face and body absolutely still. His beautiful brown eyes were locked on mine. His catalog-model cheekbones caught the lighting in the room cinematically.

I went on, not breaking eye contact with the devil. "At least return the power to the other witches. They didn't try to banish you. You can punish me, but not them."

Atom slowly settled back against the loveseat, still not breaking eye contact.

The room was quiet—extremely quiet, considering it contained five people and a loud budgie. Marzipants hadn't been put to bed with the blanket over his cage, yet he was strangely quiet. I had the urge to check if the old bird had died, but I didn't dare look away from Atom.

Zoey jumped up from her seat. "I'm going to get root beer for everyone," she announced. "After we helped the firefighters put out all the fires, we had pizza at the firehall, and the feta cheese was really salty."

My mother held out her wine glass. "Refill, please. Wine, not root beer."

Zoey took the wine glass, shot me a nervous look, then left the room.

Atom said, "Well played, Ms. Riddle."

My mother said, "Which one?"

Atom pointed at me.

"Call me Zara," I said. "There are too many Ms. Riddles around lately."

Atom said, "Zara, I'd like to return your levitation powers, but you've put me in a difficult situation. I did have a lot of fun today, first at the paintball game, then with the musicians. Getting to drive the firetruck was a major highlight. But, I wonder, is a single day of interesting experiences really a fair trade for magic powers?"

"Of course not," I said. "But it's a solid gesture. A peace offering. You might call it the beginning of a better relationship, one that can grow over time."

"Over time," he mused. "You mean until such time as you find a way to banish me for good."

"Or until you get bored and move on," I countered. "Zoey is a wonderful girl, but she's just a girl."

From the kitchen, Zoey yelled out, "I can hear you, Mom!"

"A girl with excellent hearing," I said.

"She's more than that, and you know it," Atom said. "She's half djinn. She's as much one of my people as yours."

Half djinn. As much his people as mine.

His words sent a chill to my elbows, and a splitting sensation through the middle of my chest. I experienced a mental image of my daughter being cut in half down the center.

Zoey yelled from the kitchen, "Don't talk about me when I'm not in the room!"

My mother yelled back, "Could you possibly take any longer with my refill if you tried?" To us, she said, "You can't find good help these days."

Zoey yelled again, "I'm trying, but something bit into all our cans of root beer! Something with sharp little fangs!" We heard cupboard doors being slammed as she muttered about finding anything drinkable that hadn't been bitten into by wyverns.

Zinnia returned her focus to her embroidery as she said, "I'm afraid my grocery shopping hasn't been the best this week. I've been distracted by this new development where the majority of my spells misfire."

I pressed my palms together and gave Atom a pleading look. "Did you hear that? Thanks to your punitive action, we might not get any root beer."

He nodded. "That's too bad. I've heard good things about your root beer. Where I'm from, all our soda is savory. The potato-cheddar one isn't too bad."

I still had my hands in the pleading position. "Well, Atom? What's it going to take to get our powers restored? Name your price."

Out of the corner of my eye, I saw my aunt do something magical. She was casting a sound bubble spell, but not in the usual way.

Atom scrunched his perfect face a moment before saying, "I'd like something pretty."

"I am *not* using my daughter as leverage," I replied.

His dark eyes twinkled. "Actually, I was thinking of jewelry. Something pretty that I can give to Zoey. I came to your world empty-handed, naked and covered in mud."

"You did?"

"Never mind about that," he said. "Could you locate some jewelry for me?"

All the lamps in the living room flickered like they might go out but didn't.

"Sure," I said. "I know her taste, so I can help you pick out the perfect thing. The stores are all closed now, but we can look online."

"Not just any jewelry," Atom said. "It has to be a challenge. Something difficult for you to get your hands on. You can't simply throw money at the problem. There must be effort."

"You mean something hand-made? I don't think Zoey would wear anything I made with my own hands."

Atom looked up at the ceiling and rubbed his chin.

The lights in the room flickered again, particularly the lamps.

Atom snapped his fingers.

One of the bulbs burned out with a loud pop and hiss.

"I know," he said, carrying on as though nothing had happened. "There's a bauble that people have been chasing around town. An amulet. I understand it was stolen from the local museum in January." He snapped his fingers a second time. Another bulb burned out, leaving half his face in the shadows. "That's what I want," he said. "The missing amulet."

I didn't know what to say. I'd figured the Big Day of Fun would either succeed or fail. I hadn't expected it would be step one of a multi-step process, like a side quest in a video game.

I turned to my aunt, hoping she'd thought things through better than I had.

Zinnia frowned at me, then said to Atom, "We can't do that. Even if we could find the amulet and succeed where others have failed, it belongs to the museum. We don't steal."

My mother sighed. "Oh, Zinnia. It's an *artifact*. Don't you know anything about magical artifacts? It doesn't belong to anyone in particular. I wore the darn thing for months, but I never considered it my own."

My aunt and I both jerked our heads in surprise. My mother had been in possession of the amulet?

Zinnia said, "Zirconia! Why didn't you say something?"

She replied, "When I passed it on and said they could put it on display at the museum, I assumed it wouldn't be there long. It had other things in mind. I could feel it when I wore it." She shook her head at us. "Don't you two know anything about ancient relics?"

Zinnia narrowed her eyes at my mother. "The only ancient relic I know is you, Zirconia."

Atom, whom I'd nearly forgotten was there, let out a big laugh. "You Riddles are so much better live than you are on TV."

I looked at my mother's neck. She wasn't wearing a necklace that night, but looking at her pale, bony clavicle helped me remember a necklace I had seen her wearing last summer. My memory wasn't perfectly photographic, but it was good. I remembered an ornate pendant. It might have been the same one Mrs. Krinkle had used to summon one of the Four Eves. How had I not connected the two necklaces?

Zoey returned to the living room with a tray of miniature kids' juice boxes, and wine for my mother.

"This is all we have," Zoey said apologetically to Atom as she entered the sound bubble. "I hope you like pineapple."

Atom reached for a juice box. "I don't know. I've only had it on pizza. Where I'm from, they put pineapple on every kind of pizza."

"How gauche," my mother said. "But, I suppose it *is* Hell."

Atom looked very pleased with himself for yet another amusing Hell anecdote. I still couldn't get a good reading on him. He seemed to be telling the truth, but that was the hallmark of a good liar.

If he'd been a regular teenaged boy, I could have used my bluffing spell as a lie detector. But he was no regular teenaged boy. And I didn't dare cast a spell anywhere near him. Not if it meant losing more powers. The coven would kill me.

Zoey said, "I didn't hear what you guys were saying after you cast your sound bubble." She looked at Atom. "Was it bad? Was my mother being... a witch?"

I cut in, "I didn't cast a sound bubble."

Zinnia said, "I did. I'm surprised it worked, given how our spells have been going lately."

"It was a little wonky," Zoey said. "It sounded like static." She stabbed her straw into her juice box, and gave Atom a sweet smile. "What were you guys talking about?"

Atom took a sip of the pineapple juice. "This is good," he said. "And I like the box. We have some of these where I come from, but half of the time the foil makes a hole that's just a bit too big for the straw, and the juice leaks out if you squeeze the box."

"Ours do that, too," Zoey said. "What happened inside the sound bubble?"

He said, "We had a conversation that wasn't meant for your ears, Zo."

She pouted. "Why not?"

"We talked about a research project your mother's going to do for me," he said.

"Oh?" She looked uncertain. "But research is my job, at least when it comes to magical stuff. When my mother isn't at the library, she goes around blasting fireballs and jinxing everything she comes into contact with. If you want something from a book, you should ask me."

"Your mother is going to locate something for me, and then," he paused for drama, "I'll give back the powers I took."

His words electrified me. Was it going to be this easy?

I jumped up from the couch, startling Boa, who'd been lurking on the sidelines. She raced up the stairs like a white streak.

I stood awkwardly in front of Atom, my body lightened by natural excitement. I could have floated up and bumped my head on the ceiling—if I'd been able to levitate.

With a trembling voice, I said, "Can you repeat your offer? I'm not sure I heard you right."

Slowly, carefully, Atom said, "Bring me the item, hand it to me of your own free will, and you and your friends can have your levitation powers back."

Zoey said, "What item?"

He smiled at her. "It's a surprise."

She scrunched her face. "A good surprise?"

"You can decide when you get it," he said to her. To me, he said, "Do we have a deal?"

"I'm not sure," I said.

He extended his hand.

I didn't take it. He was the devil, after all. I wasn't the smartest person around, but I was just smart enough to know I shouldn't make a deal with the devil, even if it did seem like a good one.

"I'll have to think about it," I said. "Maybe I should get a lawyer."

I turned around to check with my elders.

My mother looked bored.

My aunt looked just as confused as I felt.

When I turned back to Atom, he was lifting his extended hand into an open gesture. "The offer is on the table, whether you take it now or take it later. It's an open offer, and you can redeem it any time."

"I appreciate the offer," I said, and I slowly returned to my seat, feeling silly about having jumped up in the first place.

Zoey said to the whole group, "Now I'm more curious than ever. Do I at least get a hint?"

"No hints." Atom used his finger to tap her on the tip of her nose. "Don't ruin your surprise."

Zoey looked at me. "Mom, can Atom stay a little longer?"

I was caught off guard. She'd called me Mom, and she didn't look suspicious, angry, or annoyed.

Cautiously, I said, "Aren't you both worn out from your Big Day of Fun?"

She sipped from her pineapple juice box and gave me a pleading look. "We can hang out down here with you, and Gigi, and Auntie Z. We can all watch some TV together. Or just hang out."

I wasn't sure what to say. I really had not thought the plan through this far.

Zoey squeezed her drink box, then showed it to Atom. "See? There it goes," she said. "I swear it's more than half the time that the juice comes up through the foil." She did it again, then licked the spilled juice off her hand.

"Diabolical," Atom said.

I stared at my daughter. She was acting like her old sweet self for the first time in a week. My heart soared. Had my Big Day of Fun worked? Was this truly a new beginning? Were we already through the worst of the mess that Atom had caused?

Zoey looked at me. "Well?"

Zinnia said, "I could probably make it through one episode of a dancing or singing show before I fall asleep."

"Sure," I said casually. "It's Saturday night, so I suppose we can socialize a bit longer. Atom can stay until ten, no, eleven o'clock."

"That works for me," he said. "I have to be home by midnight or I will turn into a moldy turnip."

Everyone stared at him.

"That was a joke," he said. "I'm very adept at humor, especially dark humor. It's the best part about Hell."

My mother grabbed the remote control and switched on the TV.

CHAPTER 23

Sunday, February 26th

(The Next Day)

The missing amulet was on my mind Sunday morning.

How was I going to find an ancient magical artifact that had so far evaded the local investigators? And even if I did find it, would Zinnia let me fork it over to the devil? He'd promised he'd give it right back to Zoey, and, if I knew my daughter, she would return it to the museum, which meant finding the amulet would be a win-win deal. The museum would get the artifact back, and I'd get our coven's powers restored.

What could possibly go wrong?

After Atom had left the previous night, Zinnia and I had run a few spells for locating lost items. Our magic was buggy, though, and the only thing we accomplished was blowing out a few more light bulbs. The lamps at my aunt's house were so sensitive.

After two hours of fitful sleep on the sofa, I awoke with a few ideas in mind, but I couldn't get to them right away. I had other duties and responsibilities.

For one, I had to take Boa in for her check-up.

I tossed a piece of ham into the cat carrier as bait, loaded her up, and set off for the veterinarian clinic.

Boa serenaded me with the song of her people for the full ride.

"It's just a check-up," I told her. "Plus you'll get to see Fatima. She understands everything you say. You can tell her all about how difficult your life is."

Boa continued singing until I parked the car.

I circled around Foxy Pumpkin to the passenger side, grabbed the carrier, and started walking toward the clinic, which was two blocks over. Boa jumped from corner to corner inside the carrier, causing me to wobble and weave drunkenly the whole way up the street.

She stopped jumping around just as I entered the veterinarian clinic.

On the other side of the front counter was Fatima Nix. Our second-youngest coven member worked there as a veterinarian assistant. She was dressed in her usual patterned scrubs—all the better to camouflage the pet hair she always wore as a top layer.

The petite, dark-haired witch looked up from her computer screen with a perky expression, then saw my face, and said with disappointment, "Oh. It's just you." She scrunched her nose, and her oversized white-framed glasses slid down.

"No need to be professional on my account," I said.

"Huh?"

I sighed. "It's nice to see you, too," I lied.

She pushed the too-big, cat-eye glasses up her nose. "You didn't have to come by in person. I saw your text message in the group chat last night. I'll help however I can, but I don't know where the amulet is. You should be talking to your friends at the police station, not me."

Fatima was petite enough that she couldn't see what I was carrying.

I hoisted the cat carrier onto the counter between us.

"I'm not here about that," I said. "Boa has a checkup today. I almost forgot, with all the excitement going on lately, but I got the automated reminder."

Fatima's expression changed from surly to radiant. "Boa!" She stuck her fingers through the openings in the door of the carrier.

Boa rubbed her chin on them. She rubbed her chin on them like she'd never seen fingers before, much less been shown any human affection whatsoever. Boa twirled within the carrier, trying to touch every part of her fluffy body to Fatima's fingers.

We were joined by a clean-cut man in a white jacket— Dr. Katz.

"Hello again," he said. "What a treat, having our star cover girls here in person. Did Fatima tell you? We sent out the calendars in December, and I've heard nothing but positive feedback about all the months, especially the one for October."

I pretended to be surprised. "Oh! Is that the one I posed for with Boa?"

Fatima snorted.

Dr. Katz said, "How's your father doing?"

I gave him a wary look. "You know my father?"

"He stopped by when he was in town back in January. He wanted to thank me in person for the work I did last spring, when you brought him in. You do remember, don't you?" He gave me a knowing look.

"It does ring a bell," I said with an equally knowing look.

The veterinarian was referring to the time I'd found an injured fox in the woods and brought it in for treatment, not knowing at the time that it was my father.

Dr. Katz was doing that funny thing supernaturals did, where they dropped hints that it might be time for a full introduction, including the disclosure of powers. I'd always suspected Dr. Katz had some gifts—besides being quite attractive in his white jacket—but Fatima hadn't disclosed any details.

I reached my hand over the counter between us. "It's high time for a full introduction. I'm Zara Riddle, and I am what you probably already know me to be."

Dr. Katz shook my hand. "That you are," he said. "I'm just a minor mage, specializing in blood-based organic systems." He turned to the cat carrier and unlatched the door. "Hello, pretty girl. What a nice pink nose you have."

I felt a pang of jealousy that the cat's nose was being given such compliments. How had I not noticed that Fatima's boss was such a hunk? I must have been distracted by all my father's foxy shenanigans.

As the veterinarian stroked Boa, he casually asked, "Zara, are you part of Fatima's book club?"

Fatima answered for me. "She is. Now you know all of them." She had a snippy tone. "All six members of the book club. Are you happy now? Everyone in this town is so nosy."

Dr. Katz said to me, "I apologize for my assistant's tone."

"Please don't," I said. "I'm used to it."

He chuckled.

"Plus she has every right to be upset," I said. "I'm afraid I did something recently that's messed up her abilities."

"I may have heard a little about that," Dr. Katz said. "It's still no excuse for a bad attitude." He shot Fatima a stern look.

Fatima made an exasperated sound, then declared that she was leaving for her lunch break.

After she'd stomped out, Dr. Katz, who was holding a purring Boa, said, "Let's begin the checkup on our pretty girl, shall we?"

He led the way to an examination room.

I'd gotten heated during the interaction with Fatima, so I took off my jacket and hung it on a hook. When I turned back, I noticed Dr. Katz was looking at me, not the cat. He looked away quickly.

As he listened to Boa's heart and lungs, he said, "I was hoping to say hello to you at the Towering Inferno, but you left before I could work my way through the Monster Mash crowd."

"You recognized me? Even with the mask on?"

He smiled.

Boa rolled around on the counter, way too relaxed for a cat who was at the vet. She probably felt at home because she'd lived there a while before I'd adopted her.

Dr. Katz swiped a brush over her, pulling out an abundance of loose fuzz.

"She's releasing a lot of fur right now," he said, showing concern.

"Tell me about it. My aunt's been complaining about white fluff on everything. We might have to get one of those robot vacuum cleaners."

"Does Boa always shed this much?" He used his hand to tug on a tuft. Many strands of fur came loose.

"That might be more than usual," I said. "I think. It's hard to say." *Zara tries to be a good cat parent, but it's hard. Zara will definitely brush the cat thoroughly before any future vet visits.*

"Has she been under any stress lately?"

"Hah! She's a cat!" I genuinely thought he was joking.

He went on. "Any novel situations, such as a change in the household?"

"Oh." I counted out three fingers' worth of stress. "Our old house blew up. We all had to move in with my aunt. Plus my daughter's got a new boyfriend."

Dr. Katz raised an eyebrow. "That's a lot for a cat to have to deal with."

My skin prickled. He was right. It was a lot for a cat. I felt terrible for not providing a better home for Boa.

"You're right. It's too much stress," I said. "I should do better."

"Zara, I didn't bring it up to make you feel bad."

"Well, I do feel bad. Boa is a good cat. She deserves better. As for stress, I forgot to mention we live with a wyvern, and he hatched a son just before Christmas. The mom's not in the picture, so he's a single dad, and he doesn't keep as tight a rein on the baby as he should."

"A new baby is quite a change," Dr. Katz said.

"He's not really a baby. RJ is more of a sentient can opener that flies around."

The veterinarian nodded. "That sounds about right for a juvenile wyvern, at least from what I've seen in the literature. Nobody in my field has seen one for multiple generations. You're so fortunate to have one in your home."

"*So* fortunate," I said with an eye roll. "I spent the last hour cleaning caramelized root beer out of the pantry."

"All these changes must be causing you stress as well." He looked at my hair like he wanted to swipe the brush through it for an assessment on my shedding.

"I can take it. Riddle women are tougher than we look."

"It's okay to ask for help," he said.

"I agree. Since you offered, have you seen an ancient-looking amulet around? It's got a big, amber gemstone. It's technically not a gem, since it's not a stone. Amber is fossilized resin, but you know what I mean."

"I haven't seen anything like that around," he said, glancing around the minimal exam room. "Do you think Boa ate it? Cats are drawn to magical artifacts, and eat them when nobody's looking. We could give her an X-Ray."

"No need for that," I said.

Boa looked up at the kind veterinarian and said, "Ham?"

Dr. Katz did a double-take. "What was that?"

Boa licked her lips. "Ham."

The veterinarian looked at me for an explanation.

"She talks," I said. "I thought Fatima would have already told you."

"It's not on Boa's chart," he said. "Is this talent for speech new?"

"Relatively new. She started talking before Halloween, right after she ate something magical. You may be right about cats eating magical stuff. This wasn't an amulet, though. It was a bird, made of clockwork."

He took it all in stride. "And her speech began after she ingested this artifact?"

"Yes. It wasn't on purpose. I didn't encourage her to eat it. The bird was a messenger. Boa caught the poor thing and had it swallowed before I could get it away from her. Fatima came by for a house call, to make sure Boa wasn't about to get cut up inside. Fatima said she'd be fine. I didn't just ignore it." *Zara tries to be a good furkid guardian!*

"I understand," Dr. Katz said in a soothing tone. "Cats get into mischief. It's not your fault. I wonder, did anything ever come out in the litter box?"

"Not that I saw."

He nodded. "If you don't mind, I would like to take an X-ray after all. No charge. It's more for my curiosity than anything, since clearly she's quite healthy."

"Is she? Are you sure? What about all the loose fur?"

"Some cats shed a lot. You might want to get that robot vacuum cleaner." He patted her on the head. "May I do the X-ray?"

"Sure. Why not? I mean, if you're not too busy."

He picked up the cat, and exited through the small room's second door. He hadn't invited me to follow him, but I went along anyway.

We entered another room, and Dr. Katz said, "Fatima usually does this part. You know about her specialty, I assume. She coaches the pets to hold still so we don't have to sedate them."

"So that's why you keep Ms. Nix around, despite the bad attitude."

"She's actually the best assistant a vet could hope for," Dr. Katz said. "Aside from her obsession with fleas."

"The fleas! Does she drive you nuts about them, too?"

Dr. Katz rolled his eyes. "It's endless."

He returned his attention to the task at hand. After a moment, Boa settled on the imaging machine, needing no sedation.

Once the scans were completed, Dr. Katz led me into yet another room—his office—where we reviewed the cat's X-rays on a large monitor.

"I knew it," Dr. Katz said, sounding excited. "See? The clockwork artifact she swallowed has been disassembled and assimilated."

He tapped the monitor—it was a touch-screen—and highlighted several spots. I had no training in reading X-rays, but even I could spot the clockwork parts and gears that were distributed throughout the image.

I imagined what it might feel like to have those metal parts inside one's body, and I shuddered. Poor Boa! A chill set into my own non-clockwork bones. I regreted leaving my warm jacket in the other room.

"Remarkable," Dr. Katz said, still reviewing the image. "It's everywhere."

"Oh, no," I said. A person did not want to hear a doctor looking at an X-ray saying *it's everywhere*.

"I've never seen anything like it," he said.

"Is she going to be okay? Do you need to operate right away?"

"Oops." He rubbed the back of his neck. "I didn't mean to upset you. This isn't bad at all. The components have become part of her structure. They're knitted into her bones."

"You're not reassuring me, doctor."

"The components have made her stronger, not weaker. When Boa first came to us, she had some injuries from an altercation with a wild animal. Not only have the fractures healed, but they appear to be stronger than ever."

I didn't feel much better. I was glad that the clockwork parts were a good thing, but now I was imagining poor Boa getting munched on by a predator. I hadn't asked about her tragic backstory then, and I didn't want to know it now.

Dr. Katz said, "I'm still not sure why she's able to speak, but that's magic for you. Magic has a mind of its own."

Boa, who'd been twirling around our ankles while we looked at the imaging, jumped up on the desk and said, "Ham?"

There was a knock on the door.

Dr. Katz answered, "Yes, Ms. Nix?"

Fatima cracked open the door, and gave me a dirty look. "Your next appointment is waiting, Dr. Katz."

"Please offer them some complimentary catnip and tuna water," he said. "I'll be with them soon."

After she left, I said to the doctor, "Nobody offered *me* any complimentary catnip and tuna water."

He chuckled. "Maybe next time."

"When should I bring her in again?"

"Next year, unless you have any..." He trailed off.

"Maybe you should drop by the house sometime and see the baby wyvern."

His eyes brightened. "Oh. I'd love that."

Boa went to the door and tried to dig her way under it.

I picked her up. "She can talk, but she's not that smart."

He grinned. "I'm sure she'll surprise you someday."

He opened the door, and we crossed the hallway to the original room. I pulled on my jacket while Dr. Katz coaxed Boa back into her cage with some toys he'd had on him.

Seeing the man pull a pink-and-green crinkle-ball from his pocket reminded me of Bentley, and how he'd carry peanuts with him for the local blue jays and squirrels. There was a dull thud in my chest, an echo of the sharp pangs of heartbreak that had been much worse a few weeks ago.

I said goodbye to the veterinarian, and he gave me a refrigerator magnet with his personal phone number on it. "In case of emergency," he said. He didn't wear a wedding band.

I left, repeating my fake-drunken walk for two blocks again while Boa got her exercise inside the carrier.

After we were loaded up in the car once more, I stared at the fridge magnet in my hand.

The world was full of people who wanted to help me in the event of emergencies.

If I didn't get my powers back from Atom, I might need to rely on those other people more. And maybe that wouldn't be such a bad thing. Some of them were single and handsome.

But I did have a duty to my fellow witches to try to get the amulet.

I started the car. While I waited for the engine to warm up, I pulled out my phone and called someone who might be helpful in my mission to find the amulet.

I'd called my half-sister, Detective Persephone Rose, but she didn't answer the call. It was her partner, Detective Theodore Bentley.

"Hello, Zara," Bentley said.

I died a little. I hadn't heard his voice since our argument in the apartment. A mental image of the holes I'd put in his drywall flashed through my mind, filling me with shame.*Not cool, Zara. Not cool.*

"Hello," I managed to squeak out. "Is Persephone there?"

"She's busy. Can I help you with something?"

I answered honestly. "I don't know."

"Where are you?"

"I'm outside the vet clinic."

"What's wrong? Is Boa okay?" He sounded genuinely worried. He'd bonded with the cat, so I shouldn't have been surprised, but I was still caught off guard.

"She's fine," I managed to say through the lump in my throat. "She just had a checkup."

"We should talk," he said.

"We're talking right now."

There was a long silence. I could see him in my mind's eye, not smiling at my joke. I missed seeing him not smile at my jokes.

"Meet me for dinner," he said.

"Are you buying?"

"I'll buy," he said. "Six o'clock. At Mary Shelley's."

I agreed, and he ended the call.

CHAPTER 24

After my phone call with Bentley, I took Boa home to Zinnia's house.

When I opened the carrier door, she stepped out then stopped and gave me a confused look.

"What is it, girl? Did you think the cat carrier was a magic box, and you were going to return to your regular house instead of this one?"

She blinked at me.

"I miss our old house, too," I said. "But Zinnia's house is nice, in its own way."

She turned around and went back into the cat carrier.

"It doesn't work that way," I said.

She emerged again, marched directly to her food dish in the kitchen, and banged on the edge to make a racket.

Other than the clanging food dish, the house was empty and quiet.

"I guess you can have your dinner early," I said as I entered the kitchen. "Since I'll be out with Bentley later."

I was putting food on her plate when Ribbons flew into the room with Ribbons Junior on his back. The wyvern made a stop on the floor, sniffed Boa, then fluttered up and perched on the spout over the sink. The little wyvern on his shoulders made cute baby squawks.

The single father blew swirling ribbons of non-burning flame from his nostrils as he commented, "The feline has been recently radiated, Zed."

"You can tell she's been radiated?"

"It is obvious."

"She got an X-ray. I took Boa to the vet for a checkup, and he wanted to do some imaging.

Ribbons blew more magical ribbons. RJ swatted at them.

"You permitted the veterinarian to radiate the feline," Ribbons said in my mind. There was a hint of accusation in his Count Chocula accent.

"It's something vets do," I said. "I would have brought you, too, but I can only imagine the fuss you would have made about getting into the cat carrier." I rubbed my chin. "Plus I'm not sure what Dr. Katz would have charged me for two wyverns. Pets aren't cheap, are they?"

Ribbons puffed up his scaly chest. "You are the pet, Zed. You are my human pet."

"That's sweet of you to say. What brings you to the kitchen? Do you want some cat food?"

"What flavor?"

"The stinkiest one."

"Open the can."

"Oh, you don't need me to do that, do you? I understand the little one is quite adept at getting into cans of root beer."

"He is," Ribbons said. "His teeth are very sharp."

"Find something more appropriate for RJ to gnaw on, will you? He made a sticky mess everywhere."

Ribbons said nothing.

"This is the part where you apologize," I said.

"You are amusing, Zed."

"I sure am." I grabbed a second can of tuna-infused mystery chunks, plopped it onto a plate for the wyverns, and brought it over to the kitchen table.

The adult wyvern launched himself from the faucet, tore across the kitchen, and skidded to a landing on the table. He tipped Ribbons Junior off his shoulder. RJ wasted no time diving into the cat food. Head first.

"Tell him to slow down," I said to Ribbons. "His eyes are still bigger than his stomach. If he keeps going like that, I'll be scraping chunks off the wallpaper again."

"He will learn when he has learned, Zed."

"Spoken like a seasoned parent," I said. "You're getting the hang of being a single dad. Good for you."

"Do not mock me, witch. I will decorate these walls with your kidneys!"

"Not before I take you to the vet and get you neutered."

He took a step back and covered his lower abdomen with his wings.

I mentally filed away the neutering threat as a good tactic for when I meant business.

Baby RJ continued eating the tuna-infused chunks. He'd slowed a bit, but was still making loud mouth-smacking noises in between warning gags. I wagered there was a fifty-fifty chance I'd have to clean some wallpaper.

"So," I said conversationally to Ribbons. "What else is new with you?"

"I do not have the amulet, Zed."

"I didn't say you did, but I do find it curious you volunteered that information without me having to ask."

"The missing amulet is all over your mind, Zed. Your thoughts are messy and chaotic."

"If you don't like the state of my mind, stay out."

He didn't comment.

We both watched baby RJ gorging himself on the chunky cat food.

To my surprise, I noticed I was feeling peckish. My dinner with Bentley wouldn't be for a few hours, so I grabbed some cheese and crackers—enough for sharing—and sat at the table.

Boa finished her food on the floor, and jumped up to check on RJ, fluffy white tail swishing.

RJ, who was possessive about food, immediately hissed at the cat.

She hissed right back at him, then swatted him with her front paw.

RJ growled, and ran at her.

She swatted him again, knocking him across the table.

The baby wyvern rolled into a scaly ball, and came to a stop at his father's feet.

That wasn't good.

As the father sniffed his offspring to evaluate the baby for damage, I nearly stopped breathing.

The wyvern talked a big talk about eviscerating his foes, but what if it wasn't just talk? What if he attacked Boa? Could I cast a magic shield in time to prevent bloodshed? Assuming I could even cast one at all without it backfiring?

Boa puffed up extra big, tail up, hackles raised, and hissed at both of the wyverns.

She wasn't backing off. Poor thing must have thought she had a chance against the mythical beasts. Bless her heart.

I jumped up, grabbed the cat, and tucked her under my armpit.

As I backed away, I said to Ribbons, "She's just a cat. She doesn't know what she's doing."

After a long moment, he finally said, "My son will face much worse foes. It is good training."

Boa squirmed to be set down. I didn't bend down just yet.

"So, are we good here? No hard feelings?"

"The feline does not currently require your protection, Zed."

I set the cat down. Boa aggressively licked one shoulder, then strutted off, tail high in the air.

"Never a dull moment in this household," I said.

"We require more cheese, Zed. The ratio of cheese to crackers is not even."

I looked at the platter I'd only set out a moment earlier. "That's because somebody ate all the cheese."

"I will eat cheese, or I will eat the cat. Your choice, Zed."

I opened the fridge. "Can we lay off on the cat-eating jokes for a while?"

"There is little else to talk of that does not bore me, Zed. Unless we discuss the Vessel of the Remainder."

"The *what-now*?"

"The amulet, Zed. It is the Vessel of the Remainder. You should know the name of that which you seek."

"I can't know what nobody told me. All I know is my mom got it from a friend in Venice, wore it until she got bored of it, and then passed it on to the folks at the museum. I never caught a name. I mean, obviously I know it's not just any old amulet. I did see an elderly woman burst into flames when she used it to summon one of the Four Eves. Not something you easily forget."

"I would like to have seen that, Zed."

I finished slicing more cheese, and returned to sit at the table.

"What do you know about this amulet? Besides that it's called the Vessel of the Remainder. Why's it called that, anyway?"

"It is obvious, Zed. The secret is the name and the name is the secret. The ancient amber contains the remainder of all human souls. The ones that are yet to be released."

"Are you saying that the amber has human souls trapped inside it?"

"Yes, Zed. Where did you think the power came from?"

"How should I know? I didn't know where my own power came from until recently. I'm not like your kind. I don't have access to some computer cloud of shared memories across all of time."

"No. I pity you for your inferiority, pet human."

"Since you know everything, oh wise one, tell me something. Why are the souls in there?"

"Where else should they be?"

"I don't know. Floating around in the clouds?"

"This world is more ordered than it appears. Everything has a place, Zed. The remaining human souls were placed in amber long ago, to keep them safe from the devil."

A chill ran up my spine. "What happens if the devil gets his hands on this amulet?"

"Don't worry, Zed. It will not be the end of the world."

"Ah, that's good to hear."

"It will be the end of humankind, but the world will continue."

I stared at the wyvern. Was he joking?

"I'm listening," I said. "Tell me about the end of humankind, or you can listen to me talk about what to wear for my date with Bentley tonight."

Ribbons flicked out his long, purple tongue, and licked over one black eye and then the other.

"Maybe I'll wear one of Zinnia's sweater vests," I said. "In case the restaurant is drafty. Oh, I should definitely layer. Layers are perfect for when you don't know how warm or cold a place will be."

"Stop," Ribbons said. "I will talk."

RJ finished licking the gravy off his plate, burped, then showed his appreciation by knocking the plate to the floor, where it shattered to smithereens.

I grabbed the broom and dustpan, and cleaned up the mess while Ribbons told me about the end of humankind.

Long story short, if the devil got the amulet, we were all screwed.

CHAPTER 25

Shortly before six o'clock, I parked in front of the boxy building for the Wisteria Police Department.

The restaurant I was heading to, Mary Shelley's, was in the lower part of the building.

I walked over to the street-level entrance for the space that had once been a cafeteria and unofficial police hangout.

The place had been shuttered for years, but now Mike Mills, Margaret's ex-husband, had reopened it as a casual dining space. Mike was a former software engineer and had no experience as a restaurant owner.

The full name of the place was Mary Shelley's Franks and Steins. I knew of the place but hadn't been there myself.

I stopped outside the entrance and read the laminated menu posted next to the door.

According to the menu, they specialized in authentic German frankfurters and beer from around the world, served in traditional German steins.

Inside, the floor was dark hardwood, the walls were rich shades of green, and the lighting reminded me of the last pub I'd been to, which had been in another world. It was a welcoming environment, showing no evidence of having once been a cafeteria featuring a five-soup buffet and all-you-can-eat soda crackers.

I was greeted by a tall, middle-aged man. He matched the interior, dressed in a green felt hat, black turtleneck, and gray slacks.

"Zara," the man said warmly, tipping his hat. "It's so good to see you again. Are you meeting Margaret? I can seat you at her favorite table."

I did a double take. "Mike Mills? Wow. I didn't recognize you at all. Must be that jaunty alpine hat covering your..."

"Bald spot," he finished with a laugh.

I couldn't look away from the stylish man. In my mind, Margaret Mills' former husband had an oblong head and a generally boxy shape. My aunt and I had joked that he resembled Frankenstein's monster standing out in the rain. But the perpetual raincloud that used to hover over the man was gone. He looked like a brand-new man.

I said, "Are you sure you're Mike Mills?"

He laughed and briefly removed the felt cap to assure me it was him.

"You look great," I said. "Being a restaurateur must suit you."

"Yes, but it sure is hard work. Physical work. I've lost twenty pounds, along with the old wardrobe." He patted his midsection. "I burned all my boring software engineer shirts. I tried to donate them, but nobody wanted them, so I put everything in a barrel and burned it up real good. Margaret gave me some special branches to throw on top of the fire to enhance the change magic."

"She did?" Had someone told Mike Mills about magic? Now that he wasn't even married to a witch anymore? That would be ironic timing. I waited for him to divulge more.

He gave me a knowing look. "I know about the book club, by the way. Margaret finally told me. I hope the rest of you don't mind. The children are getting older, so

Margaret and I both need to be on the lookout for any signs."

"That's wise," I said. "You seem to be dealing with everything well enough."

"You mean I'm dealing well for a *nothing person*," he said. "Which is what I am. A nothing person."

I wrinkled my nose. "I've never liked that term."

"It is what I am," he said. "Life goes on. Nothing ever truly ends, until it does, but you might as well live while you can, right? Who knows. It could all be over tomorrow. A giant meteor could take us out. Won't do much good for us to wring our hands over it, will it? You may as well have a beer with a friend." He grabbed a couple of menus from the dais we were standing next to. "Who are you meeting? Is it Margaret? Look at me. I'm dominating this conversation, and I haven't let you say two words. You know, I used to think I was an introvert, but now I'm not so sure."

"People change," I said.

"They sure do."

A group of people came in the front door and stood behind me.

"I'll be right with you folks," Mike said to the newcomers. He led me into the dining room, right to a raised table near the corner that he explained was Margaret's favorite.

He kept up his chatter the whole time, telling me that the two of them had been getting along better than ever, and the kids were thriving despite the adjustments, and that he had a good selection of beer on tap, but that there were supply chain issues with some of the imports that he really wanted me to try as soon as humanly possible.

I had to grab the man by the shoulders and forcibly turn him around to shoo him away.

When I turned back to the table, Bentley was sitting in the chair across from me. I hadn't seen him slip in.

"You and your sneaky ways," I said by way of greeting.

He flicked his silver eyes in the direction Mike Mills had gone.

"I thought he'd never leave," Bentley said.

"He's excited about his new restaurant, and his new life."

"And seeing you."

I sensed bitterness coming from my ex-boyfriend.

"It's nice to be wanted," I said.

"And *wanted* you are. The bachelors in this town are all drawn to you," he said. "Like flies."

I wasn't imagining bitterness. There was an implied insult in his words.

I said, "Like flies to honey?"

"Sure."

It was just one word, yet I knew exactly what he meant.

I pushed my chair back. "I don't need this," I said. "I can make hot dogs at home."

"Stay," he said.

"Don't order me around. I do what I want."

"We need to talk. Stay. *Please*."

"Not if you're going to sit there hating me. I have a teenager going through a rebellious stage right now. I've got all the hating I can handle at home."

"I don't hate you," he said.

"Then why do I feel like you hate me?"

He stared at me a moment before saying, "Far be it from me to presume to know what it is you're feeling."

"How's your wife?"

He winced.

Sensing a weak spot, I went on. "How's she settling in on Beacon Street? It's a great neighborhood. The two of you should be very happy there."

Slowly, he said, "We can talk about Larissa if you wish. Is that what you want?"

I looked down at my menu. It was just squiggly lines, not even words.

Did I want to talk about life on Beacon street, now that I didn't live on Beacon street but his ex-wife did? Not really.

"Nope," I said, having been effectively disarmed by his question. Bentley usually made assumptions, and statements. Whenever he asked a question, it made me strangely uncomfortable, like the rug had been pulled out beneath me, and I was about to fall into a trap. I wasn't going to fall into this one.

I pretended to be interested in the menu.

"You've made a lot of new friends lately," Bentley said.

"I have? What makes you say that?"

"You have friends at the Inferno, friends at the firehall, friends at the veterinary clinic, friends all over town."

"Is that your way of asking if I'm dating anyone?"

He said nothing.

"I'm not dating anyone," I said. "Not that it's any of your business."

"Things change," he said.

"And rain is wet. What do you want, anyway? I've got other things I should be doing right now, like worrying about the end of the world. Why did you ask me to dinner?"

"Zara, we can do this the hard way, or we can do it the easy way. It's your choice."

"Do what?" I had no idea what he was talking about. Was this about the sweatshirt I'd borrowed the last time I was at his place—the one I hadn't returned because I liked sleeping in it? It wasn't my fault that women's garment manufacturers never made any nightgowns that were half as comfortable as what we borrowed from our men.

He tilted his head to the side and stared at me. "Don't make me ask."

"You're going to have to ask, because I have no idea what you're talking about."

"The amulet," he said. "I know you have it."

"Me?" I let out a sharp laugh. He couldn't have been more wrong if he'd tried. I'd spent the past day thinking about little else but the amulet, and how I might track it down.

Where had he gotten the idea I was already in possession of it?

A waitress arrived with two steins of beer. The steins were ornate ceramic mugs with pewter lids.

I held up a hand to politely stop her. "You must have the wrong table, miss. We haven't ordered yet."

"Mike wants you to try these," she said. "The owner, Mike Mills. It's on the house."

"That's very kind," I said. "Please thank him for us, and tell him we don't require any special treatment."

Bentley murmured a thank-you.

The waitress said, "Your whole meal is on the house. Order anything you'd like. I recommend the truffle fries and the frank sampler for two. It's a big platter with several—"

"Done," I said, feeling relieved. I would never have been able to read the menu with Bentley acting hostile across from me, let alone been able to pick something.

"That's easy," she said with a smile.

I smiled back. "I don't know what the gentleman is having, but a platter for two always works for me."

She gave me a questioning look, then glanced at Bentley.

"My friend Zara has a strange sense of humor," he said to the waitress. "It's an acquired taste."

My friend? Was that the game we were playing?

The waitress looked from him to me, even more uncertain looking.

"My friend Bentley has no sense of humor whatsoever," I said to the waitress. "That's why any humor at all seems strange to him."

"My friend Zara can easily consume enough food for six people in one sitting," he said.

"My friend Bentley would prefer to stay hungry all the time so he can use it as an excuse for being grumpy," I said.

"My friend Zara has no boundaries, and involves other people in matters that shouldn't concern them."

"My friend Bentley is a creepy sneaker who sneaks up on people just to scare them."

"My friend Zara is a secretly powerful tyrant who makes light of serious situations, and turns pleasant interactions into conflict."

"My friend Bentley wouldn't know what a pleasant interaction was if it bit him on the backside."

"My friend Zara can be charming when it suits her, but she's also a bully who uses threats of violence to get her way."

"My friend Bentley uses his job title to assert himself as superior to others when it suits him."

"My friend Zara acts as though she's the star of a reality TV show, and that an imaginary audience is cheering for her bad behavior."

"Actually, that part is true," I said.

The waitress was staring at us with wide eyes.

I cast a bluffing spell her way. "We'll share the platter you suggested," I said, weaving the witch tongue spell between my words. "We are a normal couple having a normal dinner."

Her confused expression relaxed to a blank state as the bluffing spell took hold. "The platter for two, for the normal couple," she said. "Great choice!" She turned on her heel and walked away with a bounce in her step.

When I looked at Bentley, he was frowning.

"What?" I frowned back.

"How many times did you run that bluffing spell of yours on me?"

"I never did," I said.

"Never?"

"Well, I used to, but not after we started dating."

He stared at me like he didn't believe me.

The more he stared, the more I doubted myself. Had I used the bluffing spell on him? Even after he'd become a vampire? I must have tried. I dimly recalled it not working as well once he'd had powers of his own.

Was this why he'd invited me to dinner? Did he want to do a post-mortem on our relationship?

If so, I didn't want everyone in earshot to get dragged into it.

I cast a sound bubble spell around us. The spell had been affected by the devil's power grab, but it still worked.

Bentley watched my hand movements with suspicion.

"I'm just putting a sound barrier around us," I said. "I hope that's alright with you, Detective." As the witch tongue faded, it was replaced by sarcasm tongue. "I'm sorry I didn't ask for your full consent before using my powers. I guess that's just how we tyrants and bullies are. We never ask."

Bentley picked up his stein of complimentary beer, used his thumb to flip back the pewter lid with a crisp snap, and took a sip.

He made a sour face.

"How's the beer?" I asked.

"Taste it yourself."

"Taste it myself? What's that supposed to mean?"

"There's no point in me telling you anything, since you never take my word for it."

Oh, he was in a mood, all right. If it wasn't for the smell of food in the air and the promise of a platter full of free food, I might have stormed out.

Instead, I said, "You need to book an appointment to see a proctologist. It would appear that something has crawled up your butt and died."

His sour face nearly imploded.

That's right, I thought. *Shots fired.*

CHAPTER 26

Oh, yes, I did.

I told the town's senior detective to visit a proctologist to find out what had crawled up his butt and died.

The corner of his eye and mouth twitched. He almost smiled.

Switching to a gentler tone than the one he'd been using, he said, "You have a real gift for colorful imagery."

The weight in my chest lifted, and I celebrated internally. My jokes didn't always work, but this time I'd succeeded. I had blown up the negative energy and steered us in a slightly less acrimonious direction.

"I *do* have a gift for colorful imagery," I said. "That was technically a nice thing for you to say. See? It doesn't have to be so hard to get along. You just said something nice to me, and you didn't turn into a pile of ashes, or burst into flames, or anything."

He gave me a steely look, giving away nothing.

I took a sip of the beer. It smelled of ear wax, and tasted like what I imagined beer might taste like in Hell.

"This beer is terrible," I said.

"I know." He got closer than ever to smiling. "I would have warned you, but, like I said, you wouldn't have believed me."

"It's true. I do ignore warnings about impending peril." I took another sip. "At least it's cold." I took an even bigger sip. "Actually, it's growing on me. Once it coats the inside of your mouth, it gets better."

Bentley took two more sips. "You're right," he said.

I cupped my hand to my ear. "I'm sorry, can you repeat that? It almost sounded like you said I was right."

He turned his head and observed the crowd inside the busy restaurant. It was filling up. There were no more tables available.

A young woman in a tuxedo set up a portable electronic keyboard on a small stage, and began playing a lively song.

Mike Mills ran from table to table, chatting merrily, occasionally removing his green felt hat to show diners the top of his bald head. I imagined he was having the same conversation over and over, with all the people who'd known him only as the old, shut-down-and-checked-out Mike Mills.

The keyboardist was good, and got even better when she began singing. She had some of the same music genius my daughter, the harpist, had, and could have everyone in the restaurant stop talking and give her their full attention if she wanted to. She was holding back. She caught my eye and gave me a knowing look.

Did I know her?

Two other women—sisters—joined the keyboardist on the stage, and sang harmonies.

I did know her. The three of them were the goat shifters I'd seen breakdancing at the Towering Inferno.

Small world, I thought. And, more surprisingly, they were shifters who also had mage powers. I'd never considered such things, but of course people could hold more than one type of power. My own daughter was living proof that crossing bloodlines resulted in unique combinations.

The waitress arrived with our food.

"That was quick," I said. Only a few minutes had passed since we'd placed our order.

"This table always gets top priority," the waitress said. "I don't know why, but it does."

After she left, I said to Bentley, "This is Margaret's table. That's why. Isn't it sweet that Mike gives his ex-wife a table that always has top priority?"

Bentley stared at me impassively.

I grabbed one of the franks and put it on my plate.

After a moment, I said, "What?"

"As I was saying, we can do this the hard way, or the easy way. All I want is the amulet, so I can return it to the museum and close the case. I don't care why you have it. You can turn it over any time, no questions asked."

"I don't have it," I said. "My house blew up, remember? Aside from my car, all my personal possessions would fit inside a milk crate. If I had an amulet, I'd notice."

"And yet you do have the amulet. Zara, if there's an explanation, some valid reason you can't turn it over, some magical business I don't know about, then tell me. I'm all ears."

I held up one hand. "My word is my bond. I swear I don't have the missing amulet, which is probably for the best, since the devil wants it, too, and he has made me an offer that's hard to resist."

"The devil wants it?"

"I guess everyone who's anyone is chasing after this thing right now. Do you know why? Why everyone is after this thing?"

"No, but judging by the glint in your eye, you're about to tell me."

There was a warmth to his tone that put me at ease. We were past the worst of it, and now we were just two people who cared about the safety of the town, and everyone around us.

I had no wish to keep anything secret from Bentley. We had always been good allies. He could help me with my current dilemma.

"A few hours ago, Ribbons told me something useful for once," I said.

Bentley raised his eyebrows. "It's always nice when an ornery creature is useful for a change."

I let that one go, and continued my story.

"He says the amulet's power comes from the souls that are trapped in the fossilized resin. The stone contains all of humanity's unused souls. There's a finite amount, apparently, and when we run out, we're done. After that, people will be born without souls. Given the planet's current rate of population growth, it's not due to happen for a while, and it may not happen at all if the population turns around before the supply runs out, but if this amulet falls into the wrong hands, the endgame will happen sooner rather than later. And by endgame, I mean the end of the world." I waved my fingers and added, "For humankind. Not for the rest of the world."

"Oh."

"Oh? That's all you have to say? The end of the world for humankind might be coming, and what? You feel fine? Like the REM song? Don't tell me you've become an anti-natalist."

He shook his head. "I'm the opposite. I'd like to have children."

All my worries about the amulet wafted away for a moment. Bentley was talking about having children? That was the last thing I'd expected the vampire to say. Was it even possible for a vampire?

"You would?" I leaned forward. "Since when? Who talked you into that?" I leaned back again. "Let me guess. Is it a certain succubus who bought the Moore house for twenty percent over the asking price?"

He didn't move at all. "The future may be a moot point if you don't help me locate this amulet."

"I have to help *you*? Why don't you help me?"

"I have access to resources. If it's as powerful as you say, we need to make sure it doesn't end up in the wrong hands."

"What makes you think your hands are the right ones?"

"Zara, your own daughter is dating the devil. Your family is already so compromised that you can't even see it."

"I'm not compromised."

"Prove it. Tell me where you have it stashed. I know you gave me your word that you don't have it, but those bonds aren't perfect. Someone as gifted as you are would have rule-lawyered your way around it."

"How do I know you don't have it? The last place I saw the thing was up in Temperance Krinkle's attic. How do I know you didn't swipe it out of her ashes when you had me distracted? Maybe you switched it out for a fake, and your people sent a fake amulet back to the museum."

"Why would I be looking for something I already have?"

I shrugged. "The most evil actors are often the most sanctimonious. It's a great cover."

His nostrils flared.

He raised his hand and summoned the waitress.

She ran to our table at top speed. "Is everything okay, sir?"

"Wrap all this up and have it sent to my floor." He handed her his official WPD business card.

"Yes, sir." She took away the food without question. Since the restaurant was underneath the police department, I guessed this wasn't the first time she'd had that request.

Bentley stood, nodded for me to follow him, and led us through a fire exit shortcut that took us deeper inside the building.

We took the stairs up, and he led me to a dim room with large monitors. It reminded me of the room I'd been inside earlier that day at the veterinarian clinic, except this one smelled like cigarettes and old coffee, not antiseptic.

Bentley said, "I want to show you something."

"I bet you do." I jumped up on a table, and started unbuttoning my cardigan. "You could have picked a more romantic location."

He gave me a horrified look.

"It was a joke." I buttoned up again.

Except it hadn't entirely been a joke. Sparring with Bentley in the restaurant had reignited some feelings. We'd always been at our best when we'd been in the worst situations. Also, the beer, despite tasting terrible, was having the usual effects.

Bentley got to work at some computer equipment.

Without looking at me, he said, "I know security footage can be altered, but this has been authenticated."

He tapped his access codes into the system. He had to try three times, because typing them at vampire speed caused the system to malfunction.

I slid off the table, settled in a chair, and looked into the coffee cup that had been left next to it. There were circles of green bacteria floating on top of an inch of cold coffee.

Life was so amazing.

Someone left out their old coffee, and a new civilization had started itself.

I wondered, what would happen if humans were wiped out?

The mold in the coffee would keep growing. The weeds in the sidewalk would erupt through the concrete. Every roof on every manmade structure would cave in. Life would keep going. Without any of us.

Bentley finally got the security camera footage playing.

It filled the large screen. There were multiple views showing rooms and hallways of the museum. The timestamp was January fourteenth, the morning of my aunt's belated birthday party.

Bentley explained what we were seeing. "We don't have a clear shot of Zoey taking the amulet from the display case, because all the cameras were malfunctioning at the time it disappeared."

"That does seem suspicious," I said. "But my daughter didn't steal anything."

"We do have this image of a red fox crossing over the skylights," he said. "And we have this."

The footage showed a teenaged girl with bleached blonde hair, Ambrosia Abernathy, going from room to room in the museum.

"That's all you have?"

"This isn't a loop," Bentley said. "Ms. Abernathy completed this exact circuit five times. Either she's got OCD, and needs to visit every exhibit multiple times in the exact same order, or she's on lookout."

"What time was this taken?"

"This was one hour before I came to the house to interview Zoey."

"I don't understand why you did that. Why didn't you question Ambrosia? She's the one you have on video, walking around five times, looking suspicious."

"She's visible the entire time, and she doesn't get within ten feet of the amulet. This is evidence she didn't take it."

I gave him a *duh* look. "She's a witch."

He gave me a *duh* look right back. "The exhibits have wards against magic."

I turned to the screen and stared at it in disbelief.

He repeated the footage of a red fox crossing the skylights.

"There's got to be more to this than what we're seeing," I said. "Zoey doesn't steal, and she doesn't lie.

Ambrosia, on the other hand, is less trustworthy." I looked up at Bentley's impassive face. "We need to question Ambrosia."

"We?"

"Don't act like I suddenly have cooties now that we're not smooching on stakeouts. I'm a good partner, and you know it. We should go question Ambrosia together."

He gave it some thought, then said, "You can tag along this one time."

"Why didn't you talk to Ambrosia six weeks ago, when all this happened? Why didn't you ask her about her suspicious lookout loops?"

"I did. I talked to her at her residence later that night. She swore up and down that she didn't know anything about an amulet, and that she hadn't even been to the museum in months."

"But you have footage of her inside the museum. Why would she lie and say she wasn't even there? It doesn't add up."

He shrugged. "Teenagers can be secretive."

"But she was there. Why couldn't you get her to confess to that?"

"It's not a crime to walk around a museum five times." He logged out of the computer and shut off the screens.

"So you just gave up?"

"I got busy with other things, and didn't give it another thought until the Chief asked me about the amulet today. Any idea why Fung is interested? What's his role in this?"

"Zinnia probably asked him to look into it. We were all chipping in with our own research."

"And yet you phoned Rose instead of me."

"I *tried* to phone my sister, but then you commandeered her phone." I looked around. "What have you done with her, anyway?"

He didn't answer my question. "You should have called me, Zara. You should have called me."

"Don't have hurt feelings. Be a man, and focus on solving the problem at hand."

He raised an eyebrow.

"You heard me," I said. "Now get your car keys, and whatever it is you use to beat confessions out of people without leaving bruises. Let's go pay a visit to Ms. Abernathy."

CHAPTER 27

It was Sunday night, and since Ambrosia Abernathy had school the next day, I expected to find her at home, doing homework. My own daughter did her homework Friday night, but Ambrosia was more of a typical teen.

When Bentley and I got to the Abernathy home, Ambrosia's mother said, "She's actually downstairs."

"With all the dead bodies?" I asked. The Abernathys ran a funeral home.

"I suppose there are a few clients on the premises," Mrs. Abernathy said. "Ambrosia seems to enjoy being down there all alone."

"Why am I not surprised," I said.

"Probably because she drives that old hearse," Mrs. Abernathy said, answering what I'd meant as a rhetorical question.

The woman, whose first name was Arliss, let us into the part of the home where the Abernathys conducted funeral services. The house itself was a newer build, part of a strip mall that was an innovative mix of business and retail. The stairwell was large enough to be echoey.

"We can take it from here," I said as we reached the lower floor.

"If there's anything I can help you with, let me know," she said. "Though I am a *nothing person*, so I probably can't do much." She sighed. "I can't even keep my one and only child from getting into trouble with alcohol."

"Ambrosia's not that bad," I said. "Teens experiment. It's what they do. They test boundaries."

"She's adopted," Arliss Abernathy said. "She's not at all like my husband and me. We don't know anything about all this magic business. If you ask me, I can't see the point in any of it. Maybe it's just my personal experience as a nothing person, but it seems to me that some of you folks need to have powers just so you can deal with all the bad people who have powers, too. If nobody had powers, the world would be a safer place."

Bentley said, "Power comes in all forms."

She gave him a cheery smile and lifted her chin. "I suppose you're right! I have a half-dozen guns myself. But don't worry, Detective. I keep them in a safe place." She waved for us to go on. "Good luck with your book club business. I'll be folding laundry, right upstairs if you need me." She started to leave but paused to say, "I'm an excellent markswoman," then left.

After she was gone, I said to Bentley, "Are you guys recruiting at the station? Apparently Arliss Abernathy is an excellent markswoman."

"Duly noted," he said.

"This is fun. Just like old times."

"Sure," he said noncommittally.

The house was bigger than it looked from the outside, and the lower floor was as quiet as a crypt.

As Bentley and I walked down a dark hallway, he glanced around uneasily and said, "We must be surrounded by them."

"Who? Ghosts? No. I don't see any."

"I feel something, though. The presence of death." He pulled at his collar. "Death is breathing down the back of my neck."

"It *is* a funeral home," I said. "It would be strange if you *didn't* sense the presence of death."

He shot me a sidelong glance. "You're good at that," he said.

"Sensing death?"

"Reframing a situation. Looking at things in a different light."

"A more sensible light?"

He nearly smiled. "I wouldn't go that far."

We got to the end of the hallway, where we found Ambrosia inside the coffin showroom, dusting the display coffins.

She glanced up at us, scowled, and said, "Zoey's not here. She's probably out having fun with Atom." She paused to sneer. "Haven't you heard? He's way, way, way more fun than me." She sprayed cleaning fluid on a coffin and buffed it off with a white cloth.

Bentley nudged me to say something to Ambrosia. Something nice, probably.

I said to the girl, "I can't imagine why anyone would rather hang out with a cute boy than clean display coffins with you."

"I'm not *just* cleaning coffins." Ambrosia pointed to the large television that was on. The volume was low, but I had no doubt about which movie was playing. It was the *Wizard of Oz*.

Seeing young Dorothy in her pinafore dress gave me a sharp pang. It reminded me of the crazy real estate agent who'd sold me my house. The nutty woman used to dress up like Dorothy and carry brochures in a basket. It was her gimmick—her strange gimmick that didn't seem so strange in the town of Wisteria. Why had I not taken one look at that woman and run screaming from the entire town?

Bentley watched the screen a moment before saying, "I've never seen this movie before. Not the whole thing."

"Grab a chair," Ambrosia said. "This is the local station. They're running a triple feature because of the tornado."

I asked, "What tornado?"

"The one that's probably going to pass right by here," Ambrosia said with a weary sigh. "It's so stupid what things the people around this town get excited about. The other movies after this are *Twister* and *Sharknado*."

I turned to Bentley to see if he was as confused as I felt.

He didn't look confused at all.

He explained to me, "There is a local tornado warning in effect, but it's supposed to pass right by. They're calling a *wayward tornado*, because we don't usually get them here, let alone at this time of year."

"Why didn't I know about this? Nobody informed me about any wayward tornado."

Bentley said, "It's just the weather, Zara. Not everything is about you."

Ambrosia snickered.

"This feels like an omen." I waved at the TV screen. It was an early scene, right after Dorothy's house had been swept up inside the twister. A witch on a broomstick flew by the open window as Dorothy and Toto watched in horror from the bed. The scene cut to the house swirling through the air, then landing in a strange new land. The technicolor reveal happened, with an emphasis on the artificial flowers on the film set.

Ambrosia said, "If this movie is an omen, then just stay off your broomstick and you'll be fine. Oh, wait. You can't fly on a broomstick. None of us can. Because stupid Atom took away all our best powers. Is that why you're here? Are you going to arrest him for stealing from us?"

Bentley said, "Ms. Abernathy, that's not why we're here, but we are here on official police business. We're working together."

She gave me a puzzled look. "You two are back together?" She swung her finger from me to him, and back again.

Bentley said, "No."

I said, "Yes."

Then he said yes, and I said no.

I said, "We're working on a case together."

Bentley said, "That's all."

I said, "Not that it's any of your business, Ambrosia."

Bentley said, "We just want to talk to you about the day you and Zoey were at the museum."

Ambrosia kept cleaning the display coffin, unconcerned. "I already told you, I don't know anything about whatever happened there. If I knew where the amulet was, well, let's just say Atom would already have it in his grubby little devil hands, and I'd have all my powers back."

Bentley picked up the remote control for the television and switched it over to input so he could broadcast the security camera footage from his phone to the screen.

The yellow brick road disappeared, replaced by footage of Ambrosia at the museum.

The Ambrosia that was in the coffin showroom with us stepped out from behind the gleaming coffin, and walked slowly toward the television, watching herself walking through the museum in a circuit.

"Those are my clothes," she said. "And my face." Her face scrunched up. "Oh, no," she said, and she swore a few times.

Bentley said to her, "It seems you do know something about the theft at the museum."

"No." She waved her hands as her cheeks flushed. "I mean yes? Maybe?" She chewed on her lower lip.

"You have to tell us," I said. "It's important, Ambrosia. If Zoey is involved in something bad, you're not doing her any favors by covering for her."

Ambrosia rubbed her forehead. "Zoey doesn't know anything."

Bentley said, "Are you saying you acted alone?"

Ambrosia shook her head. "I, uh, maybe I should show you."

She led us over to a locked cabinet, and opened it with a key.

"I have to use keys now," she muttered. "Stupid Atom."

Bentley shut down his phone's transmission to the television, and the screen returned to an image of Dorothy navigating a technicolor world that must have been breathtaking to the audiences of the day.

Ambrosia got the cabinet open, and pulled out an old-looking glass bottle of green liquid.

Bentley asked, "What is that? Embalming fluid? Absinthe?"

Ambrosia answered, "You could call it absinthe, but instead of the usual wormwood, it uses a different blend of herbs."

She removed the lid and let him sniff it.

He turned to me and said, "It smells better than the beer we had at Mary Shelley's, but not much."

I couldn't take his word for it. I had to smell it myself.

As I sniffed the bottle, which reeked of an artificial strawberry scent, he gave me a satisfied look, as if to gloat over having won some unspoken bet.

Ambrosia said, "It tastes better than it smells."

"I've smelled this before," I said. "You and Zoey had it on your breath at Zinnia's birthday party. I thought it was strawberry gum, but it was this. You two were drinking this before the party?"

Ambrosia nodded. "I have to write myself notes whenever I drink it, because it wipes out a couple hours of short-term memories."

She turned the bottle to show us her notes.

Sure enough, written in Ambrosia's handwriting was an entry for January fourteenth. Both Ambrosia's and Zoey's names were listed, along with the number of ounces consumed. They'd each had two ounces.

Ambrosia said, "We must have taken the amulet from the museum, then drank this right after so we would forget."

Bentley said, "You two are a couple of criminal masterminds. That explains why Zoey was able to lie to me. She was technically telling the truth. She had no knowledge of any theft."

"That must be it," Ambrosia said. "I don't know why we borrowed it." She tapped her forehead. "Everything's gone."

I put my hands on my hips. "You don't know why you *borrowed* the amulet? Really, Ambrosia? Really? You can't remember anything about the incident, but you're sure that you *borrowed* it? Why can't you just admit you stole it?"

She shivered and brought the bottle of alcohol to her lips.

I lunged forward and grabbed the bottle from her.

"Give it back." She tried to get the bottle from me and failed. "I just want a sip to take the edge off. This whole thing is freaking me out. Why would Zoey make me do that?" She lunged for the booze again.

I put my hand on her forehead to keep her away from the bottle.

"I should hand this over to your mother for disposal," I said, shaking the bottle. "Or dump it down the drain."

Ambrosia whined, "But the ingredients are expensive! And it's winter! I won't be able to get more four-leaf clover for months!"

"You should have thought about that before you stole a powerful amulet. Speaking of which, where is it?"

She stopped trying to get the bottle, and focused on glaring at me. "How should I know? My memories are gone. Duh."

"Where do you normally hide things?"

She pointed to the cabinet where she'd had the green drink locked away. Sure enough, the cabinet was full of secrets. There was a diary, plus magical elixirs, and rare objects. But no amulet.

I said to Bentley, "Zoey must have hidden it at the house. This is going to be easy. I know all her favorite hiding spots. When she's in fox form, she stashes food around the house. We just have to follow our noses."

Bentley said, "There's just one thing that isn't falling into place. Why would the devil ask you to locate something, to give to Zoey, if she already has it?"

"Because she doesn't know she has it," I said.

Ambrosia gasped, then squealed as she jumped up and down. "That's why Atom is interested in her instead of... someone else. He must know she has the amulet. He probably senses it on her. Magical artifacts cast off energy, like radiation."

"But he's been to the house at least three times now," I said. "If he knows she has it, wouldn't he have found it by now?"

Ambrosia didn't have an answer.

I went on, brainstorming. "What's the point in him asking me about it? Is it... all just a charade? A distraction from what he's actually doing? Is the amulet just a red herring? Like when you throw a crinkle toy out of the room to keep Boa away from your dinner plate?"

"Slow down," Bentley said.

I shot him a saucy look. "What's the matter? Can't keep up with your old partner? Why so slow, Bentley? Have you been eating too many sprinkle donuts?" I poked him in the midsection, which was like poking a brick wall. So much for my donut theory.

Bentley said, "First things first. We need to search your house—I mean your aunt's house—for the amulet."

"Let's get over there right now while everyone's out," I said.

We turned and headed down the hallway.

Ambrosia ran after us. "Wait for me!"

"You can stay here with your tornado movies," I called back. "Thanks for helping us."

"I'm coming with you," Ambrosia said. "I can't wait to see the look on Atom's face when he finds out I'm the one who masterminded the whole thing. He's going to be sorry."

Bentley and I exchanged a look.

Ambrosia seemed awfully confident that she'd masterminded the museum heist. Of course she didn't have any memories of the event, so she was free to change the narrative as it suited her.

She reminded me of myself.

As we stepped outside, a gust of wind blew into us so hard that both Ambrosia and I grabbed onto Bentley's arms to keep from falling over.

"The storm is picking up," Bentley said.

"Duh," Ambrosia said. "There's a tornado warning in effect for a reason. Do neither of you have the weather app on your phones?"

"I don't need an app to tell me if it's raining," I said. "I go outside from time to time. It's different with my generation."

We leaned into the wind as we made our way from the house to the car.

I paused to pour the remnants of Ambrosia's memory-erasing booze down a storm drain.

The wind blew so hard that I feared I might get a contact buzz from the mist in the air, so I held my breath while I poured it all out.

Ambrosia checked her phone app and said, "The tornado is supposed to pass by north of town, but it's going to be windy here." She frowned. "Oops. Update. It might touch down a bit closer than they thought." She looked up from her phone. "I'm sure it's going to be fine. They're just being cautious."

A powerful gust of wind ripped the phone from her hands, and sent it skipping across the parking lot.

Ambrosia squealed and ran after her phone.

Bentley moved his body to block the wind from hitting me, though it didn't work that well. The wind seemed to be coming from all directions at once. That wasn't possible. It was probably just changing directions rapidly.

The ground was icy under my feet. I began sliding away from Bentley.

He grabbed my arm and pulled me back toward him.

"Zara, does your aunt's house have a basement?"

"Not really. There's just an old root cellar where she keeps pickled things."

"How many people will fit down there?"

"It's not very big. Why? Are you getting a bad feeling about this tornado?"

He looked up at the black sky. The sun had set, and there was nothing to see except wind-blown debris. A white plastic chair flew by, followed by a pink flamingo —a plastic lawn ornament, not Frank Wonder.

Ambrosia returned with her phone—the screen was cracked—and clung to me.

Bentley said, "We should probably take cover somewhere safe, like the police station."

"Or the library," I said. "That building is mostly cement."

"But the amulet isn't at the police station, or the library," Bentley said.

His pocket flashed with a red light.

He took out his phone. "Tornado warning," he said. "It's official."

I could tell by the faint glow inside my purse that my phone was lighting up with the same emergency alert.

"We'd better find this amulet quickly," I said. "First stop, Zinnia's house, second stop, somewhere concrete."

Ambrosia said, "Don't leave without me. Give me a minute to check on my folks."

She ran back to her house, only falling over twice in the wind.

After instructing her parents to take shelter on the lower floor, she joined us inside Bentley's car.

I'd left my own car back at the station, along with our uneaten dinner.

My stomach growled as I put on my seatbelt.

"This is like old times," I said to Bentley. "You used to tell me we were going to eat, then we'd get derailed by one of your investigations, and we'd never get to eat."

"And yet you always survived," Bentley said.

"Barely," I grumbled.

As we drove away from the Abernathy home, Ambrosia said, "This is going to be fun. I can't wait to see the look on Zoey's face when she finds out we figured out what happened to the amulet before she did."

I turned around and said, "There's a maliciousness to your glee that doesn't seem right for someone who's supposedly Zoey's best friend."

She shrugged. "I am kind of a witch."

Bentley snorted.

CHAPTER 28

We pulled up to Zinnia's house as another white garden chair skated by in front of the car.

The chair whipped up in a spin, like a figure skater in a triple Axel, before landing in a tree.

"There goes another one," I said. "Who knew the unofficial symbol of the end of the world would be plastic lawn chairs?"

"I'm not surprised," Ambrosia said. "You always see those chairs in the footage after tsunamis and floods."

Bentley said gruffly, "This is bad, but it isn't the end of the world. Yet."

I patted him on the shoulder. "Thanks for the amazing pep talk. I, for one, feel invigorated. Do you still feel the presence of death breathing on the back of your neck?"

He looked down at my hand on his shoulder, then at me. There was a hungry, yearning look in his eyes that made my breath catch in my throat. Was our connection reforming, or was it just wishful thinking?

We'd been in each other's close company for almost two hours, which was usually the amount of time required for some serious sparks to start flying. The man was tough, but he could only repress his true feelings for so long. We'd come a long way since the days I'd taunted him about rainbow-sprinkle donuts.

Ambrosia said, "Come on, you guys. Stop making googly eyes at each other. Let's get that amulet before Zoey figures out what she did."

We opened the car doors, stumbled out, and formed a human chain of three as we fought our way through the wind and debris to the door. The storm howled, pelting us with loose branches and pebbles.

Stepping inside the relative safety of the house was a massive relief.

My mother and my aunt were both home, sitting in the living room with the television on.

They were watching the *Wizard of Oz*. The scene cut to a station promo for the upcoming movies, which were —as Ambrosia had already told us— *Twister* and *Sharknado*. Hilarious.

I wiped grit from my face.

Marzipants sang a happy budgie greeting at us. Boa padded up silently, and launched herself into Bentley's arms without waiting for an invitation.

"I missed you, too, Miss Kitty," the usually-cool vampire cooed at her.

She gazed up at him with adoration. "Ham."

My mother finally took her eyes off the TV screen, looked us over, and said, "Look what the storm blew in. If it isn't the scarecrow, the tin man, and the cowardly lion."

I replied, "Which one am I?"

"The scarecrow, obviously," she said with a smirk.

"Right," I said with a scoff. "Because of the lack of brains. Ha ha."

Ambrosia said to Bentley, "You're the tin man. You need a new heart."

He scowled.

Zinnia looked up from her needlework. "Sounds like that storm's getting worse out there."

"It's bad," I said. "Bentley thinks we should all go down to the root cellar, just in case."

Zinnia scoffed. "This old house has been through much worse, thank you very much."

My mother asked, "What are you three doing here?" She waved her hand at us. "It's always nice to see you, Teddy, but this combination isn't quite right. It feels like an omen."

I answered with a joking tone, "We are here to see the wizard."

Ambrosia said, "Zoey hid the amulet here in the house. That's why Atom has been coming over. He only wants the amulet. But we outsmarted both of them, and we're going to find it first."

Zinnia reacted with surprise. "You found the amulet? Already?"

"Not yet," I said. "But it's somewhere in this house. Remember how Zoey and Ambrosia were drunk at your birthday party? They did the robbery at the museum that morning, then drank some absinthe that erased their memories. Ambrosia had a special brew. She's quite the distiller, apparently."

My aunt's eyes widened even more. "That explains a lot," she said.

My mother said, "Ooh, absinthe! I do love a nice tipple of the green fairy's brew. Did you bring it with you?"

"I dumped it all out," I said.

"Boo," my mother replied.

Ambrosia kicked off her boots and started digging around in the couch cushions.

Marzipants twittered with excitement from his cage. He loved it when there was action of any kind in the living room.

I tossed my coat to the side and started looking as well.

My mother refused to move from her seat, so I picked her up and moved her over by one cushion so I could check where she'd been sitting. No amulet. Plenty of loose change, hair elastics, and some dried-up pepperoni, but no amulet.

My vampire mother scoffed and said, "Why don't you cast an object location spell?"

I paused long enough to roll my eyes at her. "We tried that already. We did it the night Atom made the offer. Zinnia and I cast all sorts of object location spells using maps of the town. It didn't show up."

She said, "Then what makes you think you're going to find it now?"

Ambrosia answered for me. "It's *got to be* here. It's the most logical place. I already checked my hiding spot, so that only leaves Zoey's hiding places." She glanced up at the ceiling. "I'll take the bedroom."

Bentley said, "We can all take an area. A search is better when it's organized. Have you got a multi-head screwdriver? I'll check the electrical outlets and heater vents."

Ambrosia ran up the stairs, calling down, "Zoey's not that sophisticated! It's probably under her mattress!"

I said to Bentley, "You must know all the good hiding places, thanks to your on-the-job experience."

"I know a few tricks," he said.

Zinnia returned from the kitchen with a multi-head screwdriver, which she placed in his hand.

She said, "I'll check the toilets." To me, she explained, "People put valuables inside jars and bags that they hide in the tanks."

"They do," Bentley said. "Some other common hiding spots are unused purses, cookie or coffee tins, and freezers. Small objects are often sewn into curtain hems, or taped to the back of artwork or mirrors."

My mother smirked. "And there's always the hidden room behind the revolving bookshelf." She tipped back her wine. "I've seen all the classic episodes of Scooby-Doo. Plus, I know about Zinnia's secret spot." She set aside her glass, got up, and walked over to the room's sole bookshelf.

She reached behind a book and pressed a mechanism. The bookshelf swung out, revealing a second bookshelf behind it, where my aunt kept her magical tomes.

"That's supposed to be a secret," my aunt said.

I asked her, "Does Zoey know about it?"

Zinnia frowned. "I don't think so. But I didn't think my sister knew, either."

"It's a good hiding spot," I said. "I'll search here. Mom, you can finish the couch cushions. Aunt Zinnia, would you mind doing a sweep of the kitchen? You know your refrigerator better than anyone."

Everyone agreed, and got to work. Ambrosia could be heard scuffling around upstairs.

As I searched the secret bookshelf, Bentley got down on his knees beside me.

I looked down at the top of his head and said, "Awkward timing for a fresh marriage proposal, but give it a shot. You never know. The end of the world brings out my romantic side."

"I'm checking this cold air return," he said gruffly.

"Sure, you are," I teased. "There are a dozen outlets and cover plates in this room, but the cold air return right next to me is the one where you need to start?"

He tossed his head in a casual, fun gesture. "Maybe I enjoy being next to your legs."

"Admit it. You enjoy being next to *all of me*."

He looked up from the cold air return, a sparkle in his silver eyes. "I do enjoy being next to all of you."

I did a double take. So, I'd been right about him choosing to search next to me.

I thought I'd detected a vibe earlier, when we'd been in the car together. It had seemed like he might have said something to me if Ambrosia hadn't been riding along.

"Detective, is it possible the impending end of the world has stirred up some of your romantic feelings, too?"

"*Stirred up* is a good description for my feelings," he said.

I got back to my search through the magical tomes. "Let me know if any other adjectives come up."

"You're the one who's good with words. I never know what I want. Not like you." He leaned over to look inside the cold air return, coincidentally rubbing his shoulder against my leg. I could feel his hot breath through my cable-knit tights.

I was about to say something saucy when he looked up at me and said, "Why aren't we together?"

It was the most beautiful question I'd ever heard.

Slowly, I answered, "We're not together because you broke up with me so you could get back together with your succubus ex-wife."

"That's not what happened."

"That's how I remember it."

"Memories are fallible. Even the sketchiest physical evidence is more damning than a dozen eyewitnesses."

"I have physical evidence." I put my hand over my chest. "My heart, and how broken it felt after you dumped me. How's that for physical evidence, Mr. Tin Man?"

Softly, he said, "I have a heart," and, "I didn't break up with you."

"But you said you wanted time. Or space. Or both."

"When? Not at Bed, Bath and Beyond. I reviewed the surveillance footage from the store, and I said nothing like that. We only talked about towels."

I'd been slowly searching the bookshelf, but now I stopped entirely.

I asked, incredulous, "You used your detective rank to get security footage from a big box store? For me? For us?"

He looked away.

"Bentley, that's the sweetest thing you've ever done," I said.

"Yeah, well, I don't have any cameras in my apartment," he said with a shrug. "I still don't know what the hell happened the last time the two of us were there, but whatever it was I did or said, I regret it now."

"Define *now*," I said.

He gave me a confused look. "What?"

"Define what you mean by *now*. Did you regret it at two o'clock today when you intercepted my phone call to Persephone? Or at six o'clock, when you saw me at the restaurant? Or was it just now, when we were driving through an end-of-the-world tornado that kept trying to pick up your gray sedan and smash it like a toy?"

"It doesn't matter," he said. "All that matters is this now. The one we are in."

His words sent a shiver through my body. A good shiver.

I reached my hand down to him.

He had to stand up or I would have to kneel.

Either way, we were going to kiss.

Bentley smiled.

As his hand touched mine, Ambrosia yelled from the bedroom, "Found it!"

Bentley didn't let me help him to his feet. He didn't need anyone's help.

With his vampire speed, he turned and left in a blur, practically flying up the stairs.

CHAPTER 29

Bentley beat me to the upstairs bedroom, but I wasn't far behind, and I had my aunt and mother at my heels.

Ambrosia stood between the bunk beds and the dresser. The room was in shambles, the contents of the dresser and closet having been dumped on the floor.

Ambrosia's round cheeks were flushed, and her bleached-blonde hair was disheveled.

"I found it," Ambrosia said breathlessly. "Me. I'm not a stupid loser. I'm not a pathetic waste of powers. I found it."

As I heard the teen describing herself in negative terms, my heart ached for her. The poor kid was having a rough time, and I hadn't noticed. This was like the Charlize situation all over again. *Zara tries to be a good witch, a competent pet owner, and a thoughtful friend. Zara tries, but she gets caught up in her own drama.*

The teen witch was holding a lamp. It was the ugly floral lamp that my aunt had given me as a housewarming gift nearly a year ago. It was mine, in a house that wasn't mine, one of the few possessions that had stubbornly survived my home's explosion. It was the same lamp that had revealed Atom's true face to me in that very bedroom nine days earlier.

Ambrosia was holding the lamp upside down. She'd unscrewed the center of the base, revealing a cavity. That alone wasn't terribly surprising. Most lamps had a cavity in their bases. But this lamp was no ordinary lamp, so that made its cavity special.

She angled the base so the cavity caught the light from the overhead fixture.

And there it was.

Glinting inside the lamp base was a familiar-looking chain and amulet. It had been inside the lamp, right under our noses, the whole time.

"The light bulbs," I said. "The ones that kept flickering and burning out when we did the object location spells. The lamps were trying to tell us something."

My aunt was too stunned to reply.

"That's it," my mother said with certainty. "That's my old necklace. It looks even chunkier than I remember it. Now I know why I handed it off to the museum curator. I prefer a more delicate style of jewelry."

I reached my hand in slowly, expecting the lamp's cavity to grow teeth and bite me.

It didn't grow teeth, or change in any way.

I looped the chain around my fingers. It felt like an ordinary chain.

"Stop right there," Zinnia said. "Zara, don't pull it out yet."

Bentley, Ambrosia, my mother, and I all turned to my aunt.

"Why not?" I asked.

"The lamp must be shielding it," she said. "This must be why the amulet didn't come up in our searches, even though we searched from inside the house. We ought to be cautious about removing the artifact."

"Why? The lamp did its job," I said. "Zoey forgot about it, thanks to the absinthe, and Atom wasn't able to detect it before we figured it out. This lamp has fulfilled its destiny." To the lamp, I said, "I take back everything I ever said about you, Lampy. You're the most wonderful home lighting accessory that's ever existed."

The light bulb that was screwed into the lamp flickered. The lamp was still plugged in and switched on.

The lights in the nearby hallway also flickered, as did the ceiling fixture.

Was the power about to go out, or was something magical happening?

The window rattled. The storm hadn't let up one bit.

I looked around at the others, who did the same.

The wind outside howled louder and louder.

Our phones all beeped and buzzed with more tornado warnings.

"Evacuation orders," Zinnia said. Her psychic connection to her phone was still working so she didn't have to look at the screen.

Bentley said, "We should retreat to the root cellar."

"We'll have to draw straws," Zinnia said. "I'd be surprised if three of us will fit down there, let alone five."

Loose branches battered the house.

Hailstones pummeled the window.

All five of us, who should have been drawing straws over who got to hide in the root cellar, were instead standing together inside a small room at the top of the old house.

"Zara, get your hand out of there," my aunt said. "We ought to leave the amulet inside the lamp until we know what to do with it."

I reluctantly released the chain from my fingers, and slowly withdrew my hand.

Nobody made a rush to leave the top-floor room.

We all took turns peering into the lamp's cavity. The amulet wasn't glowing or doing anything magical. It looked like a piece of cheap costume jewelry.

Then Ambrosia said, "Screw you, you bunch of chickens." She thrust her hand into the base and yanked out the amulet. She held it above her head triumphantly, like a knight who'd just pulled Excalibur from a stone.

At that instant, the front door banged open downstairs.

An impossibly cold gust of wind rushed through the house.

I heard my daughter call out, "Mom? Is that Mr. Bentley's car parked out front? There's a lawn chair stuck in the tree!"

Ambrosia clutched the amulet to her chest, and held her finger to her lips. "Shhh." She whispered, "Don't tell her I'm here. You guys go downstairs, and I'll sneak out the window with it."

Zoey yelled back, "With what? Ambrosia? Why's Ambrosia here?"

"Her hearing is way too good," I said.

I heard Zoey run up the stairs at top speed.

She stopped at the doorway, framed by it. She blinked in surprise at finding five people—three witches and two vampires—standing in her bedroom with the contents of the closet and dresser strewn all over the floor.

Atom, who must have been right on her heels, stood behind her. He had loose branches visible in his dark curls, and a smear of dirt on his cheek.

Atom's gaze went straight to the lamp, which I was now holding, upside down, with the cavity exposed. I couldn't remember taking the lamp. Ambrosia must have handed it to me after she was done with it. My head was spinning like my skull had its own small tornado. Everything was happening so fast.

"The amulet," Atom said in a relaxed tone. "You found it, Amber."

"It's Ambrosia," she said.

He gave her a sideways look. "That's what I said."

She shook her head. "You called me Amber. You always do."

"I apologize," he said. "Good work, Ambrosia. You're a clever witch. I had a feeling there was something funny about that lamp, besides its powers." He held out his hand. "I'm so glad we can finish our deal."

Ambrosia said, "I'm the one who found it, Atom. What do you think of that?"

He looked at me instead of her. "Is that true, Zara? Did Amber—I mean Ambrosia—find the amulet?"

"It was a team effort," I said. "But Ambrosia is responsible. She gave us the lead we needed, and she's the one who located it inside the lamp."

Atom jerked his chin in Bentley's direction. "Who's the dead one?"

"A friend of the family," I said. "None of your business."

Atom wrinkled his nose as he turned to Bentley. "Don't worry about what comes next. I promise it won't hurt."

Bentley moved with vampire speed, right at Atom.

My eyes weren't fast enough to see what Atom did in response, but, whatever it was, it was effective.

Bentley flew away from the devil just as quickly as he'd flown at him, rising up through the air and striking the ceiling before falling to the floor in front of us. Bits of plaster rained down.

Zoey pushed Atom out of the way, and ran to Bentley.

He was face-down.

We all watched in stunned silence as Bentley struggled to get up to his knees then collapsed, eyes closed.

Power tingled in my fingertips. I wanted to fire at Atom with everything I had, but I managed to stop myself. My powers wouldn't do any good if I got them confiscated.

"Stay down," Atom said, pointing a finger at the vampire detective. "Bad dog. Stay where you are if you know what's good for everyone here. I don't want to have to hurt anyone else. You don't count, because you're already dead."

My body buzzed with rage. I was still holding the lamp, and the urge to send it flying into Atom's face was almost unbearable.

He was a monster, and now he was showing himself.

My daughter was close enough to me that I could put my free hand on her shoulder. I squeezed her shoulder and whispered, "Look at your boyfriend, Zoey. Look at who he truly is. See what he's capable of. *See him.*"

My mother said to Atom, "Young man, this is unacceptable. We—"

Atom waved his fingers in her direction, and she went down like a marionette with severed strings.

My aunt gasped and knelt next to her sister, who was crumpled on the floor next to her fellow vampire. My daughter was still kneeling as well, trying to revive Bentley by slapping his cheek.

Atom said, "And then there were three left standing." He made eye contact with Ambrosia, and gave her a dazzling grin. "What do you say? Are you ready to make a deal, Ambrosia?" He tilted his head back and gave her an appraising look. "That is a pretty name, by the way. I like it. Ambrosia. Like the only kind of salad we serve in Hell. Tell me, Ambrosia, did I place my bet on the wrong horse? Were you always the one I should have wanted?"

Ambrosia giggled.

I elbowed her to shut up, but it didn't do any good. She was under his thrall.

Ambrosia took a step toward Atom with the amulet.

I felt a blue fireball pooling in my free hand.

In my other hand was the lamp.

If I threw the fireball, it likely wasn't going to do much, except cause me to lose the ability to ever throw a fireball ever again.

So, I threw the lamp at him.

While he and Ambrosia were distracted by the flying lamp, I swiped the amulet from Ambrosia's hand.

When Atom caught the lamp, his demonic face reappeared, contorted and red. He let it fall from his hands. It smashed, cracking up the center of the base. The lampshade protected the bulb, though, so it remained lit.

A devil with horns and a tail glared back at us.

"Yikes," Ambrosia said. "That's, uh, not a cute look, Atom."

"That's his true face," I said. "Take a good look, girls. Is he still the cutest boy in school?"

"Uhh." Ambrosia took a step back.

Zinnia and Zoey were watching quietly, clinging to each other. Zinnia was chanting a protection spell—protection from demonic forces. It was a bit late for that, but I couldn't fault her for trying.

Atom pointed at me. "Give me the Vessel of the Remainder, witch."

I clutched it tighter. "No. You're just an entitled brat, Atom. Here on earth, entitled brats don't snap their fingers and get their way."

His hideous red face contorted even more. "I'm not... I'm not... how dare you, witch! After everything I've given you!"

"You've never given me anything but trouble," I said. "Furthermore, it's a school night. Time for you to go home. Right now."

More plaster rained down from the ceiling.

Bentley had opened his eyes. He tried to get up, but couldn't get his feet underneath him. He was bleeding from the back of his head. He needed help. He needed me. But I couldn't take my attention off the devil in the room.

The wind continued to howl, and hail pelted the window. The ceiling plaster continued to rain down.

And then, there was a strange ripping sound.

The room went dark.

The plaster stopped coming down.

The air changed from hot to cold.

My hair flew up and around my face, obscuring my vision.

I looked up at the blackness of the sky.

There was no roof above me.

The storm raged around us, louder than ever.

Atom yelled, "Give me the amulet now, before it's too late!"

Zinnia looked up from my mother's crumpled form. "The roof," she said. "It's gone."

I said to Atom, "Who took the roof? Was that you, or the tornado?"

"It wasn't me," he said.

"But you have to admit the timing is pretty convenient."

He wiped his nose with the back of his hand, which was the most human thing I'd seen him do. His nose was... bleeding. It was hard to tell, given how red his demonic face was, but the fluid was dark. Blood.

Seeing the devil with a nosebleed was, weirdly, more disturbing than just seeing the devil.

I looked up at the black sky. What was next?

"I'm not the only one after that amulet," Atom said, answering my unspoken question. "Give it to me, witch, and at least you'll have your powers back. You'll need everything you can get for what comes next."

"No," I said. "You can keep trying to negotiate, but I won't give it to you. No deal, Atom. No deal."

"What makes you think I won't take it from you?"

"The fact that you haven't taken it yet," I said. "Something tells me you have to be given this amulet. Is that right?"

He said nothing, but the fury in his yellow demon eyes said everything.

The blood coming from his red nose flowed over his snarling lips, and stained his pointy yellow teeth.

The magic lamp had flashed out when the roof had been torn away, yet his true demon face remained, barely visible yet unmistakably grotesque under only the wan moonlight coming through the stormy clouds.

Atom said, "I'm not the only one after that amulet, but I am the only one who plays by the rules."

The others were silent, so I kept doing the talking.

"Who else is involved? Is it Mahra? Or one of the other Four Eves?"

His monstrous face gave away no clues. "Guess again."

Before I could, the wind grabbed hold of me like a pair of strong hands.

With its invisible hands, the darkness itself wrenched the amulet from my grasp.

The amulet hung in the air before me.

The wind snarled and whipped around us, swirling away more of the house. A wall crumbled. The bunkbeds skidded across the floor and teetered on the edge.

The amulet began to rise, moving skyward.

Atom said, "Now you've gone and done it." He shook his head. "This is on you."

My daughter, who'd been leaning against my leg, suddenly turned into a fox.

The fox jumped onto the top of the bunk bed, then through the air.

She caught the amulet in her mouth.

The fox hung in midair, as the amulet had.

And then the wind changed direction, and she was sucked straight up and away, into the darkness.

I felt a hand grasp mine. Bentley's hand.

Bentley stood before me, his face in front of mine.

"Zara," he said hoarsely.

I was stunned. A tornado had just sucked my daughter, the fox, into the sky.

With a croaking voice, I managed to say, "Zoey."

"My vow," he said.

The storm was so loud in my ears.

Had he said something about a vow? What did he mean?

"Zoey," I said again.

Bentley's silver eyes turned dark. They became bottomless. They were the pits that held more sorrow than any mortal could bear.

He turned, used his vampire speed and strength to jump onto the top of a crumbling wall, and then shot into the sky.

He disappeared, like Zoey had.

CHAPTER 30

I would have jumped into the dark sky, too, but my aunt grabbed my hand and held me back.

"You can't fly," Zinnia said.

I pulled my hand away. "Neither can Bentley," I said.

She grabbed my arm at the elbow, and held it tightly. "Don't you feel that? The wind's dying down."

She was right. The worst of the storm had passed. Even if I could jump in the direction my daughter had gone, I would immediately fall back down to the ground. Even if I'd been able to cast a buoyancy spell to lighten my body, the wind had died down to where it wouldn't even take away a dry leaf, let alone me. And I couldn't cast that spell, anyway.

I stared up at the sky. "Zoey," I said, my voice weak and raspy. "Bentley."

My aunt slowly released her grip on my arm.

"Zara, your daughter will be unharmed," Atom Wick said. "She has the amulet in her possession. It will protect her."

I turned to the devil, fists raised in anger. "Nobody asked you, Atom."

He gave me a surprised look.

"You did this," I said angrily, pointing my finger at the boy, and then around us, at the destroyed house. "This is all your fault."

"Me?" He took a step back, into what was left of the hallway. Most of the walls were gone, along with the doors, and even some of the flooring.

I moved forward, advancing on him. I didn't dare use my magic on him, lest I have it confiscated, but I'd be happy to try an old-fashioned attack.

Atom moved back again, stumbling over loose boards.

My mother groaned, bringing my attention back to my family.

Zinnia and Ambrosia were helping my mother get to her feet. My mother was stunned, moving slowly, but still alive.

"This is unacceptable," my mother said.

I'd never been more relieved to hear her complain.

"Hurry up," I said to the other women. "We have to find Zoey and Bentley wherever the tornado set them down."

"Hang on," Zinnia said, checking my mother over.

I stamped my foot impatiently.

The floor replied with what seemed like a protest to having been stomped on.

The wind had died down, and now we were able to hear the creaks and groans of the damaged house. It seemed to be growling out a warning to us.

Ambrosia said, "Is that the house?"

I stomped again, as a test. The house groaned and creaked even louder.

"We need to get out of here," Atom said. "This charm-filled residence has been structurally damaged. It's such a shame."

My mother looked up at the empty sky. "The roof is gone," she said. "Zinnia! Your roof is gone!"

I snapped, "Welcome to five minutes ago."

Atom said, "Without the trusses in place, this old house could fold in on itself like a house of cards."

Zinnia scoffed. "This house has been here over a hundred years, thank you very much."

She might have said more, but the floor beneath her gave way at that exact moment.

Zinnia fell through it, into the living room.

The rest of us raced downstairs.

We found Zinnia on the sofa, surrounded by crumbled plaster and shattered wood. She was shaken up, but unbroken.

My mother checked Zinnia over, inspecting her sister as Zinnia had done for Zirconia a moment earlier.

As touching as the scene of sisterly caring was, we didn't have time for much more.

Zoey's absence was pressing on my mind, like a foot on my gas pedal.

"Everyone out," I ordered. "Out! Out of the house! We're evacuating right now!"

Boa was there, circling my legs, so I picked her up.

The ghost of Mrs. Pinkman dashed into the destroyed living room, waving her hands. Her ghost hair was in ghost curlers.

"I see you," I said to the ghostly woman. "I haven't forgotten about Marzipants. Ambrosia, get the bird cage."

Ambrosia, who could also see the ghost, followed Mrs. Pinkman to the bird cage, and lifted the cage from the base.

Atom, who was wisely keeping his mouth shut, led the way out the front door.

The five of us—three Riddles, one Abernathy, and one devil—got to the front lawn with Boa and the bird cage.

We were met by several concerned neighbors.

Everyone talked at once.

I took a minute to get my bearings and survey the situation.

There was no sign of Zoey or Bentley.

From what I could see, my aunt's house wasn't the only one on the block that had been hit by the tornado, but it had been hit the worst.

There was damage all around, and more neighbors emerging from their houses. The streetlights were out on one side of the street, along with the lights in the houses, but the other side of the street still had power.

My aunt put her hand on my shoulder. "Don't worry," she said. "We'll find Zoey. She's going to be okay. She's got Bentley with her, and we all know how tough he is."

"That man is indestructible," I said, then I turned to Atom. "Take me to her."

He shoved his hands in his pockets. "What makes you think I know where she went?"

His devil face was no longer visible. It must have changed around the time we exited my aunt's house, as none of the neighbors were screaming. He looked like a normal boy again. His nose was still bleeding. The blood looked like regular, human blood. It was just as unsettling.

"Work with me," I said to the boy. "Your stock is currently tanking with the Riddle family, but you can still save it. Work with me, Atom. Help me find Zoey and Bentley. Take me to them."

Atom pulled his hands from his pockets and held them wide. "I don't know what's happening. My usual thing is I act like I know everything, but the truth is... I don't know what's going on. Nothing I've seen or done before has prepared me for this." He crossed his arms and shivered visibly. "I'm cold."

"You're useless," I said.

He flinched as though I'd shot him with an arrow.

Ambrosia said, "I know how to find them."

My mother and aunt were standing with us. We all turned to the teen witch.

Ambrosia waved her cracked phone screen. "This app will show us. Everywhere the tornado touched down, the power went out. We just have to follow this map of all the power outages." She showed us the screen. Even through the cracks in the screen, I recognized the familiar map of the seaside town. There were red highlights showing the tornado's path of destruction as power outages.

I asked, "Which way should we go? This map doesn't say what direction it was heading."

Ambrosia said, "We'll split up. Two groups."

The other neighbors were still milling around us, their frightened voices threatening to drown out our conversation.

A neighbor who I recognized took Boa from my arms, and offered to take care of her for the night. Another neighbor was arranging with Ambrosia to take Marzipants.

Everyone's faces lit up with red flashing lights. A siren sounded. The fire trucks were there.

I felt a lump in my throat.

The crowd.

The chaos and destruction.

The flashing red lights lit up the night.

I got a powerful sense of déjà vu.

This felt an awful lot like the night my house blew up. The night I shot two people. The night Zoey was almost ripped in half by...

I couldn't think about it.

This was not the time for memories.

I had to stay focused.

She would be okay.

Bentley was with her, and he was tough, plus she was tough, too.

We split into two teams.

Ambrosia took Atom and Zinnia, and I took my mother. I loaded the power outage app on my phone, and we set out on foot.

We searched.

The destruction had caused unfathomable damage to the town. The cost would be in the millions. Some streets would never be the same.

I noted the scenes we passed with detachment, like an insurance adjuster.

All that mattered was finding my daughter and my whatever-Bentley-was. My boyfriend? We had gotten back together that evening, had we not? I remembered him smiling at me. Kneeling next to me, and smiling.

We searched.

My mind was numb.

One hour later, we still hadn't found any sign of either of them.

Zinnia told me to stop calling her because I was draining her phone battery.

My phone rang with an incoming call from an unknown number.

I signaled for my mother to stop searching the darkened alley and come closer. She leaned in and listened with her ear next to mine as I answered the phone.

"Hello?"

A male voice on the other end said, "Zara? Zara Riddle?"

I was panicked and distraught, yet I managed to reply, "This is Zara."

"It's Dr. Katz," the veterinarian said in a calm, cool manner. "I've had an emergency patient come in that I believe belongs to you. A fox. Are you missing a female fox? She's red."

My voice squeaked up. "Is she okay?"

"I'm sorry. She, uh..." The phone line crackled as he trailed off.

"What? Dr. Katz? Speak up. I can barely hear you."

My mother said, "What? What is it? Is she okay?"

"Sorry, I got distracted," Dr. Katz said. "Your fox is here at the clinic. Fatima just got here to help out. We've had a number of injuries tonight. You can come see her. Let yourself in the front door. The lights are off, but it's unlocked."

I stared into my mother's eyes. What did he mean? We could see her?

I couldn't talk anymore. All that came out was a croak.

Dr. Katz said, "She's going to be okay, Zara. Someone brought her in. She's got a broken leg, and a few cuts, but other than that, she's going to be okay."

I fell to my knees, gripping the phone.

My mother pried the phone from me, and told the veterinarian we'd be there soon.

As luck would have it, we weren't far from the clinic.

CHAPTER 31

One Hour Later

Bentley stood in the corner, quietly observing while the veterinarian told me and my mother about the extent of Zoey's injuries.

Another witch, Fatima Nix, stood to the side as well.

I could barely look at the unconscious fox on the examination table. It hurt so much to see her this way.

Fighting back my emotions, I laid my hands on my fox daughter's leg.

"As far as bone breaks go, this isn't a bad one," Dr. Katz said. "The cast I'm going to put on may be uncomfortable, but..."

He trailed off in stunned silence as my healing powers activated.

A regular person wouldn't have noticed, but Dr. Katz's mage powers gave him enough insight to know what I was doing.

My healing magic didn't work the way it used to, but it still worked.

I paused and asked, "Mind if I help out?"

He nodded for me to go ahead, and he stayed quiet.

I closed my eyes and focused entirely on letting my power flow out of me.

Under my hands, I felt the bone reconnecting, and the broken skin from the compound fracture knitting together again.

When it was done, I pulled my hands away and stepped back.

Dr. Katz inspected the leg, then looked up at me in astonishment.

"You healed her," he said. "The bone is unbroken."

My mother shook her head and said to me, "This man is an idiot. He has a witch for an assistant, and he doesn't know what witches can do?" Then she looked at Fatima, who was standing off to the side with Bentley, and said, "Shame on you, girl. Taking people's money for subpar treatment."

Fatima's jaw dropped. "But I... I can't... I'm not..." Fatima gave me a pleading look.

"Easy now," I said to my mother, stepping between her and Fatima for everyone's safety. "We witches have different levels of powers. I'm sure Fatima does her best to help the clients, in her own way."

I glanced over my mother's shoulder, at Bentley. He raised an eyebrow in amusement, but wisely chose not to weigh in. When it came to my mother, he gave her a wide berth.

"I do help," Fatima said. "I do as much as I can."

"She does," Dr. Katz said, coming to her defense. "My patients heal much faster in Fatima's care. Just not," he looked down at Zoey's paw in amazement, "instantly. Wow. That really is something." He flashed a friendly grin at me. "If you ever decide to leave the library, there's a job waiting here for you."

"I appreciate the offer," I said.

"You do have my number," Dr. Katz said.

"The fridge magnet? I sure do. I stuck it on the fridge at..." I looked at my mother. "Hey, am I mixing up reality and nightmares, or did that tornado do some damage to Zinnia's house?"

"Zarabella, the tornado tore away half the house."

"But we can fix it," I said. "There's still half a house there. We can rebuild."

She took my hand and looked into my eyes. "The house is ruined. I told you ten minutes ago, when I spoke to the fire department."

I was so confused. "There was a fire?"

She squeezed my hand. "No, Zarabella. There was no fire, but Zinnia's house is ruined."

"That doesn't work for me," I said. "Where are we going to sleep tonight?"

Dr. Katz said, "We have one cot here, and you're welcome to it."

My mother scoffed. "A single cot? Are we to hot-cot it, like a couple of submariners?"

Fatima said, "The cot is really comfortable. I've stayed here plenty when we have a client giving birth. It can get a little noisy at night, with the various nocturnal animals, but—"

My mother raised her hand, stopping Fatima. "I'm sure we can find appropriate accommodations on our own. There's at least one adequate hotel in this town."

Dr. Katz said, "The insurance on the house probably covers a hotel stay for a few nights. I'm sure you can get reimbursed."

He went on, talking about insurance and paperwork.

His words became meaningless noise.

My head was swimming with stars.

This was all so familiar. He was saying the same things people said to me the night my house imploded, or exploded, or whatever it was called when a vengeful genie sets off explosives in the magical tunnels underneath your sentient dream house.

I picked up a nearby bottle of water and took a sip.

Was I dehydrated, or just drained from healing Zoey's leg?

I didn't feel right. I wasn't myself. There were things in my head I didn't want to have there.

A chair was being nudged against the back of my legs. I sat.

While the others talked, I sipped my water and tried to find myself inside the blackness.

Eventually, someone said my daughter's name, and I came back to reality.

Dr. Katz was saying, "You can take Zoey to your hotel with you tonight, but I want you to call me any time, day or night." He was looking at me, and only me. He didn't take his eyes off me. "Call me any time. For anything."

There was something he wasn't saying. A strong implication.

"Dr. Katz," I said with a head shake. "You are absolutely shameless." I shot a look over to Bentley, in the corner, and whispered a silent apology on behalf of the flirty veterinarian.

Zoey remained completely still on the table, breathing steadily, her fox form resting. She'd been given enough sedatives to keep her sleeping until morning. I longed to see her human face as soon as possible, and I might have had the strength left to force a change—something I hadn't done since I'd forced my father to change—but I didn't dare try. I would let her rest. She could change back to human form on her own time.

My mother unsnapped her purse, which she'd had the presence of mind to grab from the house, along with mine.

"How much?" She pulled out her wallet, and looked back and forth between the veterinarian and his witch assistant. "How much are you charging us for the one hour of babysitting you did before we could get here and fix everything?"

"No charge," Dr. Katz said, bristling visibly. "Though I did a lot more than babysitting after your granddaughter was unceremoniously dumped on my doorstep, practically at death's door. Between the sedatives, the IV fluids, the imaging..." He paused, frowning. "That reminds me. I'd like to go over the imaging again, if you have time."

I glanced over at Bentley. He nodded to say we could take all the time we needed. Then he walked over to stand next to Zoey, keeping a watchful eye over her.

Fatima, my mother, and I went with Dr. Katz to his office, where I'd reviewed Boa's scans not even twenty-four hours earlier.

An image of a fox's bones flashed onto the monitor.

The broken leg bone was clearly visible.

I turned away quickly, but not quickly enough.

The revulsion was as surprising as it was fast.

I grabbed a waste bin, and held it under my face as my mouth filled with salty water. The room was spinning.

"Oops. My fault," Dr. Katz said. "I'm sorry, Zara. I shouldn't have just flashed it up there like that, without any warning. Hazard of the trade."

I swallowed, then wiped my mouth with the back of my hand. "False alarm," I said. "I'm okay. I'm not going to barf."

"Are you sure?"

"She's fine," my mother said with a hand wave. "We Riddles have very strong stomachs."

"It's true," I said, returning the waste bin to its spot under the desk. "I guess I wasn't prepared for seeing my daughter like that. As a collection of bones."

Dr. Katz said, "You don't have to look at the imaging, but I thought you'd like to see how the magical artifact has integrated with her system. Forgive me for being curious, but I wonder, did she eat one of those messenger birds when Boa did, or was it something else?"

There was a magical artifact inside my daughter?

An image of the amulet, hanging in the air, flashed through my mind.

Then Zoey, jumping off the upper bunk, catching it in her mouth.

Did she...?

My mother leaned in, blocking my view of the screen. "It's the amulet," she said. "The so-called Vessel of the Remainder. I recognize the chain."

I pushed her out of the way so I could see for myself.

I was looking at my daughter's bones, and also at the amulet. The Vessel of the Remainder.

"That's not a clockwork bird," I said. I explained to the veterinarian that we'd all been searching for a magical artifact. I didn't tell him why, or what it was, but told him how the last time I'd seen the necklace, it had been when Zoey caught it in her mouth.

Fatima, who'd been relatively quiet, said, "She must have swallowed it."

That was our Fatima. Always the best at stating the obvious.

My mother said, "But this area here," she waved at my daughter's fox limbs, "This is not her digestive system. I see bits of it here, here, and here. How can that be?"

Fatima said, "The legs are not part of the digestive system."

Her tone and her words rubbed me the wrong way.

I glared at her. Fatima could be irritating, but I usually didn't react as strongly. I must have been frazzled from the day's events.

Fatima glared right back at me. "What?"

My mother said, "Something strange is going on. Zoey ate the amulet. She *ate it*. Why does that sound so familiar?"

Fatima said, "Foxes eat plenty of things."

The three of them started talking to each other about strange things that pets sometimes ate. It was as though I wasn't even in the room.

After several minutes of their inane nattering, I said, "She's The Soul Eater."

The other three turned to me.

"She's the Soul Eater," I repeated. "That's what Zoey is called in the prophecy."

"I thought that was a metaphor," my mother said. "A colorful version of something else." She frowned. "Is that what it meant? That she was always destined to..."

Fatima's eyebrows shot up. "Zoey is the Soul Eater! That's why she ate the amulet. It contains the souls."

"That's what I just said."

"Ah," Dr. Katz said. "Wait. The amulet has a soul in it? Who does the soul belong to?"

"Long story," my mother said. "It's all the souls for the remainder of humanity." She shrugged. "Not a long story after all."

Dr. Katz frowned. "This is some end-of-the-world stuff, isn't it?"

They all looked at me.

"Zolanda Daizy Cazzaundra Riddle is the Eater of Souls," I said. "And now she has fulfilled her part in the prophecy."

Nobody spoke.

A chill rippled through me.

My daughter, the Soul Eater, had swallowed the amulet containing the remainder of humanity's souls, and now they were... part of her?

CHAPTER 32

Friday, March 3rd

(Five Days Later)

My coworker, Frank Wonder, came around the corner, spotted me, and said, "Oh, it's just you."

"It's just me," I replied. "You were expecting someone more exciting? Maybe a leprechaun? Joke's on you, Frank Wonder. Saint Patrick's Day is still two weeks away."

I was sitting in the library's cozy reading corner, the one that caught the sun at the end of the day. We patrolled the area most afternoons so we could wake up the nappers before they started snoring. I had nodded off once myself, but was wide awake now, curled up in the leather club chair known affectionately as Harry's chair. The sun I'd been enjoying was nearly gone, setting for the day.

Frank explained, "I was trying to close up and activate the security system, but I kept getting an error message that the library wasn't empty." He looked around us at the empty lower floor. "What are you doing here? You finished your shift hours ago. I heard you clock out."

I held up my book. "I'm enjoying some *me* time. You may find this hard to believe, but when you're sharing one hotel suite with three other people, two wyverns, an old lady ghost, a cat, and a talkative budgie, quiet reading time is hard to get."

Frank unbuttoned his conservatively stylish suit jacket, and took a seat on the less-comfy wooden chair across from me.

He sighed.

"Don't let me keep you," I said. "I can lock up."

"Would you like to come to my apartment for dinner? I wasn't planning anything fancy, but you could hang out there for a change of scenery. The couch pulls out into a bed. You could even stay over." He smiled and ruffled his snowy white hair. "We'll have a sleepover party, and do each other's hair."

"That's an appealing offer, but I'm going to stay here until Bentley swings by after he's done work."

The smile fell off Frank's face. "What?"

"He's been dropping by here lately in the evenings," I said. "It's sort of our new routine, now that I'm crammed into a hotel suite with the whole zoo." I set aside my book. "Speaking of the zoo, did you know Nick Lafleur takes naps with the cheetahs? They curl up next to him, just like little cats, except, you know, *big*."

"That is... um... I did not know that." Frank got up again, and held out his hand toward me. "Why don't we lock up together, and go somewhere for dinner? We don't have to sit around my apartment if you don't want to. I know my building gives some people the heebie jeebies. There are an awful lot of old spirits lingering around—not that there's anything wrong with spirits lingering around, but it's not for everyone. So, what do you say to dinner? With your best friend, Frankster the Prankster?"

"Can I take a rain check?" I nodded at the window. "It's raining, and I'd rather stay dry in here until Bentley comes by."

Frank nodded and backed away. "Sure. If you change your mind, I'm just a phone call away."

"Have a good night. See you Monday."

His right eye twitched. "I'll see you this weekend, at *the thing*. You do know about it, right? You remember?"

"Yes," I said. "I haven't forgotten." I made an exaggerated frown. "So sad."

"So sad," he agreed, and he left.

For the next two hours, I enjoyed the silence of an entire library all to myself.

When Bentley finally came by, we agreed to head over to his apartment.

He took his own car, and I drove Foxy Pumpkin.

He must have stopped for some errands along the way, because I got to his place ahead of him.

I couldn't use my magic to open doors anymore, so I fished around in my purse for the spare key, and let myself in.

As soon as I entered the building's hallway, I realized something was wrong.

Bentley's door was open.

I walked into the apartment, and found a crew of people going through all of Bentley's things. They wore uniforms from a moving company. These were not uniforms from a fake company, like organized thieves might use to commit broad daylight heists. I recognized them as the same moving company that had moved my possessions to Wisteria.

I even recognized two of the men as the movers who'd unloaded my things at my new home.

"Gary," I said to the nearest one. "What are you doing here?"

He pointed at me. "Hey! Redhead lady with the nice kid. Librarian, right? Eliza?"

"Zara," I said. "Zara Riddle. I'm sorry to have to tell you guys this, but your office must have made a mistake. The owner of this apartment isn't moving out."

"I know," Gary said. "We're working for the building management company. The contract is for any time this month. We had some free time this weekend, and my crew could use the extra cash, so we're getting things done ahead of the deadline."

"All of that would be great, if your services were actually required," I said.

He gave me a confused look. "Are you with the management company? I thought you were a librarian."

"As a matter of fact, I am the building manager," I lied, selling it with a bluffing spell. "Tell your crew there's been a mistake. I'll see that you all get paid for your time, and we can sort out the mistake in the morning."

He bought it, his eyes taking on the glassy look that confirmed my spell was working. The devil had hampered my powers significantly, but I could still do a trick or two.

Gary apologized for causing a fuss, and got the crew to stop what they were doing. They didn't take much convincing. It was a Friday night, after all.

No sooner had they left than Bentley arrived.

He looked around at the cardboard boxes with a detached curiosity I found hilarious.

"You sure know how to roll with the punches," I said. "Nothing can ever get you down for long."

He shrugged, as if to say he didn't think it was a superpower, and he couldn't understand why other people weren't as level-headed as he was.

I looked for the groceries he must have stopped to pick up, but couldn't find them.

"Nobody could find anything in this mess," I said, stacking a box of professionally-packed stemware out of the way, on top of a larger box.

Then I dug around in the refrigerator for something to eat.

The dairy products were all expired or moldy.

"You're such a bachelor," I said, and I prepared a quick meal of pickles, crackers, and mini marshmallows.

When it was time for bed, we discovered that the entire bedroom had been packed up and removed, including the bed.

We found some blankets and pillows in the living room, brought them to the bedroom, and curled up on the floor, camping style.

The apartment was quiet.

No other Riddles, no cat, no budgie, no wyverns.

Just peace and quiet.

Nobody whispering about me when they thought I couldn't hear them.

No sympathetic, pitying looks.

No gentle voices saying things I didn't want to hear.

There was only the quiet, and Bentley.

CHAPTER 33

Saturday, March 4th

(The Next Day)

I woke up to the sound of banging on a door.

That alone wasn't unusual. For most of the past week, I'd been sharing a hotel suite with three other women, and the suite only had one washroom. The sister who was pregnant was often in conflict with the sister who wasn't, about who needed the bathroom more urgently.

Fun times at the Cerulean Lagoon Hotel and Spa.

At least we still had Bentley's apartment, a place to get away from everything and everyone.

I got up from the pile of pillows on the floor where we'd slept.

There was no sign of Bentley. He must have gotten called in to work, and left without waking me. As the girlfriend of a detective, I was accustomed to that sort of thing happening. Criminals didn't stick to a sensible nine-to-five schedule. They did, however, cut back on their outdoor work when the weather wasn't good, so if it was raining at night when we went to bed, I could expect to wake up with Bentley still around. Not this morning, apparently. I hoped whatever had happened wasn't too serious. The town had already suffered so much from the tornado. How much more could a town take?

I opened the apartment door to find my daughter standing in the hallway. She was holding a zippered garment bag, like the kind you'd get from a dry cleaner.

"Good morning," I said.

"There you are," she said. She was wearing a black dress.

"Look at you, all dressed in black," I said. "Not jeans and a T-shirt. Who died?"

"That's not funny." She came into the apartment and glanced around. "They don't mess around in this building, do they?"

"Oh, this. Don't worry about this. I'll get it sorted out."

"Good." She handed me the garment bag. "Put this on."

"So bossy!"

She leaned forward and sniffed me. "It's been three days since you bathed. Either get in the shower willingly, or I'll call for reinforcements."

"You are such a weird kid," I said. "I can't believe you ever thought you could pass for normal."

She pointed at the hallway. "Shower."

I did as I was told, though I didn't see the point. Just because my daughter, with her super sensitive nostrils, could detect some scent on me, that didn't mean I was in violation of social norms.

I wondered if her bossy behavior had anything to do with the fact that she'd consumed an ancient magical artifact containing the rest of humanity's souls, and now the amulet itself was part of her bones. Something like that could change a person.

After my shower, I dried my hair with a spell—a simple spell that worked as it was supposed to—and pulled on the dress. It was, like my daughter's, black.

"This is fun," I said through the door. "Putting on an outfit that I didn't have to pick out myself. I miss my old closet that picked out my clothes for me. I miss my old house."

"Me, too," she said.

I opened the door and struck a pose. "Voila. How do I look?"

She frowned. "Mom, are you going to be okay today?"

"I promise I'll be on my best behavior."

"That's not what I meant."

"What about you? Is your friend Atom coming?" Atom was still around, but Zoey had put him into, in her words, "the friend zone."

Zoey said, "He didn't think it would be appropriate for him to be there."

"Is that so?" I scoffed. "The devil is worried about his appearances being *appropriate*. How quaint."

Solemnly, Zoey said, "He feels responsible, even though it wasn't his fault." She looked into my eyes. "You don't blame him, do you?"

I shrugged. "He is the devil, Zoey. I don't know how you can even be in the same room as him after seeing that ugly face of his, not to mention the tail." I paused to shudder. "But since you and the devil are... *friends* or whatever, you should probably get used to hearing him get blamed for stuff."

"You may be right," she said.

"I'm your mother. Of course I'm right."

"Let's go." She nodded at the door.

"Where are we going? Is this the thing Frank was talking about?"

"Frank will be there," she said. "I'll drive."

We went out to the car, and I did let her drive, since she seemed to know a lot more about my schedule for the day than I did.

We went to the Abernathy Family Funeral Home, which explained the black dresses.

We were there for a memorial service for one of the victims of the tornado.

It was a nice enough service. Better attendance than the last two I'd been at.

People kept staring at me as they dabbed their eyes with tissues, which I found unsettling, but it wasn't like memorials were my favorite events anyway.

After the service, people gathered in the community room for light snacks.

I didn't see the point in sticking around much longer, so I slipped out the back without Zoey, and went for a drive.

I drove to the ocean, parked the car in the nearly-empty parking lot—early March wasn't quite swimming weather yet—and stared at the sea for a long time.

I don't know how long I was there, but when I got up from the driftwood seat, my joints were stiff.

I got in the car again, and started driving with no particular destination in mind.

When I pulled onto Beacon Street, I realized I'd been heading there the whole time.

I parked in front of the construction fence surrounding the pit that used to be my house, and got out to peer through the gap in the plywood hoarding, as was my routine.

I'd been standing there for a while when I felt a hand on my arm.

"Zara," said a pleasant female voice. "You must be freezing. Your lips are blue."

I turned to see a face I'd practically grown up with.

It was Larissa Lang, the actress who'd been a child actor on my favorite show, *Wicked Wives*. She'd grown up into a gorgeous woman who was currently starring in a reboot of the same series.

"Larissa Lang," I said, momentarily confused about her knowing my name. Had we met? Was I dreaming?

She took my hands in hers and blew on them. Her breath was very hot.

"You're one of my favorite actresses," I said, gushing like a true fan. "I should get your autograph. Do people still do that, or is it all about photos now?"

She gave me a charming smile. "Are you still cold, Zara?"

Her question surprised me. My feet were quite cold. And my legs. How did she know?

"A little bit," I admitted. "I could cast a spell to warm up, if I need to. You know about spells, don't you?" Bits and pieces of our previous meeting were coming back to me. We had met before. I wasn't dreaming. This was real. "I remember. You know my father, and you know what I am." I pointed at her. "And you're a succubus."

"I am," she said plainly. "Would you like to go somewhere more private, where we can talk?"

"Sure. I don't have anything else going on today. Not until my chauffeur tracks me down again. My daughter is friends with the devil, but I suppose you know all about that. You strike me as the kind of person who always knows what's going on."

Larissa said, "I would say the same about you. What's going on? I saw you at the memorial, but you got away before I could talk to you. How are you?"

"Fine."

"Fine?"

"Maybe just okay," I said. "Normally I'm more on top of my game, but my life's been in a bit of upheaval lately, ever since this." I waved at the pit. "My daughter's been extra bossy lately, sixteen going on sixty, treating me like I'm the kid and she's the parent."

Larissa turned and started walking away.

I skipped to catch up with her.

She led me up the stairs to the familiar blue house that used to belong to the Moores.

I remembered that she had bought the house. I also remembered that I'd been furious about her doing so, though I couldn't recall why.

She was such a talented actress, and seemed like a nice lady in person. We'd met for the first time at the hotel. Yes. I had been rude. I'd probably been projecting my irritation about my father onto her. That wasn't fair of me.

As she prepared a pot of tea for us inside her house, I told her as much, and apologized.

She accepted my apology with grace.

"Your father is a lot of fun," Larissa said.

We were sitting at a small table in the breakfast nook that overlooked the back yard. I'd envied that breakfast nook the first time I'd seen it, because my house only had a potting shed. Now my house didn't have anything.

"Zara, did you hear me? I said your father is a lot of fun."

I searched her pretty face for clues. "How much fun are we talking about? Are you going to be my new stepmother?"

She laughed. "Not that kind of fun. But I do wonder if you got your wild sense of humor from Rhys."

"If you met my mother, you'd know for sure that I did." I waved both hands emphatically. "Mystery solved."

She lifted a delicate teacup to her famously perfect lips. "The gifts we receive from our parents will never be fully revealed to us. We pass many of them on, unopened." She sipped her tea then set it down. "That's a line from the show," she said. "It's a bit on the nose, don't you think?"

"I don't know. I like it. We do get gifts from our parents, and we don't unwrap all of them. It's a nice idea. Maybe it's for the best that some things stay sealed up. Secrets revealed are trouble unsealed."

"That's a good line," she said. "Mind if I pass it along to the writers? I'm an executive producer, so I can give notes." She wrinkled her nose. "They love it when I do that."

I didn't say anything. I didn't quite know how to take her. Why were we having tea together? What was going on? I couldn't put my finger on it exactly, but some part of me was screaming that she was the enemy.

"Cookie?" She pushed over a plate of gingersnaps.

An enemy who offered me cookies wasn't so bad.

I gobbled down three of them. I hadn't eaten anything all day.

As I chewed, I turned and looked back into the house, through a pair of open double doors.

I surveyed the kitchen, looking for changes. Larissa had upgraded several things since the Moores had owned the place. The kitchen looked less interesting but more stylish, like a photo spread in a better magazine. Chet's concrete countertops, which he'd been so proud of, were now gleaming white marble. The marble wouldn't be nearly as low maintenance as concrete, but Larissa didn't have Corvin and his pepperoni fingers to worry about.

My gaze settled on a shelf of cards. They weren't birthday cards.

I pointed to them. "What's the occasion?"

"Someone died," she said.

That got my attention.

I turned to her face. Her eyes were gleaming. She looked more beautiful than ever. That was the thing about famous actresses. They never got ugly and red-eyed when they cried, like regular people. They only became more captivating. Was it something in the chemistry of the tears themselves?

I looked down at her clothes. She was wearing a black dress, like me. I'd seen that dress earlier, at the memorial. We had both been there.

I looked up at her shining eyes again.

With a growing lump in my throat, I asked her, "Who died?"

"My ex-husband," she said.

"I'm sorry for your loss," I said automatically. "Were you two close?"

The corner of her mouth twitched. "We were divorced."

"Right. Dumb question." I glanced at the cards again. There were an awful lot of them.

"Zara, he loved you," she said.

I kept my focus on the cards. I didn't dare look at Larissa. She was too good of an actress. If I looked at her, I would start feeling what she was feeling, and I didn't want to. She was grieving, and I would have none of that.

"He was always yours," she said softly. "I had a crazy idea that things might be different a second time around. We would be on even footing. Me with my powers, and him with his. But I was wrong. He loved you, Zara. He chose you."

I got up from the small table in the breakfast nook, and walked through the double doors into the kitchen, to the shelf of cards.

I took one off the shelf and read inside.

Underneath the printed poem was a handwritten note: *We loved Theodore like a son. Much love and prayers to you at this difficult time.*

"Theodore," I said to Larissa. "Was that your ex-husband's name?"

She didn't answer me.

She stayed where she was, in the breakfast nook.

I picked up another card at random.

There was that name again.

Theodore.

And another one.

Teddy.

And another one.

This one had the full name.

Theodore Bentley.

The other handwritten sentiments were all variations on a theme. *Our thoughts and prayers are with you in this difficult time.*

We had some of these cards at the hotel suite. I kept getting rid of them, but they kept coming.

The cards never stopped.

I swept them off the shelf.

They fluttered to the floor.

The room blurred.

When Larissa Lang finally joined me in the kitchen, I was ripping apart all of her lovely cards.

I looked up from what I'd done.

"Sorry," I said. "I'm sorry." I couldn't explain what I was doing.

She knelt down next to me, picked up a card, and ripped it down the middle.

"You've got the right idea," she said.

She put the torn pieces together, and ripped them again.

Then I tore apart a fresh one with gold leaf highlights.

She did the same to a pale watercolor.

We tore up beautiful cards together for a while, and then she was holding me, or I was holding her, and maybe we were laughing, or maybe we were crying.

CHAPTER 34

Sunday, March 26th

(Three Weeks Later)

"Find me," I called out from my hiding spot behind the sofa. "Find me!"

I popped my head up so Marzipants, the elderly green budgie, could see where I was, then I ducked down again.

"Find me!"

It took a couple more head pops, but Marzipants finally strutted around the sofa, found me, and waited for praise and a head rub.

"Now it's your turn," I said.

The bird said, "Find me!" in his mimic bird voice, and waddled off. "Find me!"

I closed my eyes and counted to ten before I started looking.

Several minutes later, when I still hadn't found the budgie inside the hotel suite, I started to get worried.

"Marzipants? Where'd you go, little buddy?" I whistled. "Marzipants?"

The room was silent. Usually saying his name got the little guy excited enough to chatter, but he'd gone silent.

"No hints? No chirps? What's gotten into you?"

There was still no response.

I felt a chill, and then a rush of heat.

This was it.

Marzipants, who was a very old bird, had died.

I just knew it.

That was why he wasn't chirping.

It was my fault for trying to teach him so many new tricks.

How could I be so selfish? These new games were too taxing on an old fellow. It was bad enough he had to live with so many other creatures who were more powerful than him. I'd pushed him over the edge with my games. I'd given him a heart attack.

From behind me, there was a tiny, muffled cry of "find me!"

I turned around slowly.

"Marzipants?"

Another chirp. Still muffled.

I checked behind the curtains.

Under the couch.

Then I saw it.

A plastic drinking glass that was upside-down on the coffee table.

Slowly, I lifted the drinking glass.

It wasn't empty.

The green-and-yellow budgie that had been hiding inside stretched out his wings in pride.

He sang, "Find me, find me!"

"You little brat," I said. "How did you get yourself in there?" I looked at the cup, mystified.

Marzipants flitted over to the curtains and climbed them to the top, where he triumphantly chirped one of his favorite tunes, a radio jingle for a local furniture store.

Boa, who'd been sleeping during the whole hide-and-seek game, stirred in her sleep. She woke up just enough to yawn before going back to sleep again.

Twenty minutes later, I was putting Marzipants back in his cage when my daughter let herself into the hotel room.

She was in jeans and a T-shirt, the sight of which always gave me relief, because it meant we weren't going to a memorial service. We'd only been to three memorials that year—her father's, Mrs. Pressman's, and Theodore Dean Bentley's—but three was far too many. Two of the men I'd loved, nearly seventeen years apart, were now gone from my life. I never wanted to see another black dress ever again.

Zoey paused, looked around the room, and said, "What's going on in here?"

I had moved some of the furniture around, hoping to find a better layout that gave us more space.

"I was playing games with Marzipants," I said. "Did you know he can hide himself under this?" I showed her the plastic tumbler.

She pulled at her T-shirt collar and chuckled. "Who do you think taught him the trick?"

"You should have warned me," I said. "I couldn't find him anywhere. I thought he'd crawled under the armoire and died." I held my hand to my chest. "I feel like a crazy woman."

"You're not crazy," she said. "He's an old bird. He could go at any moment."

"Thanks," I said flatly. "That's very reassuring. Why are you here? I thought you were playing harp at Dreamland today."

"I'm on a break," Zoey said. "I came to get you."

"To get me what? A coffee? Sorry to break it to you, but you're empty handed. You forgot my coffee."

"Mom, you have to leave the hotel room."

"Why? I've got everything I need here. Food. Running water. TV." I waved at the sleeping cat and the bird cage. "My crew."

She took my hand and led me to the sofa, where she tried to get me to sit. But this wasn't my first rodeo. People had been trying to give me interventions for a while now. I slipped away, and didn't stop fleeing until she caught up with me in the hotel suite's single bedroom.

I backed up to the window and started to undo the latch.

"Not another step closer, or I'll jump," I said, mostly joking.

"We're over top of the awning," she said. "Go for it. I dare you to open that window, climb out, and jump on the awning like it's a trampoline. Get some sunlight on your face for once."

"Leave me alone. You've got your cool circle of friends, with your devil friend, and your band. Go play your harp, and don't worry about me."

She sat on the edge of the bed.

I abandoned the pretext that I might open the window, but I didn't sit. I leaned against the cool wall, and ran my hands over the wallpaper. It was flocked wallpaper, an abstract pattern, and I enjoyed the sensation of the fuzzy shapes on my palms.

Zoey twirled her long, red hair between her fingers and looked at me with a sad expression.

She asked, "Do you know what today is?"

"It's not your birthday," I said. "Not until tomorrow. You're still sixteen for one last day."

"Today is the one-year anniversary of the day we moved here." She looked around the hotel suite bedroom, which was cluttered with the clothes and hair-styling products of four women. "Well, not *here*, but you know what I mean."

"One year," I said. "You're right. It's been one whole year."

"A lot has changed," she said.

I didn't say anything.

"Mom, I want to tell you something."

I waited, aware of my heart beating faster than it needed to beat. Why was I nervous? Was it because I'd just had a nervous breakdown over not being able to find the budgie, and now I was worried my daughter was about to break some terrible news? Was it because lately it felt like every bit of news I got was bad? That good news had ceased to exist? That was probably it.

"I think we're winning," Zoey said.

I slowly slid down the wall, to the carpet, and hugged my knees to my chest. What was she talking about?

"We're actually winning," she said. "Even if it doesn't seem that way."

I found my voice and asked, "Winning? At what?"

"At life," she said. "I'm glad we moved here. Even though we've had a lot of bad things happen, I think that, overall, we're doing okay."

"Bentley died," I said. "He died."

"I know." She bit her lower lip. "But I think it could have been a lot worse."

A nasty, insolent, bitter response came to me, but I swallowed it, unspoken.

My daughter was only sixteen, and she thought about life with a sixteen-year-old's brain.

She was trying to be reassuring. She was trying to help me, to coax me out of my sorrow.

She was doing a terrible job.

Just terrible.

"We can't bring him back," Zoey said. "Mr. Bentley is gone."

She was right about that. When he'd saved her from the worst of the tornado, shielding her body with his own, he'd made the ultimate sacrifice. His life for hers.

The stranger who'd found the wounded fox, and taken it to the vet had mistaken the debris around her for... clothes, shoes, and mud. Not a person. Bentley had been torn apart by the tornado's fury. The world's top necromancers—who probably lived in Wisteria—couldn't have put him back together.

"He's gone, but we're still here," Zoey said.

I continued hugging my knees to my chest. I didn't want to be there. But I couldn't tell her that. That would make me the worst kind of mother—the one who didn't even want to be there for her child. The fact that I'd even had that thought sickened me.

Zoey checked the time on her phone. "My break is almost over. I have to get back."

"Okay."

She stood and crossed her arms. "I'm not going without you."

"You have to go. Your fans are waiting. People lost a lot in the tornado, and it cheers them up when you play your music. Everyone says you play like an angel."

She reached down for my hand. "Your logic is impeccable. My harp playing *does* cheer people up. That's why I have to insist that you come with me." She flexed her fingers.

"Okay."

I let her help me to my feet.

As I stood, I felt something happening in my body.

It was like a magical spell, the one that made witches lighter so they could take flight.

As my daughter helped me put on clean clothes, and we left the hotel room, I felt lighter and lighter.

Was it a spell? Was my levitation magic returning?

I tried casting movement on the spring flowers that had pushed up through the dirt in tidy rows at the front of the hotel.

No dice. I couldn't even pluck a single petal. That magic ability hadn't returned.

And yet, as we drove together to the coffee house, I felt buoyant.

When we got there and stepped inside, into the warmth, and I saw strangers gathered together, laughing and talking and waiting for the band to come back from their break, I felt lighter still.

In my lightness, I still missed Bentley. He should have been there. I looked around. Maybe he was there. I couldn't see him, but he didn't feel as far away as he'd been the last few weeks.

I didn't know many of the people gathered inside the coffee shop.

There were two small children there with their families. The kids toddled their way into the middle of the open area, near the band stage. It was clear to all the adults watching that they were meeting for the first time. They grabbed hands, shyly at first, and then began twirling each other around, giggling as they tossed their heads back, encouraged by the warm smiles all around.

I spotted Zinnia across the crowd, sitting in one of the comfortable wingback chairs, rubbing her belly. She didn't see me there, watching her, watching the children, both of us thinking about the little one who would be joining us soon.

My body felt so light, so free.

Then, when my daughter sat at the harp and began to play, I soared.

Before she'd even finished the song, I heard what she'd been trying to tell me.

We were going to be okay.

We were going to keep on living.

There would be bad days, but there would be good ones, too.

Not just memorials, but birthdays, and weddings, and spontaneous gatherings for no reason whatsoever.

We wouldn't be able to keep everyone we'd ever loved around forever, but we would always have their memories.

And magic.

And music.

We still had so much.

Maybe we were winning, after all.

For a full list of books in this
series and other titles by
Angela Pepper, visit

www.angelapepper.com

www.ingramcontent.com/pod-product-compliance
Lightning Source LLC
Chambersburg PA
CBHW072205030726
47501CB00015B/647